CW01203110

Text Copyright
© 2021 Brynne Asher
All Rights Reserved
No part of this book may be reproduced, scanned, or distributed in any printed or electronic form without permission from the author. Please do not participate in or encourage piracy of copyrighted materials in violation of author's rights. Only purchase authorized editions.

Any resemblance to actual persons, things, locations, or events is accidental.

This book is a work of fiction.
Deathly
The Dillon Sisters Duet
Brynne Asher

Published by Brynne Asher

BrynneAsherBooks@gmail.com

Keep up with me on Facebook for news and upcoming books
https://www.facebook.com/BrynneAsherAuthor

Join my reader group to keep up with my latest news
Brynne Asher's Beauties

Edited by Edit LLC
Cover Design by Simply Defined Art
Interior Print Design by Christina Smith

Other Books by Brynne Asher

The Carpino Series
Overflow – The Carpino Series, Book 1
Beautiful Life – The Carpino Series, Book 2
Athica Lane – The Carpino Series, Book 3
Until Avery – A Carpino Series Crossover Novella

Killers Series
Vines – A Killers Novel, Book 1
Paths – A Killers Novel, Book 2
Gifts – A Killers Novel, Book 3
Veils – A Killers Novel, Book 4
Scars – A Killers Novel, Book 5
Until the Tequila – A Killers Crossover Novella

The Montgomery Series
Bad Situation – The Montgomery Series, Book 1
Broken Halo – The Montgomery Series, Book 2

Standalones
Blackburn

The Dillon Sisters
Deathly by Brynne Asher
Damaged by Layla Frost

Dedication

To Layla Frost

Thank you for trusting me to help bring these sisters to life.

Deathly

BRYNNE ASHER

One

THE BEHOLDER

Aria

*B*RAVERY IS IN the eye of the beholder.

I know the idiom is *beauty*, but beauty won't get you anywhere in life. I don't care how you spin it, how poetic you drone on about it, or how deeply you reach inside your soul to find it.

I'm sick of beauty and the weight our society puts on it.

I'll take bravery over beauty any day.

Some might think *bravery* is the important piece of that puzzle.

They would be wrong.

Bravery is only the act. The beholder … that's the key.

They shoulder the power, the fight, and, when they come out on the other side of the battle, the consequences.

In any plain-Jane, sappy fairy tale, courage, and heroism are romanticized, polished, and dusted in glitter to shine through the darkness. They scream, "Look at me! I'm perfect. Normal. Winning at life!"

But for those of us who are not normal—let alone perfect—who are struggling to catch our breaths, bravery looks very different.

Bold, daring, and, yes, even audacious. This is the type of bravery required to walk in my designer-dupe heels and off-the-rack cocktail dress, since the real deals aren't in my budget.

Yet.

I'm working on it.

Most wouldn't think bravery would be required for a night out with your only friend, who isn't really that close of a friend. But for me, it is.

Psychoanalyzing every detail of every moment until I'm bleeding from my nails is a curse. It's how I'm wired and impossible to turn off. But when I manage to, things don't turn out well.

At all.

"Hot and cute have collided, creating a burst of beauty. I'm telling you, my heart and lady bits can hardly take it. I thought for sure I was here just for the eye candy, but I might have to dip into my 401k to make a bid."

I look over at Kate, who has become one of my only friends in the Pacific Northwest aside from my sister. "No way. We're here to check off a major task on my list to become a well-rounded human. Don't ruin it for me. We're here to be social—but just you and me, not with anyone else. We need to sit back and appreciate everything going on around us. My plan is airtight if we stick to it."

She hikes her perfectly manicured brow. "Don't lie, Doctor Shrinko. You're drooling over these beautiful specimens that God sculpted just for us—I've had my eye on you and you've had your eye on a certain tall, tan, broody man. Either that or the chocolate something-or-other with curly hair he's got on a leash."

Dammit. I'm not usually transparent. I excel at drowning every emotion that claws its way to the surface. My father made sure I hid my feelings. "Emotions showcase your weaknesses," he said.

My insides tense just thinking about it.

I turn back to Kate. "Of course, I'm looking. I'm like every other woman in the room. There are plenty of men and muscles here to appreciate, Kate. We're here for the experience, but that's it."

I've lost her attention. She takes a sip of her green apple martini, zeroing in on a man across the room who's being attacked by a Dachshund trying to lick his face off.

From the looks of it, I bet Kate wouldn't mind tasting him too. Lust is dripping off her like the perpetual Washington rain.

I grab her forearm to stop any crazy ideas running through her head. If I'm cautious by nature, she's the exact opposite. "We made a pact. Tonight is about getting out and doing something new, but only observing from afar."

When she levels her gaze on me, I know I've lost all control because she starts talking to me like I speak to my patients. "That doesn't mean we can't introduce ourselves. Aria, it's time to cross something else off

2

your list besides going to an event only to hide in the shadows. You can do this. It's your day. I feel it!"

My face turns to stone. "Don't you dare—"

"It's going to be okay." Her words bleed with sarcasm as she twists out of my grip. "Drink your wine, hang back, enjoy the scenery if you insist on living your boring, horrid life. But you could also talk yourself out of your hole and speak to someone who isn't a colleague or a wacko. Like a hot guy with a dog."

"Don't talk about my patients like that."

She waves me off. "I'm on my second martini and I'm not letting our scheduled Uber or this buzz go to waste. I'm going to fuss over stray dogs and drool over firefighters."

"You're the worst friend ever," I hiss under my breath, but it's pointless. Her long, blond waves swish to the rhythm of her hips. And that swish is strong as she moves across the ballroom, disappearing into a sea of shirtless firefighters wrangling homeless canines, all in the name of philanthropic cuteness.

I pull in a big breath and take a bigger sip of my merlot. Then I take a step closer to the wall and into the shadows. As I survey the room, it's not hard to forget why I'm here or why tonight was a biggie in all the things I need to cross off my list.

A slew of firefighters roam, each with their own homeless pup.

Dogs and Dates.

The annual fundraiser for the Redmond Rescue, a no-kill animal shelter. I doubt there's anything that melts panties quicker than bare-chested heroes and puppies. Along with their annual calendar, these half-naked men and their canines will be auctioned off after the cocktail hour designed to loosen the pockets of single women. The highest bidders will be the proud owners of a puppy and a date.

Kate is right. I do have a list. It's long and carefully curated. It's made of things I was never allowed to do because they were beneath me. Or, rather, beneath our family name.

Rescuing an animal was always a big, fat *no*. Owning anything less than a pure-breed from a distinguished bloodline would definitely be beneath my family, *if* we would've been allowed to have a pet. I won't even go into paying for a date—especially with a man who fights fires for a living. My father would have a fit and my mother would slur on about how impossible it is to live on a salary less than the top one percent of pretentious Americans.

Tonight is definitely at the top of my list, even if I'm only here to observe and experience it from afar.

Now that I have a moment to myself, I look for that curly-haired chocolate doodle who was rescued from a puppy mill. They're nowhere to be seen.

The firefighter and the popular hybrid pup are likely being eaten alive by women with healthy bank accounts who aren't working to pay off student loans that rival a jumbo loan.

My wine sloshes when something hits my bare-skinned legs before a deep voice I've never heard before rumbles beside me, "Been waiting for you."

I'm forced to catch my breath as I blot the wine off my chest. His eyes—as dark and oppressive as the black nights I've become familiar with since I moved to this part of the country—might as well claw through my skin.

They're *that* intense.

I feel *that* transparent.

I look away and push the jumping dog down. "Waiting for me?"

"Woof!"

I keep my attention on the puppy who looks like it belongs on Instagram more than in its homeless reality. Because it's easier to focus on the fur ball than the man, I run my fingers through its thick, floppy hair. "Hey, you."

The man's bulky fire pants ride low on his hips, only hanging on by the suspenders strapped over his wide, bare shoulders. The only other thing he's wearing north of his waist, is a simple gold cross hanging around his neck. He gives the leash a tug and the puppy wiggles at my feet trying to get to me. "Been waiting for you. It was easy to see from across the room you liked what you saw."

I look from the dog to the man who's wearing a five o'clock shadow from yesterday. His hair is long on top and tight on the sides and back—all but a few strands are trained to sit obediently in place. I'm jealous of the rebellious hairs that kiss his olive skin and strong, thick brows. "Excuse me?"

I work hard to focus on anything other than the faint scar that mars his right brow. I try so hard, my gawk falls to his pecs, and then farther to his rippled abs, but I force myself to stop there. This is awkward enough and not a part of my plan for the evening, so I focus on his square jaw that couldn't be more tense at the moment.

His irritated stare matches his tone. "The dog. You couldn't take your eyes off it from across the room. Look, I got roped into this. I don't want to be here, but I do want him to find a home. I had to drag my ass through all these women, so if you're not serious about him, just say the word, and I'll move on."

I squat as best I can in my cocktail dress that was designed solely for foreplay. It might be off the rack, but off the rack in black is easy to perfect, and this dress fits like a glove in all the right places.

The man gives the pooch enough slack to attack me and I instantly understand my childhood friends' obsession with pets. My mom never wanted dog hair marring her pristine house, so Briar and I never experienced the unconditional love of a canine, or anyone else for that matter. Briar rectified this childhood injustice and surrounds herself with animals by working for Redmond Rescue. Despite her frequent attempts to get me to adopt, I've resisted.

"I've never had a dog."

"So you're a chick who likes cats. Got it. I'll move on."

He starts to pull the puppy away, but both the dog and I resist. "I'm not a *cat chick*. I've never had a pet and I work long hours."

The beast of a man stops and I set my wine next to me to properly give this pooch the attention it deserves when he asks, "Your parents hate you or something?"

I pull in a breath but don't look away from the sweet, furry face. "Or something. Is it a boy or girl?"

"Boy."

As much as I don't want to, I look up to keep the precious doodle from licking off my makeup. Crouched at the firefighter's feet, my view does not suck as he lifts a bare shoulder. I try not to think about what other things might be like from this view. "Does he have a name?"

"I don't know."

I press my lips to the dog's head and stand straight on my heels. "Why would you volunteer your time if you're unhappy about being here?"

I'm too fascinated for my own good by his irritation and the way every movement and tick creates a ripple through the rest of his muscles, like a never-ending wave lapping at the shore. He pulls a big hand through his dark hair before spearing me with his intense scrutiny, gritting his words in a way I have a feeling he'd rather spit them at me. "Only so many single firefighters. I was guilted into it."

I tip my head and ignore the puppy vying for my attention. I can't focus on anything else but the half-naked, angry man in front of me. "I'm sorry."

His expression barely shows any patience. "Why are you sorry?"

"Because I know firsthand it's not fun to be guilted into anything. It's stressful."

"This isn't stressful." He lifts his chin toward the chaos around us. "It's irritating."

"I stick with my earlier sentiment—I'm sorry."

He shakes his head and starts to turn. "If you're not interested—"

"I never said I didn't *want* a pet," I interrupt and he halts mid-turn. "I said I never had one. I work long hours, but my sister works at the shelter and loves animals."

He hikes a brow again and this time there's condemnation laced through his tone. "So you're going to guilt your sister into taking care of a dog you don't have time for?"

If I were sitting in my office in my favorite chair where I'm most comfortable, I'd be able to handle this … handle him. Instead of deflecting whatever frustration or anger he's not trying to hide, I say nothing. For the first time in a long time, I'm at a loss for words.

He shakes his head. "Got it. I'll keep roaming the damn room until he finds a home and this shit show is over."

With nothing on my mind but my damn list—its top item blinking like a neon sign in my brain reminding me why I'm here—I swallow my nerves and steady my voice before he has a chance to turn away from me for good. "Maybe I need a pet."

His dark eyes narrow, questioning every word I utter. I don't blame him, I'm questioning my judgments, motives, and words, as well.

"I just … see, all I do is work. My sister doesn't need me as much as she used to. Being needed will give me balance. At least that's what I tell people. Might as well live by my own advice, right?"

"Don't make commitments you can't keep."

They might be simple words, but, from him, they feel like a slap and a warning. Little does he know, I made a vow long ago I'd never allow anyone to control me by delivering power plays like that. I've learned how to draw the line.

I deliver my words with a bite. "I've never made a commitment I haven't kept. Ever."

By his expression, I must've caught him off guard, but I don't wait for a response. I look back to the excited pup at my feet, pulling this way and that, not knowing what to focus on with all the activity. I bend at the knees again and he comes straight to me, flopping on his back for a belly rub.

"He likes you—" the hero starts, but we're interrupted.

"Oh-Em-Gee, look at this one!"

I'm forced to stand when we're surrounded by a group of women flashier than a disco ball. From platinum locks to fake bronze to high-pitched squeals, I've lost the attention of the dog as he has a slew of new women to dote on him.

The one in red slithers between me and the firefighter. "What station are you with?"

I take a sip and expel a relieved sigh when I realize his disdain isn't only directed at me. "Sorry, not into sharing where I work."

"But isn't that why you're here? To be auctioned off?" Long, highlighted hair sways in front of me and her crimson painted index finger taps him on the pec. "There might just be a bidding war over you."

"That'd be a waste of your money," he mutters and turns to leave with the dog.

I watch him walk away, every lat moving in symphony with one another, as he stalks through the room without stopping to speak to another soul until we lose sight of him altogether.

"Wow, what's with him?" one woman complains. "Every other man we've talked to is chasing ass as much as we are."

The rest chime in and start to gnaw on him like vultures would roadkill. Since I listen to people for a living, I have no desire to hear them talk about the man's less-than-winning personality. I decide it's time to find Kate before I do something rash, like bid on a dog I have no time for and end up on a date with an intimidating man who wants no part of this.

I head to the bar for one more glass of wine because Kate is right, there's no point in wasting an Uber. Everyone in this room is vying for the attention of the opposite sex—it will be easy to blend into the background.

With a fresh drink, I spot Kate across the room sidling up to the blond with the Dachshund. She might be fawning over the dog, but she definitely has puppy eyes for the man standing at least eight inches taller than her. Unlike the only man who's given me any attention tonight, hers might as well be oozing sex from his perfectly-smooth skin. He leans in to say something but stops when the emcee booms across the ballroom speakers to announce the auction will start in five minutes.

All canines and heroes make their way to the front of the room and disappear behind a curtained wall next to the stage. The doodle and his handler are one of the last pairs to disappear, the man not giving one ounce of attention to any woman he leaves in his wake.

It doesn't take long for Kate to find me. Excitement is etched all over her face as she hurries across the room through the crowds of women who have their bidding paddles ready to wave.

"I don't give a shit about our pact," she starts before she even reaches me. "I'm going to do it! His name is Clay. When he's not fighting fires, he's a carpenter. And when he's not building bookshelves for his mom, he's trying new recipes because, get this—" She grabs me and it looks like she might shed happy tears. My wine sloshes for the second time tonight as she gives me a little shake. "He likes to cook. Do you hear me, Aria? He. Likes. To. Cook. You know how much I love food! I think it's meant to be!"

I pull out of her hold to salvage what wine I have left and shake my head. "Everyone loves food. That doesn't make you soulmates."

"But I *really* love food and I *really* like when someone else prepares it."

I roll my eyes. "You're a match made in the kitchen."

She lowers her voice and turns to stand next to me so we're both facing the stage. "I saw you talking to Mr. Broody. Please tell me you talked about something other than your job."

I frown. "I don't always talk about my work."

"Not the good stuff anyway … just random shit about how busy you are. You need to get laid more than anyone in this room."

"I'm trying to get my practice going, but thank you for reminding me about my lack of *life*," I mutter and take another gulp.

Kate nabs my thin purse from under my arm and digs out the bidding paddle I received when we checked in. I smashed it in there as best I could since I knew I wasn't going to use it.

Kate shoves my clutch back at me and smooths the wrinkled paddle. "You're checking something else off your list tonight. We're gonna find you a man."

I grab the paddle from her. "A man is not on my list. Besides, have you seen the women here? They're exhaling money. Even if I had the time or the inclination to bid, there's no way I can afford it. Not with my rent and student loans."

"That's what credit cards are for," she argues.

"No. Credit cards are for emergencies."

She stares me straight in the eyes. "This is an emergency, Aria. A nine-one-one, four-alarm, all-hands-on-deck emergency. This is me saving you from your pathetic life. It has to happen."

"No." I shake my head and turn back to the stage that looks like something between a dog park and the set from *Magic Mike*. Lights bounce around the stage like a pathetic Vegas show and fire hydrants glow bright red. Music, reminding me of a strip show from a bachelorette party I once attended, vibrates from the monstrous speakers.

There's no way I'm bidding. I came here to watch, that's it. Nothing more.

Kate snakes her arm through mine. "Get ready. By the end of the night we'll both be dog owners with the potential of love on the horizon."

Shit.

"If not love, then at least maybe some rocking orgasms," she adds.

If I follow any of Kate's advice, the only thing on my horizon will be an ulcer.

The Auction

Aria

"GOING ONCE, TWICE, three times…"

Kate bounces on her toes as she looks across the room toward her main competition. The woman who ran up the bid on Kate's newest obsession glares back.

"Going to the pretty blonde in the red dress for three-thousand, five-hundred, and twenty dollars. Paddle number six-four-two-seven. Congratulations, little lady, you've got yourself a Dachshund and a date with Clay."

Kate screeches as she throws her arms around my neck. "I won!"

"I can't believe you just did that. So much for paying off your debt."

"I don't care! Okay, I've got to go pay. Shit, I hope I have enough credit and I'm not denied the transaction." She doesn't stop bouncing. "You're next. I had no idea your guy would be right after mine. Don't let me down, Aria. You *need* this. If you chicken out, I'll literally kill you myself!"

My lids fall shut and I pull in a calming breath. At least twenty dogs and firefighters have been auctioned off. The dollar amounts are staggering and Briar will be ecstatic since she works at the shelter. At least as ecstatic as Briar is capable of being. My sister's range of emotions fall between sarcasm and the driest of humor.

"Do it," she demands and pushes the bidding paddle to my chest. "Don't think, don't examine your feelings, don't focus on the consequences. Just raise your number, dammit. It's all you have to do. Your brown, curly fur ball is waiting on you and the broody man isn't bad either. Who knows? Maybe he's broken, and you can fix him. Just think about how much you'll get off on that."

"I don't need to fix everyone."

"If you say so, Miss Fix-It."

"Ladies, are you ready?" The announcer's voice rumbles through the room and I look from Kate to the stage. "Get those paddles ready. We have one last dog and date to auction off. Remember, one hundred percent of your donations go toward caring for animals like these, making sure they have happy, forever homes. Redmond Rescue never turns an animal away. From food to medical care, we're determined to find each one a loving human. And, bonus, tonight you big spenders will get a night out with one of our bachelor firefighters who have donated their ... ahem, time to the cause."

Kate pokes me in the ribs harder than necessary. "Be a strong bitch, Aria. You can do it! Now, say a prayer my credit card isn't denied."

And, with that, she's gone.

I finally breathe a sigh of relief. If I weren't sharing a ride home with Kate, I'd escape right now. I came, I did what I wanted to do, and can check tonight off my list, once and for all.

"His name is Brando, but he goes by Brand, and he's thirty-seven years young," the announcer starts.

Brand.

I look left to the stage. There he is, this time holding the doodle at his side, his bicep flexing with every move.

"I mean, he looks like a Brando. Right, ladies? When he's not fighting fires or performing mouth-to-mouth, he's ... ah ..." The announcer tips his head and flips this card over and back, then shrugs. "Well, Brando is somewhat of a mystery, I see. The highest bidder will just have to figure him out on their own. More fun for you."

Jealousy eats at me. All of a sudden, I hate the highest bidder and the bidding hasn't even started.

"Brand's little pooch won't be little for long. The vet thinks he might grow to be about fifty pounds. He was rescued from a puppy mill and our volunteers tell us this little guy is friendly and loyal to everyone he meets. He's almost housebroken and probably not a guard dog, but he'd be perfect for a family."

Well, there you go. Another reason I don't need to bid on a dog or a man. I don't have a family, nor do I plan on starting one in the near future, or far one.

"One thousand!"

I turn and find a woman who looks older than Brand raising her paddle. Probably in her mid-forties, she's beautiful—dripping in diamonds, bursting with Botox, and radiating self-esteem.

"Two thousand!" another voice comes from across the room.

"Twenty-five hundred!"

"You ladies are anxious." The announcer's bright smile shines and he eggs on the crowd. "Remember, this is the last date and dog of the night. You won't get this chance again until next year. And who knows, Brand here might be snatched up by then!"

Brand glares and isn't doing anything to raise his bids, unlike the others who played to the audience. It doesn't look like he's going to allow anyone to *snatch him* anytime soon.

"Four thousand." I turn and the cougar looks as serious as Brand as she ups the bid.

I look back at Brand and my breath catches. Even through the bright lights, his dark eyes find mine. He hitches the doodle up in his arms and his frown deepens.

"Six thousand!" is shouted from across the room.

Shit.

"Now, this is exciting!" the announcer bellows into the microphone. "We haven't seen six thousand all night. Seems the ladies are into broody, and Brand here might just be your golden ticket. Do I hear seven?"

"Seven."

My head whips around. The cougar is not happy as she lowers her paddle and crosses her arms.

"Give me eight thousand! C'mon, let's do this for the homeless animals."

A murmur blankets the room as women glance at one another, waiting for the next diamond to drop.

"Seven thousand," the announcer warns. "Going once..."

I look back at the cougar. Her lips tip on one side. Damn. She's smug as hell.

"Twice."

I turn back to the stage and Brand looks as if he couldn't be more miserable.

Fuck.

You don't not need to fix everyone, Aria.

"Three—" The announcer's voice rises.

"Eight thousand."

The announcer squints through the stage lights, into the crowd. "Where did that come from?"

My stomach drops.

I raise my paddle and stares from around the room weigh heavy on my soul.

I'll have to work more overtime to pay for this and I'm already at sixty hours a week. Not to mention, Briar is going to have words for me. I have no business making a commitment to a pet right now.

I clear my throat and speak clearly—it's been ingrained into me ever since I could remember, after all. "Eight thousand."

Brand stares me down, not a hint of emotion etching his beautiful olive skin.

"Nine thousand."

I turn, and unlike Brand, emotion is bleeding from the cougar—anger pouring off of her in waves.

I turn back to the announcer and raise my paddle with conviction this time. "Ten!"

A whoop, a holler, and a bit of applause erupt around me, but I pay them no attention.

"Ten thousand, five hundred."

I don't give the cougar the satisfaction of a glance. I'm committed to the game at this point and push all thoughts of how many hours I'll have to bill to pay for this…

This …

Obsession.

I'm not proud of it but there's no other way to describe it.

I raise my paddle again. "Eleven."

It's small but I don't miss it—Brand shakes his head.

"Eleven-five."

Damn the cougar.

"Twelve," I counter, refusing to give her the satisfaction of my attention.

Her bid is swift. "Twelve-five."

I expel all the air in my lungs and scrutinize the man and the dog, both of whom I'm allowing to control my future. Money I can't afford to spend on anything but student loans, or saving for a small down payment on a tiny house. Or, who knows, maybe a splurge on a good pair of shoes that aren't dupes.

My paddle—bent, wrinkled, and crushed since I had no plans for it to see any action tonight—finds the space above my head. "Fifteen thousand."

Brand's eyes narrow and the doodle, as if understanding the worth of the hard-earned dollar, barks.

I don't dare turn to see what my competition is doing and pray the small fortune I pledged is enough since my one and only credit card maxes out at sixteen thousand.

"Well, I'll be!" The announcer waves his hand in the air and I remotely wonder if he doubles as a Southern Baptist preacher. "When they asked me to volunteer to lead tonight's auction, I never—*never*—thought it would get as exciting as this. Fifteen-thousand dollars for a floppy-eared puppy and a date with a local hero. This is drama made for cable TV, if I've ever seen it. Do I hear sixteen?"

Please, no.

"Fifteen-five?" he eggs.

I swallow the bile that bubbles in my throat like the cauldron I'm about to dive into headfirst.

Female murmurs return and the hair on my arms stands straight. I hold my breath waiting for something.

Anything.

"Fifteen. Going once…"

Holy shit.

"Going twice…"

What have I done?

"Three times!"

I gasp as a beacon of light blinds me and I curse the audacity that masked itself as bravery just hours ago.

Bravery, my ass.

Consequences can be life changing. I fear I've tickled the beast.

I jerk at the slam of the gavel, sealing my fate. "The broody Brand and happy pup go to bidder six-four-two-eight, the lovely lady in black with a philanthropic heart."

Philanthropic my ass.

As cheers erupt around me, I don't waste any time. With the damn paddle in my sweaty grip, I turn on my cheap heel and head for the back of the room.

When I exit the ballroom doors, Kate is nowhere to be found, but there is a line at the table where I'm supposed to pay for my overwhelming obsession. I ignore every woman waiting and cut straight to the front. "Excuse me, I'm a doctor. I've been called out on an emergency. I need to pay for the damage."

The young woman can't be older than Briar. I hand her my paddle, ignore the comments from the line behind me, and turn and scan the area for Kate or, worse, my new dog and my date.

Dammit. I don't even know what to do with a dog.

"Wow." I look to the woman who is now staring wide-eyed at the tablet in front of her. "You're a big spender! That will be fifteen-thousand dollars."

My stomach roils as I hand over the credit card I keep only for emergencies, even though this does not qualify. She swipes and I sign— my gritty signature the only hint of the frayed nerves I'm barely clinging to.

"I need to leave. Please have the rescue organization contact me about the dog—"

She interrupts with a smile, reminding me of the hell I've just gotten myself into. "And your date."

"Yes, that too." I wave her off, stuffing my abused credit card back into my small clutch.

"Thank you for your donation," she calls but I'm already halfway out the door, my dupes not carrying me nearly as fast as I need.

I type out a quick text to Kate, lying to my only friend about my non-existent emergency, telling her to take the Uber, and that I'll call her tomorrow. She's used to me putting my patients first—it isn't the first time I've dumped her in the middle of a night out.

The cool night air fills my lungs as I move as quickly as I can around the corner of the building. I barely get ten feet into the dark alley before it happens. I drop to my hands and knees, ignoring the bite of rocks and wet, cold concrete on my bare skin. Appetizers, wine, and the protein shake I chugged on our way here haunts me as the contents of my stomach empty and splatter in front of me. Poor decisions chased by dry heaves are the very physical reminders of what I've done.

I tremble but it has nothing to do with the cool, moist air seeping through my barely-there cocktail dress. It offers no protection from the elements or my own self-absorbed and sick fascination.

I cough and spit as I drag myself to my feet. The buzz of my phone vibrates through my purse. I'm sure it's Kate, but I don't dare look. Instead, I move through the dark passageway between buildings, a place I have no business lurking by myself.

I need a taxi.

I need my treadmill.

I need a shower and definitely a toothbrush.
But what I need now more than anything…
Is a plan.

Three

Bad Memory

Brand

"YOU NEED TO be careful, son."

"I'm thirty-seven. Don't *son* me."

The sunrise is struggling to peek through the clouds—the weather shifted last night. A walk by the lake usually brings me clarity like nothing else, but today it's a pain in my ass since I'm stuck with a dog. The big spender ghosted both of us last night.

My fucking life.

"Ruff!"

The dog pulls at his leash and barks at fuck knows what—probably the wind. If only my problems could be as easy as his. I have no time for this. He bites at the leash, as chipper as a rodeo clown.

I learned my lesson last night when I cracked the door and he took off. I chased the little shithead all the way to the water and up the shore to the next property—a good thirty acres away. He was a muddy fucking mess. I had to put him in the tub and wrestle him clean. My master bathroom now looks like a warzone dusted in dirt, though it's seen worse.

A breeze mingles with the sounds of the city through the phone as my father does what he does best—*be* my father. "I'll *son* you as long as I'm stalking this earth. Your mother would be crushed if she heard you talking like that."

It's early and my dad is out for his morning walk to my mother's favorite coffee shop. He hasn't strayed from his morning ritual for as long as I can remember. He loves the city—Seattle has been his life since we moved here when I was two.

My parents give new meaning to a functioning-dysfunctional relationship. He makes life a soft bed of feathers for her and she pretends he doesn't keep a piece on the side—a piece that changes, sometimes with the seasons. Mom spends half her time back in New York with her family, spending every penny of his she can manage. It's the normal we're used to.

That is what love looks like, or what they've made it look like. I know firsthand true love is nothing more than a business and political arrangement. Where my father and I differ is he lucked out—my mother is a fucking saint and goes along with the charade. She knows what she signed on for. Nothing like the she-devil I was expected to love, honor, and cherish, 'til death do us part.

Or at least pretend to.

Catholics can be sticklers on that last point. Annulments might come easy when every priest and bishop in a four-state radius are in your back pocket.

But family on the other hand…

They take the *death do us part* so fucking seriously, you'll be fearing for your life if you even think about taking a break, let alone uttering the D-word.

Divorce is never an option.

A bell clanking against glass replaces honking traffic as my father continues to speak. "It's been six months. You've done your part—you've grieved publicly. You're pushing forty and your mother wants more grandchildren. Hell, God gave me one son and a slew of girls. Eventually you need to step up and do your part to carry on the name, but now is not that time. Things are hot."

"I know—"

"You think you know, but you're not in the day-to-day business," he bites. "That little show you took part in last night is getting chatter and the sun is barely up. Your mother doesn't get it and said just last night that she has a friend from church who has a granddaughter she wants to introduce you to—"

"No fucking way," I interrupt.

"I agree." He pulls the phone away and in the background I hear him say, "Good morning, beautiful. I'll take my normal order, but throw in a couple of those muffins for the love of my life." I sigh—same bullshit, different day. "Keep the change."

"I don't have time for this. I understand. Look, I've gotta be at the station before eight, but I got a call late last night. There's been a delay on the Realm project. An inspector blocked the permits."

"Fuck," he hisses. "Who the hell would do that?"

"I don't know. The money was paid—my source is clueless. I'll make some calls once I get through check-in at the station."

"Hang on, Brand. Thanks, love. See you tomorrow." The bell rings and sounds of the city streets replace tree-hugging, coffee-shop music. "Stay on it and let me know who's standing in our way. That building is already behind schedule."

I tug the leash to get the dog back up the hill to the house. "Will do."

"And call your mother. Break it to her gently that you're not ready."

"You don't need to worry about that. She's not setting me up with anyone."

"It won't be like this forever. When it's time, it'll be different. You've done your part for the family. We need this shit to settle with all parties— I'm as anxious as anyone for that to happen. I need the Vitale name to carry on and it's your responsibility."

"Ruff!"

"What the hell? Is that a dog?"

"Yeah." I sigh and wrestle it with the leash. "I'm dog sitting … sort of. I'll call you later."

"A dog might be good for you. Soften your image with the press—"

I've had about enough of him trying to manage my life crisis. "Later."

I double-time it up the stairs from the boat dock. The dog finally gets with the program and is on my heels—panting and yapping. When I get to the wall of windows that cover the back of my home looking over Gray Mountain Lake and we get inside, I unleash the beast. He goes straight to the food I had to stop and buy last night on the way home.

I pull up a number on my phone I've called at least ten times now—a number I never thought I'd be calling. But the chick shelled out fifteen Gs, you'd think she'd at least be interested to know where her damn dog is.

"You've reached Dr. Aria Dillon. Please leave your name, number, and a message. I'll return your call as soon as possible. If this is a patient and you're in need of immediate assistance, you know how to reach me."

After the tone, my words are not cordial or friendly. "Aria Dillon, you're a shit doctor if you can't check your messages. I've got your

21

damn dog and I'm not happy about it. I have a shift at the station in—"
I check my watch "—exactly forty minutes. The dog is coming with me
because I refuse to leave him in my house alone. He's a needy son-of-
a-bitch which means I'm the worst person you should leave him with.
I don't do high maintenance. I'll be at Station Six on the west side. If
your ass isn't there to claim him in the next twenty-four hours, I'll take
him to the pound myself."

I slam my cell on the marble and hear a whine.

"What?" I look at the mutt sitting on my boot, staring at me like I
didn't just threaten to take him to a place where rescuing is not the goal.
I shake my head. "You're at the end of a long line of pains in my ass,
you know that?"

He wags his tail. *"Ruff!"*

ARIA

"...I'LL TAKE HIM to the pound myself."

I squeeze the water from my hair and listen to the message again. I've
lost count how many times he's called and how many irate voicemails
I've collected.

After I taxied home last night, I hit my treadmill harder than normal. I
ran for over an hour straight until my body and mind were so exhausted,
I knew I'd sleep.

Turns out I stopped too soon. I was restless for most of the night, but
like I've done every Sunday morning since we moved to Washington, I
woke before dawn and was in the pool swimming laps by seven.

Being below the surface has a calming effect unlike anything else.
The quiet, the solace, and quite literally, the utter beauty of peace. I've
counted on its protection for as long as I can remember, drowning out
voices and demands and demons that have nipped at my heels for most
of my life.

Even if its protection only lasts as long as my held breath, I still crave
it.

If only it worked like it used to.

Today, being under water drowned out the messages from *him*.

So many messages.

When I ran out of the auction last night, I assumed I could collect
my expensive new dog from the rescue organization. The hero attached
to him certainly wasn't interested in being there and probably wanted

out of his end of the bargain. But when I started getting calls last night from an unknown number, I realized I should have signed over the small fortune, grabbed my new dog, and ran.

Now, I've got a bigger problem on my hands.

I have to see him outside of the auction, a place I would've had the security of the crowd.

If he takes my new dog to the pound, I don't know what I'll do, and that's if Briar doesn't kill me first.

He's at work. I might not have the buffer of a large crowd, but we won't be alone. Station Six isn't far from my neck of the woods. I'll get in, get out, and never see him again.

I'll go home, shower, then hit the pet store on my way, to get who knows what my new dog needs, and then face my consequences. I'll do it like any self-respecting adult would who considers herself a health professional. I need to suck it up and do the hard shit, as I tell my patients daily.

Maybe I'll luck out and he'll be putting out a fire somewhere, saving someone's life, or pulling a cat from a tree. Though, it sounds like he doesn't like animals, which I find hard to believe.

Who doesn't like dogs?

Well, other than my parents.

I push that thought away because I hope he's nothing like my parents. I've got less than twenty-four hours to get my dog. Then I can put this behind me once and for all.

Brand Vitale will soon be a bad memory that will fade into the landscape of my life, just like the rest of them.

Then I can get on with my fresh start with the dog that was never a part of my plan, but that's okay.

I think I'll name him Muppet. He looks like one.

Muppet and I will be just fine.

Four

HAPPY LIFE

Aria

*M*Y CREDIT CARD is officially maxed out. Unexpected pets are expensive.

I pull into an empty parking lot across from Station Six. My ten-year-old Merc is bursting at the seams with puppy food, toys, dog shampoo, treats, and everything else the kid at the pet store informed me my new dog needs to live a happy-go-lucky life. I, on the other hand, will not be happy or lucky while I'm paying off one bad decision after another. If this stuff doesn't provide Muppet with the lap of luxury, I give up. And since I never give up on anything, that's saying something.

The enormous garage doors are open and heroes are scrubbing trucks and restocking an ambulance. It looks like they just returned from something big. Some of them are wearing their gear. But unlike last night when their job was to seduce stupid, tipsy women such as myself, today they're dirty and covered in soot.

Which means I missed my window of opportunity. Had I not stopped for coffee on my way to the pet store, I might have missed them, grabbed Muppet, and been able to avoid another confrontation with Brand Vitale altogether.

I guess I could wait it out, hope for another fire, medical emergency, or a time-consuming highway pileup where they have to break out the jaws of life.

My phone vibrates.

A text.

Unknown Number – Are you going to come and get your dog or sit in your car across the street all day? I'll walk him to you if I have to.

My heart drops as I look toward the station. He appeared out of nowhere, standing at the curb across the street glaring at me.

Damn.

I hold his glare as I flip off the engine and climb out of my car. Waiting for traffic to clear, it's all I can do to stand tall and not let it show how much the man intimidates me. People take advantage of weaknesses. I should know, my father has lived his life doing just that to everyone around him.

Right now, I need to hide every simmering emotion, so I hold my head high as I make my way across the busy street.

Get the dog, get out. Simple, quick, easy. This will all be over in no time.

My hair flutters as a truck rumbles past. Every step I take closes the gap between me and Brand. With each of those steps, it's harder and harder to keep my mask of confidence secured in place.

His arms cross and eyes narrow as I join him on the sidewalk. He's wearing his uniform pants again, but today they're dirty and he smells like a bonfire.

Oddly, it doesn't smell bad, but rather elevates his masculinity to levels I've never encountered. I'm wearing my old-school Adidas instead of heels. He's got at least six inches on me and I'm not a short woman.

His jaw tenses before he snaps, "Not sure how you missed the memo, but when you bid on a dog, you actually take that dog home with you."

I hitch my purse up my shoulder. "I had an emergency."

"That's what they told me." He motions to the fire station behind him. "I have a job, too, and it always involves emergencies. I do not have the time, patience, or inclination to babysit your dog."

"Well, I'm here now. Where's Muppet?"

His head tips. "Muppet?"

"Yes, Muppet. The dog." I exhale. "My dog. If you point the way, he and I will be out of your hair and you can tend to all your emergencies."

Brand shifts his weight and analyzes me, but not as if he likes what he sees. I shiver as he studies me like a complicated riddle, one he doesn't care what the solution might be. "You just want the dog."

I roll my lips in to wet them and sharpen my tongue—I need to be done with this. "Yes. I paid handsomely for him, after all."

"About that, why the hell would you pay that much for a dog?"

I shrug. "Muppet and I had a moment. It was short, but we bonded. I didn't want to see him go to anyone else. He belongs with me."

"That's it?" he demands.

I ignore his question. "Where is my dog?"

He lifts his chin. "In the station. I'll take you to him as soon as you answer my question. What are you after besides the dog?"

"Why would I be after anything else?" With blank eyes and a quick shake of my head, I move around him on the sidewalk. "Never mind. I'll find him myself. How many dogs can there be in one fire station? Unless you're stereotypical and have a dalmatian."

Boots clomp behind me in unison with the swishing of his bulky pants. I ignore it all and stalk straight to the front door. I find myself in the middle of a reception area with no one in sight.

"Aria," Brand growls, but I don't look back. A door marked *Authorized Personnel Only* stands in front of me.

Well. Desperate times call for desperate measures.

I really need to quit telling myself that.

I push through the door even though I'm not authorized and enter a large room filled with sofas and chairs arranged for prime viewing of an enormous TV mounted on the old brick wall. Beyond is a kitchen with miles of counter space and a huge range that looks like it should be in an old diner instead of a firehouse. Everything is clean and tidy even though it is ancient.

"Can I help you?"

I look to my left and another firefighter is standing in the doorway to the bays dressed exactly like Brand. "I'm here for my dog from the auction last night. Brown, curly, friendly. Do you know where he might be?"

A hand wraps around my bicep and my face instantly warms when Brand butts in. "I'm taking care of this."

"You're the big spender?" The firefighter breaks into a grin. "I hope Vitale's worth it."

I try to pull my arm out of Brand's grip, but he's having none of it. "Shut your trap, Moreland."

Moreland does not shut his trap, and the grip on my arm tightens. "Brand better up his game for the price you paid."

I shake my head. "I just want the dog. I'm happy to skip the date—"

"Come on," Brand interrupts. "The shithead is in the laundry room. I had to lock him up when we got a call."

I don't have a chance to convince Moreland or Brand of anything, but I do manage to twist my arm from Brand's hold and turn to glare at him as he pushes me through the massive space to another set of doors.

"What is your problem?" I hiss.

A deep voice rumbles so close to my ear, a chill slithers down my spine. "Aside from the auction, your dog, and you ignoring my calls, my list of problems is long and varied. Don't piss me off any more than you already have, Ms. Dillon."

I don't dare correct him, even though I worked damn hard for the title of *doctor*.

With one hand plastered to the small of my back pushing me forward, he reaches around and throws another door open. In the middle of a room lined with washers and dryers, my new long-term, spur-of-the-moment commitment is beside himself with excitement, despite the fact he's tethered to a leash. He's also sitting in a puddle since his water dish is tumbled next to him upside down.

I know nothing about dogs and even less about puppies, but that isn't his fault. I silently apologize to him for the long hours I work and hope that his new Aunt Briar will make up for my shitty life choices.

I go to him instantly. Thank goodness he's just as excited to see me as he was last night and doesn't understand that I actually ghosted him. "Hey, buddy. I'm here to take you home."

He barks.

Brand grunts.

And I'm reminded of my goal—get the dog and run away.

I untie his leash. "Let's go. I don't have a yard but I'm working on it. I'll do my best, I promise."

"He's a runner—I was cursed with the experience last night when you skipped out on him. And he likes mud. My bathroom will never be the same."

I stand and square my shoulders. "I appreciate you taking care of him."

Brand's broad frame fills my only escape route and the need to put this behind me, once and for all, increases. I ignore Muppet's excitement because the hero's dark eyes pierce me. "We have another issue to address."

I jut my chin to the doorway he's standing in, trapping me in the laundry room. I'm in varied levels of hell. "I came to collect my dog so he and I can start bonding. That's it. I know you wanted no part of the auction—you spelled that out quite clearly last night. Consider yourself off the hook. I'm not dating right now anyway—I don't have the time or the energy for anyone."

"I don't need to be let off the hook," he bites. "I wasn't happy to be there but that doesn't mean I'm not going to follow through. I never hedge on a commitment."

"Really, it's okay."

His dark eyes narrow. "It's not."

"But it is." Muppet's wet paws are seeping through my jeans since he continues jumping on me and I regret already swimming laps for an hour this morning because I think I'm going to have to start running with my new dog to tire him out. I take a deep breath and unglue my feet from the floor. "Excuse me."

Brand proves once again he doesn't care about manners or social cues because he doesn't budge. His arms drop to his sides and I wonder if he's fisting his hands because his biceps flex. I focus on his sharp eyes when he bites, "You don't know me, Aria Dillon."

Hmm. I disagree, but will never express that aloud. As in never ever, for the rest of my days walking the earth. "No, I don't. I'm also too busy to know you. See, I don't usually attend auctions or any other type of social events because, as I said last night, I work a ridiculous number of hours building my practice. The way I see it, I did you a favor. You don't have to go on an absurd, fake date, and I get the dog. Win-win and I'm the one who paid for it. Either thank me and move out of the way, or just move out of the way so I can get on with my Sunday. It's my only day off and I'd like to enjoy the rest of it with Muppet."

"Ruff!"

Feeling more powerful than I have in a long time, I hike a brow and smile. "See? He already knows his name. Get out of my way, Mr. Vitale."

Despite the small space separating us, he breaks eye contact and examines my body. This is surprising for so many reasons. He didn't do this last night when my dress screamed *sex me up*, but now, while in jeans and a hoodie, he takes the time to look.

"For someone who wanted no part of the auction, you sure are dragging this out," I add.

He shakes his head slowly before drawing his gaze back, lingering on my lips before finally making eye contact.

Deliberate.

Scrutinizing.

And so very, very depraved.

For the first time, I witness a smile from Brand Vitale. It's small but telling. Instead of feeling warmth, the way a human normally would from such a gesture, the small act of his lips tipping on each side chills my blood.

He lowers his voice. "I had a feeling you'd be interesting."

"I'm really not."

"Ruff!"

I've had enough. Allowing him to analyze me will make me go mad. Damn my curiosity.

I tighten Muppet's leash in one hand and push my hero out of the way with the other. Brand allows it and shifts. It doesn't matter how much I workout, I'd never be able to move a mass like his on my own.

He follows as I escape.

I don't look back. Not when I pass Moreland, make my way back through the empty reception area, out the door, and across the street. I ignore him the entire time despite knowing he's still watching my every move.

"Up in the car, buddy." Muppet jumps into the front seat, not at all concerned by who I am or where his journey will take him next. I could be a dog-napper for all he knows.

I don't look back until I'm pulling out of the parking lot. There he is, Brand Vitale, standing in the middle of the wide drive, his heavy stare glued on me.

I steal one last peek before I whisper for only Muppet to hear, "I hope you have a happy life."

Brand keeps staring.

"Or, happier."

Traffic clears and I turn to leave.

I'm done.

And I don't look back.

Five

SHRINK THE SHRINK

Aria

NO SOONER DO Muppet and I get to my apartment, my phone vibrates. I unhook his leash and he takes off to explore his new home, as small as it may be.

Unknown – I've decided you're going to get your fifteen Gs worth. Be ready tomorrow night, eight sharp. That'll give you time to work your long hours.

My heart spasms.

No!

Me – No.

Unknown – Yes. And be ready on time. I don't like to wait.

Shit. For once, I'm at a loss for words.

Me – No.

Unknown – Eight. Sharp.

Me – No. And I'm not going to tell you where I live.

Unknown – Finding you will be the easiest thing I've ever done. And wear a dress.

My breathing shallows.

Unknown – A dress as short as the one you wore last night.

I swallow over the bile creeping up my throat.

Bubbles appear and disappear on the screen.

Then, nothing.

My ass falls to my sofa and Muppet jumps in my lap, his tongue connecting with every inch of my face.

"What did I get us into?" I ask him, scratching and petting until he settles into my lap.

I look back to my phone and select a different text string. One I haven't needed in at least a couple months.

Me – Do you have any time tomorrow? I'll take anything you've got. I'll switch my patients around if I need to.

It doesn't matter how long it's been since we've spoken. He's just like me and responds to his patients immediately.

Russ – My schedule is full and sounds like yours is too. Can you do Tuesday at lunch?

Me – Yes. Thank you.

Russ – See you then.

I lean back, close my eyes, and focus on deep, even breaths.

When I get to the point I need someone to shrink the shrink, I know I'm in trouble.

Six

GASLIGHT

Aria

MY TIME IS split between Redmond Mental Health Center and my new private practice.

The center keeps me booked thirty hours a week. My five-year plan is to have my private practice going full-time, so I can quit the center. Seeing patients in my private office is more beneficial to everyone. I like working one-on-one. Sure, group sessions have their place—hell, I was in group therapy as a patient back when Briar was going through cancer treatments. There's comfort knowing you're not the only one living through your season of hell.

But private practice is my end goal. I rented a two-room unit the moment Briar and I rolled into town. It has a small reception area and an office where I get to do what I love most—help people help themselves.

My office is a beautiful space.

Serene, neutral, welcoming, comfortable. It has to be. My patients sit here for an hour at a time—that is if they're not pacing or circling the caramel-colored leather sofa. I always sit in the same linen chair. The walls are a warm white, the window coverings are light and airy, and I put great thought into every accessory. It's an extension of me and I want my patients to be comfortable in every way—physically and emotionally.

"You sound like you're doubting your own feelings, Marin."

Marin's husband, Eric, runs a hand down his face before expelling the largest sigh I've ever heard from him. And that's saying something.

She dabs one eye as she struggles to hold back her tears. "There are days I wonder if this is all my fault."

"Here we go again," Eric mutters.

I focus on Marin. "In what way is Eric having an affair with his co-worker your fault?"

"Are you fucking serious?" Eric clips. "I knew this was a bad idea. I'm paying you to take sides now?"

"I'm not taking sides, Eric. I'm simply stating the facts and want to know why Marin is owning responsibility for your actions."

Marin lets out a small sob. "I wasn't giving him the attention he needed. I'm busy with work and the kids and the house. It's a lot but I could've tried harder."

"This is new." I jot this in my notes for later. "You've been coming to me individually and as a couple for over a month now and this is the first time you've expressed this. What's changed?"

Patients speak candidly when alone, but Marin is tense when they're here as a couple. Eric has been on my schedule twice and has canceled both times because of work, yet he's the one who instigated couples counseling as a last resort.

"Nothing's changed," Eric answers for her, which has become a trend in our sessions. "Same shit, day in and day out. If she's not with the kids, she's on her phone for work. If it's not that, she's exhausted and busting my ass because I don't help around the house. I told her we could bring someone in to clean, but I'm paying for this." He lifts his chin toward me and seals it with a deadly glare. "Waste of time and money."

"This," I motion to myself, "was your idea, Eric. I'd like to stay on topic as to why Marin is bearing the weight of your infidelity."

Marin shakes her head and sniffs. "Exactly what he said."

Seems there is some gaslighting going on at home. It's not professional to think of your patient as an asshole.

But, asshole.

I nod. "Have you been doing the exercises I recommended? Pinpointing your stress triggers? Choosing one night to unplug everything after the kids go to bed to focus on each other?"

Marin shakes her head and looks away.

"See?" Eric motions to his wife. "I just want my life back."

"You have a life, Eric. We just need to find a way for everyone to find happiness in this season."

"We unplugged last week," Marin admits. "Or we tried to. It ended in a fight like it always does."

I make another note. "What did you fight about?"

Marin looks to her husband, but he doesn't offer an answer. When she does speak, it's hesitant. "Her."

"*Her*," I repeat and tap the end of my pen on my notebook. "What about her?"

"He was with her," Marin states on a hiccupped sob. "Again."

Eric doesn't look contrite when I ask, "You were unfaithful again?"

He throws his arms out. "I just want my life back. A normal life."

"You mean sex," I state.

"Yes." He raises his voice. "And adult conversation that isn't about daycare or the electric bill!"

"So you want to be a teenager?" I challenge, because it's time. If I don't, there won't be progress, whatever that progress may look like. The three of us have been treading water far too long.

Marin stands and walks to the window.

"Fuck you," he growls, glaring at me.

There are days I think my father prepared me for this job more than my Harvard education, because I have no problem holding his angry stare. "I'm trying to get to the bottom of what you want out of life. Because you continue to be unfaithful, and your wife seems to think it's her fault."

Marin turns to me and is all-out crying now. "Please stop."

I look at the clock on the wall next to the window. "No need to stop now. We still have twenty minutes." I turn my focus back to Eric. "When was your latest encounter?"

He tips his head. "I don't have to tell you shit."

"Then why are you here?"

He shrugs and stays silent. I know what he's doing. He's going through the motions, doing all the right things. When he gets the divorce he wants, he can prove on paper this was his idea and how he tried.

"You agreed to stop seeing her while you and Marin were in therapy. I have the contract you both signed during our first session."

"Your bullshit contract is about as official as the stop sign in a Target parking lot, and you know it."

Marin continues to cry.

"Then why did you sign it?" I ask. "You don't seem to be the type of person who agrees to *bullshit*, as you say."

His glare darkens.

"Why did you go back to your mistress?" I press.

"You really want to know?" he grits, turning a deep shade of crimson.

Unlike his, my expression remains stoic. "I do."

Without looking away, he stands and motions to Marin. "Because she deserves it. For checking out. For being a cold bitch. For ignoring me. I'm not sticking around for it." He raises his voice and points at me, then Marin. "So fuck you, fuck your therapy, and fuck her too. I'm over this shit."

He stalks out and slams the door in his wake.

Marin turns back to the window and whimpers into her tissue.

I give her a moment before asking, "Do you feel unsafe at home? Physically unsafe?"

She hesitates before shaking her head.

"Your children?" I add. "Marin, this is important. Has he threatened you or your children? First and foremost, I need to know you're physically okay. If your home is not a safe place, I can help you and the children. I can do that right now."

She turns and sighs—her makeup smeared and ruined—and shakes her head. "He's never laid a hand on us."

"Do you think he would?"

She shrugs but shakes her head. "I don't think so."

"He's turning this on you. Making you feel responsible for his adultery. No one is pushed into having an affair. That is one-hundred percent his responsibility."

She sits again and stares at her mangled tissue.

"Marin," I call for her. She finally musters the courage to look at me. "It's not your fault."

She nods. It's small, and I doubt she believes it.

"Do you need a ride home?" I ask.

She starts crying again, and I take that as a yes.

I go to my desk to retrieve my phone from the drawer and search for my Uber app. "I'll get you a ride, but we need to meet again soon. Call or text anytime. I can step in at a moment's notice. Before you leave, we need to establish a code if you need immediate help."

They're my last session but I can't offer her a ride. Going to a patient's home is a bad idea. Plus, there's my looming date I never agreed to. *Eight o'clock sharp* has been nagging at the back of my mind all day. It will be here before I know it.

Briar was supposed to stop by and walk Muppet for me today. I bet my new dog is going to ditch me to go live with his new aunt. I really need to figure out a way to balance my life. Maybe I can start dropping him off with Briar before work a couple days a week when I have evening appointments. She can be my doggie daycare and take him to work with her.

First, I need to update my patient files while my day is fresh in my mind. Maybe I'll hide out in my bedroom and pray Brand Vitale can't manage what he said would be easy.

Find me.

Seven

LIGHT HIS NIGHT ON FIRE

Brand

D R. ARIA LAKE Dillon.

Did her undergrad at Stanford on a swimming scholarship. She even went to the Olympic Trials and failed to make the team by the literal skin of her teeth—three hundredths of a second, to be exact.

Earned her Ph.D. in clinical psychology from Harvard.

One year in practice.

Drowning in student loans because, from the look of her grades, she was smart, but not the cream of the crop which is what it takes to land a Harvard scholarship.

Daughter of the infamous Miami-based plastic surgeon, Dr. Astor Dillon. Old Astor looks like he's worth a fucking mint. I'd wonder why she'd be struggling financially if it weren't so clear she's estranged from her parents. I didn't need to dig deep to figure this out, a blind man could see it in full color.

Aria's mom is deceased after losing her fight with a rare cancer. It seems prior to biting it, Bette Dillon was known to make a hobby of sampling the best prescription drugs she could get her hands on and washed that shit down with top-shelf vodka. When you're married to millions, that's an easy rabbit hole to dive into.

Aria moved here a year ago with her sister, Briar. Unlike the highly-educated psychologist, the younger Dillon has no record of higher education. Despite living paycheck to paycheck, the hot doctor is a generous donor to Redmond Rescue and the new owner of the little shithead who muddied my house.

Interesting how I know everything about her and still feel like I know nothing. What I do know about Aria Dillon is the shit I don't care about. I want to know what makes her tick. What motivates her. Why she shelled out money for a dog she could've paid a small fee for at the pound, because she sure as hell doesn't want anything to do with me.

And I don't like that.

I jog the three flights of stairs to her barely-less-than-shitty apartment and rap on the door.

Shithead starts barking, but that's it.

I knock harder.

No one. Only a dog who wants out as much as I want in.

Hell yeah, I want in.

Aria might have started this by bidding on me, but I'm damn well going to finish it. The moment she laid a hand on me to push me aside and marched her sweet ass out of the station, I made a decision. The timing isn't great. Even I can't deny it and don't need my father to remind me of the flames nipping at my back. I feel the heat.

But the good doctor opened a door. I'm not only going to walk through it, I'll make the thing mine and lock it behind me until I get what I want out of her.

I knock again. "Aria—"

"You're early."

I turn, her voice hitting me from behind. She's trudging up the steps weighed down with approximately half-a-million bags.

I frown. "I told you eight."

She pushes by me to get to her door and I'm reminded of her doing the same thing at the station yesterday. "You can *tell* all you want, Brand, it doesn't mean your every wish is going to come true. It's been a long day and I had files to update while details were fresh in my head."

I take her in from top to bottom. Even dressed for business, I wonder if her patients fantasize about fucking her, because I know I would if she were my doctor. Her sweater is skin tight and her pants might be wide-legged, but they're like a second skin on her ass. Every curve and swell is on display. My need for therapy just reached epic proportions. "Get changed and we'll go."

She stabs a key in the door handle and twists. "I told you, you're off the hook. I'm tired and have to be out the door before the sun rises. I can't stress enough, you're off the hook from your date duty."

She opens the door carefully and pushes the jumping bean of a dog back. I wonder if he's run on her too. She deserves the experience after ditching us after the auction.

I don't give her the chance to shut the door in my face or tell me to get lost again. I move in and slam it behind me. She drops her bags to the floor and her ass follows. I cringe as the dog attacks her face.

"You weren't invited in," she mutters, trying to not be tongued by a canine.

I cross my arms. "You two look like you're going to live happily ever after. My condolences."

She pushes him away from her face and flips him to his back in her lap. He pants happily as she scratches his belly. "You don't like dogs?"

"I don't have the patience for anything that needs my time right now. Puppies are a time suck I refuse to invest in."

She continues to scratch her dog as she studies me. Or, who the fuck knows, maybe psychoanalyzing me.

"Get changed," I repeat. "We can't be late."

She kisses the shithead on top of his head and reaches for a ball, tossing it down the short hall of her apartment. He scrambles after it and Aria climbs to her feet. "I'm not going anywhere, and you're leaving. I'm hungry, exhausted, and need to call my sister." The dog returns and drops the ball at her feet. "And I need to walk Muppet."

I can't believe I offer, but there's no way I'm leaving. "I'll walk him. Get changed and call your sister. We have a reservation, and someone did me a favor to get it last minute. We can't no-show."

I turn and nab the leash off the knob. She starts to argue, but I hold my hand up. "It's just food, Aria. You paid fifteen grand, the least I can do is feed you one meal."

I'm not used to being around a woman who doesn't want something from me and I'm really not used to anyone letting me off the hook for something I owe them. I'm a Vitale—there are no favors in my world. Everything has a price tag.

"Get a move on. We're already late." I hook the leash on the dog and we're out the door before she can argue further.

There's one other thing about being a Vitale—we always get what we want and I'm no exception.

ARIA

"YOU'RE TELLING ME you paid fifteen thousand dollars—money you do not have—for a dog I could have gotten you for free since I work at the rescue? And now you don't want to go on the date that comes with the dog? I thought I was the fucked-up one, Aria. What the hell's wrong with you?"

I yank a midnight-blue dress out of my closet. It's classic enough that it's not out of style even though I've always hated it. The last time I wore it was when Dad forced me to attend a public event with him when Mom was too smashed to scrape herself off the floor. The dress already has bad juju. A stressful night out with Brand Vitale and it might land in the dumpster.

"You're not fucked up. Stop talking about yourself like that. I explained what it does to your mind and the toll it takes on your body. Speak positively about yourself. You're perfect the way you are."

"I'm positive you should go out to a perfect dinner. You won't see many of those in your near future now that you have to pay off your expensive doodle. Maybe you'll luck out and it'll involve salsa."

I put her on speaker, set the phone by the sink, and yank the dress over my head. "I'm going, okay? I just need a little ... I don't know. Pep talk?"

"The person who hates talking on the phone and has all the pep of an emo cheerleader?" Briar deadpans, but then again she pretty much deadpans everything. "You called me for a pep talk?"

"You're my person. I have no one else to encourage me."

"Go get 'em, Aria. You're the shit, Aria. If you can't do *him*, no one can, Aria. Light his night on fire." She puts so little effort into it, I even hear her flipping the channels in the background.

I grab my mascara out of my drawer because he'll be back any moment. "Thanks. You're a lot of help."

"You should do a deep-breathing exercise. Picture yourself being a strong woman at dinner. Make a list of all the ways you're awesome."

She's mocking me.

"I hate you," I lie.

"Then it really sucks for you that I'm your person."

"It doesn't suck." I twist my mascara shut, toss it on the counter, and stare at myself in the mirror. "Because I love you ... even if you're a smartass."

"Let me pick Muppet up in the morning. I can take him to work to play with the other dogs."

I'm not surprised she dodges all talk of emotions, but me voicing them was enough of a push so I let her change the subject. "Really? That would be great. I hate that he's alone all day. I'll grab him on my way home."

"I'd say you could repay me by taking me out for Mexican, but thanks to your expensive pup purchase, I think you only have the budget for Taco Bell."

"And only if they have a dollar menu."

"Seriously, though. Are you gonna be okay? Between loans and starting the practice ... I can give you some money."

That surprises me. We never talk finances, but only because we have none to talk about. Before I can think twice, I ask, "How do you have extra money to lend?"

She laughs, but it comes out forced and fake. "I'm a hermit who hates shopping."

I drop the subject and sigh. Brand will be back any minute. "I'll be fine. You know, eventually."

I hope, anyway.

"Let me know if that changes. I don't want you to stress when I can help." Reaching her limit of seriousness, Briar jokes, "Just don't drop ten K on a parakeet."

The door to my apartment slams. I look back to myself in the mirror and curse the consequences I'm about to endure. "I have to go. Wish me luck."

"It's dinner. You don't need luck. But if you happen to lose your panties on the way home, then good for you."

I flip off the bathroom light. "See you in the morning. Love you and I know you love me back."

"Later."

I pull in a big breath because never, ever, ever, ever, did I think I'd be going somewhere with none other than Brand Vitale.

One dinner. That's it. I can do this.

"Aria!" he bellows.

Shit.

Shit, shit, shit.

Eight

TAILGATE

Brand

I DRAG MY middle finger around the rim of my water glass and stare as she finishes her last bite of cheesecake.

For someone who didn't want to go on the date she paid a pretty penny for, the woman sure took advantage of dinner.

Besides her thanking me when I opened a door for her, ordering her dinner, and asking me to pass the bread, Aria hasn't uttered a word.

Not one fucking word. And we drove all the way to Seattle.

She wipes each corner of her plump, blush lips—lips I've studied more intently than I did her background.

Chewing. Pursing. Licking.

When she paid enough attention to find me watching her, she'd pulled that bottom lip between her teeth before focusing back on her medium-rare filet. Props to her, she even ordered the ten ounce.

And a loaded potato, burgundy mushrooms, oysters on the half-shell, and a Caesar salad.

Seems she's set on getting her fifteen grand worth out of our date after all.

Interesting.

I like a woman who doesn't starve herself.

She clears her throat. "That was good."

I hike a brow. "Good?"

"Very good." She checks the time on her phone again for the millionth time since we left her apartment.

"I'm sure my godparents will be pleased to hear it."

"Godparents?"

"Vinny and Marie. They own the place." I throw my hand out to the crowded restaurant they opened before I was born. "It's a Seattle hot spot and difficult to get a table."

"I've never been here. I appreciate you following through on your end of the bargain. Can we go now?"

"No."

She crosses her arms under her tits. It's not lost on me from studying her all night, she's in good shape. Graduate school, a doctoral program, and working sixty hours a week hasn't made her soft. The woman does not spend her extra time at the mall or getting her nails done. I find that refreshing since every woman in my life—down to my own mother and sisters—do just that.

"What do you mean, no?"

"You're a therapist."

Her blue eyes narrow. "Psychologist."

I nod once. "What made you want to become a *psychologist?*"

Instead of asking how I know what I know, she proves she's got a set of lady balls. "I'm fascinated by what drives people. More specifically, what inhibits them. I want to help people help themselves and do it without the use of medications, if at all possible."

I throw my napkin on the table and lean back in my chair. "Interesting."

"Is it?"

"*You're* interesting," I specify.

"I work, sleep, work some more, and swim and run when I can squeeze it in. And I'm now a dog owner. I'm the least interesting person I know."

"Why Redmond?"

"It's the best of city and nature combined."

"A lot of places offer that," I point out. "Which makes me wonder further, why Redmond?"

She lifts her wine glass to her mouth and I watch the last drop disappear between her lips, thinking of other things I'd enjoy her lapping up. She's had two glasses, and since every employee in this restaurant knows who I am, like always, the pours were heavy-handed and free, just as the meal will be. My godparents don't fuck around when it comes to taking care of family.

Her damn tongue sneaks out to lick her lips again as she slides her glass to the middle of the table. "Redmond Mental Health Center made me the best offer. It included partial student loan forgiveness when I reach my five-year commitment. It won't come close to paying it all off, but I need all the help I can get. I'm ready to go."

"I'm not."

"I want to go home, Brand. If I need to call an Uber, I will."

"For someone who talks for a living, you sure are short on words," I note.

"My job is to get other people to talk," she points out.

"Yet, you haven't tried to get me to talk at all."

"You're not my patient."

I shrug. "Maybe I should make an appointment. I'd like to know what you think about my deep-seated issues."

Calm, collected, and poised, she studies me. Not even the two heavy glasses of cab seem to have loosened her. "You're irritable, pushy, and closed tighter than a tomb. I have no doubt you have issues, but I do not take on friends or acquaintances as patients. Should you need a reference, I'll be glad to help."

"I want you."

Her nostrils barely flare and her full, firm tits rise a centimeter with her intake of air. Other than that, stoic.

And sexy as fuck.

Our server appears. "Can I get you anything else, Mr. Vitale?"

I raise a brow to Aria and she shakes her head.

"We're good. Tell Vinny it was perfect, just like always."

He nods and disappears, leaving me to the conundrum that is Aria. I've never seen a woman as a challenge … I think I could get off on it.

And her.

I turn my focus back to the first dinner date I've had in forever. "There's something about you. You're confident in your skin. You're straightforward. You don't rattle off bullshit conversation just to fill space, which makes every single word you utter mean something. Come to think of it, I've never clung to anyone's words like I have yours, Aria. Ever."

She's as cool as the nip in the crisp fall air. "Take my word for it, those are not the qualities to look for in a doctor. But they are qualities of a shitty date, which doesn't say much about you."

"See there? I'm finding you more tempting than the top-of-the-line Porterhouse I just inhaled." I lean forward. "Let's play the hypothetical game. If I were your patient, I'd tell you how I haven't slept with a woman in over a year. And despite being a single man for the last six months, the last woman I was with was not my wife. I'd also tell you I hadn't fucked my wife for so long, I've lost count of how many years it's been. As a psychologist, what would you say about that?"

She chews on the inside of her lip before answering, "I'd say you should've invested in some marriage counseling a long time ago."

"That ship has sailed. I'm not married anymore."

"That's good," she retorts. "Since you auctioned yourself off and insisted on taking me to dinner. I wouldn't be very happy if you were still married."

I lean back in my chair. "Sarcasm doesn't look nearly as good on you as that tight-ass dress and those fuck-me heels."

"I guess that's why I'm the psychologist and you're the hero. You don't know the difference between sarcasm and flat-out honesty. Psychologists are rarely sarcastic. Stay in your lane, Brand."

I let my lips tip on one side. "I think I'd very much like to be in your lane, Aria. Heed my warning, I tailgate."

"Are you threatening me?"

I shake my head. "Informing you. I don't play games. Everyone in my life knows exactly where they stand with me."

"Ask for the check. I'm ready to go home," she demands.

I stand and pull out my wallet. After tossing three one-hundred-dollar bills on the table for the tip, I hold my arm out. "There's no check. But I will take you home now."

She hesitates and I wonder what she's going to do. If she were any other woman, she'd either jump my bones, order an Uber, or dial nine-one-one because I've rattled her to the core. She should pick the latter, but I'm not going to tell her that.

Instead, the good doctor stands, collects her wrap, and allows me to lead her out of the restaurant with my hand firmly glued to the small of her back—my fingertips flirting with the swell of her ass. Even though every single eye in the place is on us, she isn't fazed, holding her head as high as a beautiful thoroughbred.

But given her bio, she's been trained as one, which is exactly what I need.

ARIA

OF COURSE HE couldn't just take me to the Olive Garden down the street.

No, the man drove me all the way to Seattle.

On the ride back, Brand allows us to fall into the awkward silence I initiated when we left for my paid date hours before. I want to thank him in the parking lot and put this whole thing behind me, but he insists on walking me to my door like a proper hero. I climb the three flights of stairs as fast as I can in my heels. I hear him casually keep up with me, taking two stairs at a time for every one of mine.

I'm ready to shut Brand Vitale out of my life, once and for all, by slamming the door in his face. My key is in the lock and the knob is half turned, when he snakes an arm around me and wraps his big hand over mine.

The heat of his body presses into me and I'm forced to fight off the chill that runs over my skin. His other arm wraps around my midriff and his lips hit my ear through the blanket of my hair.

"The only thing that kept me from touching you at dinner was the fact we were in public, and despite my age, my godmother would still whack me over the head for being brazen in her restaurant." His hold tightens under my breasts. "I liked watching you eat."

My hand squeezes the doorknob in unison with my thighs. I don't dare move for fear my body will defy and humiliate me. "That's odd."

He shifts and his every muscle that touches me tightens. "Do psychologists often call people odd to their faces?"

I pull in a deep breath and try to ignore his erect cock pressed to the top of my ass through his trousers and my dress. "Sometimes."

"That surprises me." He drags the tip of his nose over the curve of my ear. "But what do I know? I've never been in therapy."

"I call it as I see it."

"Hmm. Is this more normal?" He stresses the word as he presses his hips into me, the underside of his cock pressed between my ass cheeks. "I liked sharing a meal with you and I want to do it again soon."

"There's no such thing as normal," I mutter through a shaky breath. Brand Vitale has broken through my shield—the one I use so often to prove to the rest of the world how normal I am, even if I am secretly a fraud.

I'm surrounded by the grumpy hero—a beast of a man who seems to get whatever he wants, eats five-star meals for free, and tips three-hundred dollars like it's no big deal. My father doesn't even do that. But, then again, he's an asshole.

The jury is still out on Brand. He has asshole qualities, but to reach the level of my father is a whole other beast.

His tone rumbles down my spine that would be directly connected to his cock if it weren't for our clothes. "That's good, because I'm anything but normal."

I swallow over the lump in my throat. "It doesn't take a psychologist to figure that out. Don't bother wasting your money on therapy."

A smile forms against the skin below my ear as he inhales. I have a feeling a smile from Brand is so rare, I'm sorry I don't get to see it. "Thanks for the tip."

He presses his hips into me again. Hmm ... tip. I'm too busy struggling to stay vertical to form an answer.

"I'll call you tomorrow."

"Don't," I plead.

"Why not?"

"I don't want you to."

His arm around my midriff shifts and he brushes the underside of my breasts with his thumb. "Your body disagrees."

"My body doesn't know what it's talking about."

He ignores me. "Tomorrow."

Then he leans in and presses his lips to my jugular and leaves them there. I gasp and I'm sure he can feel my pulse racing. He is a paramedic, after all. Though, I doubt they're taught how to take someone's pulse with only their lips.

I force my brain to crank over and do something. "Thanks for dinner. Or, you know, tipping so generously."

"Watching you eat was a sexual experience I'm looking forward to again."

"Brand," I beg.

"Aria," he challenges.

My body tenses. "You seem nice enough now that you've gotten over your initial irritability. I hope you have a nice life."

"My life has been a pain in the ass recently, but things are looking up now that I'm focused on my mental health. I have high hopes, thanks to my new psychologist."

Shit. I need to put an end to this. Once and for all.

"Goodbye, Brand."

Grabbing his splayed hand below my breasts, I unglue him from my body. It takes all my energy to turn the knob and push my door open, but I manage, and don't look back.

Muppet attacks me, but I push him back and slam the door in Brand's face, fumbling with both flimsy locks that wouldn't deter a mouse if it wanted in badly enough.

I just hope he's smart and doesn't follow through. Because, after tonight, I have no doubt what Brand wants, Brand gets.

Kicking my shoes off, I silently pad through my apartment to my bedroom with Muppet on my heels. I lock us in, putting one more barrier between me and the man I never should've provoked.

Muppet digs in his dog bed and starts turning circles.

I fall to my mattress and cross my thighs over my drenched thong. I haven't felt this way in … in …

I don't know when.

Ever?

I try to calm my heart, but the pulse between my legs refuses to cooperate.

Brand Vitale is a force. I had a feeling he might be after he barked his first word to me at the auction. He's the type of intensity I don't need in my life right now.

But his eyes.

His body.

His *hands*.

The way he surrounded me just moments ago almost made the rest of the world melt away. No one has ever come close to doing that for me. It was freeing, and had I not untangled myself from his touch when I did, I might've let him have his way with me…

Even yank my dress to my waist and do whatever he wanted right in the breezeway for all my creepy neighbors to see. How can being confined and utterly surrounded by an almost stranger feel so liberating?

Lord knows, the world is heavier than an anvil bearing down on my shoulders right now. I could use the escape.

I open my eyes and stare at the cracked ceiling of my bedroom as my body wars with my head.

The last thing I need is a fantasy mingling with a dreary reality.

But this pulse…

I raise my feet to the bed and allow my knees to fall apart. I rip my thong to the side and groan as I imagine my fingers are his. My other hand mauls my breast the way his was itching to—I could sense it.

I imagine his dark eyes studying me, turning molten as he focuses between my legs. My clit—needy and swollen and begging him for more.

My ears tunnel and I barely hear myself gasp, my fingers moving relentlessly, wishing they were his. That the cock he just teased me with was bare, hard, and ready to pound into me until I was so sore, I couldn't walk.

I come.

For the first time in a long time.

And definitely for the first time fantasizing about someone.

Without taking my hand from between my legs, I roll to my side.

As my heart calms, I realize what I've done.

"Damn, Aria," I admit to no one but myself and Muppet. "How many lines are you going to cross before this explodes in your face?"

JUGGLING MY BAGS and largest travel mug, I trudge down the stairs to the parking lot.

After the most surreal dinner in the history of meals, and then ashamed of fantasizing about a man I should be running away from, sleep was better than I thought it could be. Even with my frayed nerves, I didn't have to run miles to pass out. The fantasy, the orgasm, and the filet proved to be the cocktail I needed for a good night's sleep.

That doesn't mean I should've ever agreed to dinner in the first place. All it took was dipping one toe into the cyclone, and now I'm lost and dizzy and have no sense of direction.

I need to stop making excuses—I have to find my way out. The longer I ride this twister, the harder it'll be to make it out unscathed.

I'm almost across the parking lot to my car when two men dressed in off-the-rack sport coats and dockers exit the car parked next to mine.

"Ms. Dillon?"

I stop in my tracks and step back three paces. "Who are you?"

One of them reaches inside the breast of his jacket and produces a badge. I can't read it from where I'm standing, but it does come with a set of credentials. "Detective Trudeau from Redmond PD. This is my partner, Detective Osborne. We'd like to ask you some questions."

I hitch my strap up my arm and try to calm my speeding heart. "About what?"

Officer Osborne tucks his badge back into his pocket. "Your association with Brando Vitale, Jr."

For once, I allow my expression to define my true feelings, because surprised is an understatement. "I don't have an association with him. I only met him a couple of days ago."

They give each other a look before Trudeau adds, "If you could follow us to the station, this shouldn't take long, Ms. Dillon."

"Doctor," I correct. "And I have patients scheduled back-to-back today." Not to mention my own emergency session at lunch. I'm now going to need it more than ever.

"Dr. Dillon, this is important. We'd appreciate it if you could shift your schedule for us."

I move around them and flip the locks on my car. "I don't have to answer anything."

"Is Mr. Vitale one of your patients?"

I turn in my open door and tell the truth. "No, but even so, I refuse to blindly go to the police station to be questioned about someone I hardly know when you haven't told me what this is about. I respect my patients' time and won't disrupt their schedules while you're being vague."

"Dr. Dillon." Detective Trudeau takes one step closer. "We should have specified. We're from homicide. We've been working on an unsolved murder for months."

I lean into my car door for support. "Whose murder?"

"Mrs. Marcia Vitale. Brando Vitale's wife."

Nine

LIES

Aria

I ONLY SORT of lied when I told Brand why I moved to Redmond. It's true I took the only position that offered a small student loan forgiveness program. The reimbursement isn't life-changing. But when I'm carrying six years of graduate and doctoral loans, I couldn't turn it down.

The full truth is, my offer from the center was the farthest I had from Miami. For Briar and me, Redmond was our ticket out from under the very sticky thumb of our father. I grabbed my sister and we got as far away from Florida as we possibly could. He knows where we are, but he also knows to leave us the hell alone. All she and I have are each other, we don't need his toxicity.

I love nature and being outside. Briar loves the clouds and rain. She lived with me until she found a job that makes her happy with Redmond Rescue. She prefers animals over humans any day of the week. Now she lives five minutes from me in an apartment that makes mine look like the mansion we were raised in. But for the first time in her life, she's independent and happy… *ish*.

As happy as Briar will allow herself to be at this point in her short, delicate life.

Redmond has been a win-win.

Until recently.

I've never been in a police station, let alone sat in an interrogation chair for any reason. Honestly, I'm a bit disappointed. It looks nothing like it does on TV. It's not dark or dingy, and there's no bright lights blinding me. It's clean, simple, and the coffee smells good. I would have accepted a cup had I not brought my own in with me.

And no one is playing good-cop, bad-cop. Rather it's their curiosity that puts me on edge.

"So you went to an auction and bid on Mr. Vitale—"

"No. I bid on the dog. A date with Brand Vitale just came with it. I told him I didn't want any part of the date, but he insisted I get my money's worth, so I went. We had dinner last night."

"Did he mention his wife?"

Doctor-patient confidentiality is the groundwork for trust. Even though Brand is definitely not my client, it still feels weird to speak about his sex life. There's something about our dinner and brief conversation that I want to protect. Not to mention I already said I knew nothing about him so it would come across odd that I knew he hadn't had sex with his dead wife in years. Truth and lies fog over like a cloudy sunrise on water. "He informed me he's been single for six months. I didn't ask anything further because I don't plan to ever see him again. It was none of my business."

Detective Osborne leans back in his chair and studies me. "Six months ago, Marcia Vitale was found dead, floating in the lake behind their house."

My eyes widen. "That's horrible."

"Yeah, it is," Osborne agrees. "She drowned and we have reason to believe it was not accidental."

I look from one detective to the other. "Really?"

"Yes. Vitale's house sits on thirty acres and there's enough surveillance and security cameras on that land to rival The Pentagon. But during the projected time frame of her death, the feeds from the security cameras went dead. Or they were deleted. Whatever it was, we were told there was no footage."

My palms are so sweaty, I have to white-knuckle my coffee when I take another sip. "You think Brand Vitale killed his wife? And how did the security feed disappear?"

"There was a storm and power outage that night. Vitale insists he doesn't have his cameras on any type of backup power source." Trudeau rolls his eyes. "Vitale is our main suspect and the only person with motive. They weren't known to be ... happily married."

I'd say so. No sex for years on end certainly screams *troubled marriage*, but I don't express that. "That is horrendous, but lots of people are not happily married. I should know, I counsel them. What I don't understand is why you're telling me this."

Trudeau leans forward and points to me. "Because you're the first woman he's been seen with since her death."

I frown and shake my head. "Our meeting was a chance encounter. Do you really expect me to know something about his marriage or this poor woman's death? And how do you know I'm the first woman he's been with?"

They glance at each other and Trudeau shrugs, taking the lead. "He's our only suspect. We keep close tabs on him."

"But he's a firefighter. A paramedic. You really think he could kill his wife?"

"His alibi is … murky."

"How can an alibi be murky?" My words are rushed, edging on anxious. "An alibi is black and white. Either he has an alibi or not, right?"

"He had a shift during the time the coroner estimates Marcia Vitale was killed. His unit had a call, but Vitale didn't go. He wasn't feeling well—it was a small job and they could spare him. He stayed behind. Everyone on duty that night confirmed it."

I lean back in my chair. "That sounds like an alibi."

"By himself," Osborne stresses. "His cell phone shows he was there the whole time. But he was alone. See? Murky."

"You consider that murky?" I pull in a big breath and try to keep my heartbeat from racing out of control. "Wait. What do you want from me? I don't even know him. Why am I here?"

"We told you—you're the first woman he's been seen with since his wife's death. And we wanted to give you the heads up. The Vitale family…" Osborne trails off without finishing.

"What about the Vitale family?" I ask.

"They've managed Marcia's death in the media. They can be influential, to say the least," Trudeau says.

"Influential?" I echo.

"That's putting it mildly," Osborne deadpans.

I tell them the truth. "I don't know what to say."

Osborne digs through his wallet and slides a business card across the table. "If you think of anything, or if Vitale starts acting … odd, let us know. But be careful."

"I don't plan on seeing him again. My schedule is hectic." I take the card and drop it in my bag. "I especially don't have time for someone who may or may not have an alibi during the time of his wife's murder. I appreciate you bringing this to my attention."

Detective Trudeau has not stopped scrutinizing me since I sat in this chair, so his words don't match his demeanor. "It was the least we could do. It's our duty to make sure this doesn't happen again. Just being vigilant."

I stand and shake both their hands before gripping my travel mug to my chest. "I rescheduled my first patient of the day to this evening, I really need to get going. I have a long day ahead of me."

Detective Osborne gestures toward the door. "Thanks for making time for us. I'll show you out."

I hurry out of the police station and hope it was a once in a lifetime event. I have no desire to return.

Ever.

In the early hours of the morning, police were called to the home of Brando Vitale, Jr. where his wife, Marcia Vitale, was found dead. A call to 911 reported a body washed ashore at the prestigious Gray Mountain Lake. The body was found approximately one-half mile from the Vitale home. Preliminary reports from the coroner suggest Vitale drowned in shallow waters twenty-four to thirty-six hours prior to being found. Evidence shows there could have been signs of a struggle and police are investigating her death as a murder.

Arthur Ramos, Vitale's attorney, has made a statement on behalf of the family. "We are devastated by the loss of Marcia and expect whoever was responsible to be charged to the fullest extent of the law. We appreciate privacy during this time."

Saul Ricci, Marcia Vitale's father, has not minced words and wants Brando Vitale, Jr. investigated in his daughter's tragic death. Vitale is a decorated firefighter of Redmond Station Six and was on duty during the time of his wife's death.

The investigation is ongoing.

One Google search is all it took. I have memorized every detail of the investigation into Marcia Vitale's untimely death.

I can't lie. It haunts me.

"When you texted me for an appointment, it sounded urgent. Now you're here and haven't said a word."

I stare out the window of Russ's office and wonder what it feels like to drown. I've been a swimmer for as long as I can remember and competed for the majority of my life. I find being submerged in water peaceful. Quiet. A place I can turn everyone and everything off.

When I'm underwater, I'm weirdly focused.

I haven't been able to stop wondering...

Unlike my office, Russ's is dark and masculine and smells like a freshly-showered man. I'm surrounded from head to toe in dark-stained wood. The leather club chairs are old and wrinkled, the kind that get softer and more beautiful as the years wear on.

Russ is just like his chairs and I love him for it. He's also a Harvard grad and we met through a mentorship during the last year of my doctoral program. We might've been long distance, but he was integral in helping me through the toughest year of school. He became a friend, and despite carrying a full load of his own patients, has made room for me and refuses to accept payment.

He's basically the dad everyone deserves.

I'm so comfortable when I'm here, I allow myself the nervous fidget my father would demean me for. Chewing on the skin around my thumbnail, I will my body to stop fidgeting.

Russ calls to me in a fatherly tone—or what I guess is a loving, fatherly tone. Certainly not one Astor ever used. "Aria."

I exhale loudly, drop my arms to my sides, and turn to him. "I'm sorry. A lot has happened lately. First, I need your opinion on one of my cases."

He nods.

I speak in code, the way we were trained to when referring with colleagues about patients. "It's a couple. I'm afraid patient A wants to harm patient B. But I don't have proof. Patient A is a classic narcissist. I'm trying to get to the bottom of it. I have a bad feeling, but not solid enough to go to authorities. Yet. But I'm also afraid I'm waiting too long."

"You haven't had to do that yet. It's rare for psychologists to experience this often in their careers, but you never want to dismiss anything just in case. You're good at reading people—what is your gut telling you?"

I sink into one of the club chairs across from him and let my foot dance freely. "I think patient A is playing me—goading me. And that worries me more. I'm struggling to find the truth in anything patient A says. I'm not sure they could be more of a textbook narcissist. They like the attention and I'm pretty sure they want to keep me guessing."

"Narcissists get easily distracted by the next shiny object that puts them in the spotlight. Any chance this is a phase?"

I shake my head. "No."

Russ leans in and rests his elbows to his knees. "You managed your parents for most of your life. You'll know if and when to step in. Don't question yourself."

I sigh. That's easy for him to say.

He sits back in his chair. "What else brings you here?"

"I'm doing it again. Trying to fix everyone … everything. You know, personally. Not professionally. It's getting out of hand." I mumble around my index finger, chewing on my nail this time.

Calmly, he speaks without judgment, because he's pretty much perfect. "We've addressed this once in the last year. You seemed to be controlling it. Is this about Briar? I thought she was doing better."

"Briar is doing…" I think about the effort she's made to have dinner with me more often, and how she not only answered my call, but tried to help me too. "She's doing well. As well as I've seen her, at least. Going to individual and group therapy. I don't know her group counselor well, but the fact that she's going is major. This isn't about her." I tap my foot, not wanting to tell him about my new-found debt, my curiosity masked as bravery, or the man who stirs things in me, much less how that same man is being investigated for his wife's murder. Because when I put all that together, it's embarrassing and proves I shouldn't trust my own judgment—ever. Instead, I keep it vague. "I went on a date."

"Really? That's good." Russ offers a genuine smile. I wish I could share his enthusiasm, but instead I'm anxiety-ridden by the fact a man I should have nothing to do with makes my panties wet. "I've been encouraging you to do something for yourself. To invest in you outside of work or exhausting your body so you can sleep. This is a good thing, Aria."

If he only knew.

Lies. They're as delicate as the finest crystal and as powerful as our next needed breath.

My conscience delivers a punch to the gut and my stomach churns.

"Why do I have a feeling you don't think this is a good thing?"

"It's a distraction I don't have time for. You know my schedule. I told him I wouldn't see him again."

Russ frowns. "Was it that bad?"

That's the understatement of the century.

Russ doesn't wait for me to answer. "I think you should give it another chance. Even if you aren't interested, it will be good for you to break this cycle you're in. We've discussed it. You're either obsessed with Briar or your patients. How about accepting a challenge in the name of personal growth?"

There's no way I can tell him that personal growth isn't a priority when murder is thrown into the mix. I cross my arms to keep from chewing on my finger and my teeth instantly find the inside of my lip. "I don't know."

"Think about it, Aria. Now is a good time to push yourself."

I turn to look at the clock behind me. "I shouldn't take your whole lunch hour, plus I have a patient in thirty minutes. Thanks for making time for me. It's always good to see you."

He stands and follows me to the door. "Call anytime and keep in touch. I want to know how your second meeting with this man goes."

I turn and force a smile as he moves in for a hug. In the short time I've known Russ, I'm positive he's hugged me a thousand times more than my own father ever did. "It was good to see you too. Next time I'll make sure it's of a social nature instead of my being needy."

He waves me off. "We all need someone. I'm happy to be here for you."

When I walk out of his office, I feel marginally better. Just enough, I manage to hold my head high and focus on my long day, now even longer since I had to move my schedule around. Thank goodness Briar took Muppet to work with her today.

I wonder if joint custody of a dog is a thing? I could use all the help I can get right now.

I need to focus on my patients, paying off my debt so I can get Muppet a backyard sooner rather than later, and making up for lost time with Briar.

I'm done with everything and everyone else.

Ten

FRAUD

Aria

BRIAR – *YOUR NEW baby is home. He's walked, fed, and thoroughly loved on. We bonded and I'm sure he'll like me more than you by noon tomorrow. Mostly because I bribed him with treats.*

Me – This is why I love you and I'm sure Muppet will love you more than me by noon tomorrow. You're the best.

Briar – Oh, yeah. Taking care of the sweetest pup—what a hardship.

I toss my phone into my bag and collect everything I need because I'll be back at the center tomorrow.

It's almost eight. My stomach is complaining after only a sandwich on my way back from Russ's so I wouldn't be late to my next appointment.

My files are updated and the only things I want are a frozen dinner and my bed.

I swing open my office door to the reception area that barely holds a few stiff, uncomfortable chairs.

I stop at the threshold and barely catch the tote that falls from my shoulder.

"You always work this late?"

Shit.

Filling the small space, he hasn't even bothered with the uncomfortable chairs. Like a statue of a Greek god, he's standing between me and the exit to the hallway—my only escape route.

My gaze darts from him to the door that I *swear* I locked after my last patient left.

"What are you doing here?"

His large frame comes to life, closing the gap to my now-erratic heart. I take a step back and grip the door. "I tried to call you today. Over and over and fucking over. I've texted you so many times, I'd be surprised if I still have fingerprin—"

"Interesting," I interrupt. "I didn't get them."

"Yeah, I know. You know what else is interesting? You don't seem like the kind of woman to ignore people. Sometimes when people don't respond, it's because—" he steps forward as I try to slam the door on him but his big boot might as well be a boulder "—a certain someone blocks you."

I push on the door for the sheer fact I'm no quitter. "Someone blocked you?"

"Stupid is not a good look on you, Aria. I've had nothing but respect since the moment we met. Don't disappoint me and prove that you're some average bitch who likes to play games. I've experienced enough of that in my thirty-seven years."

I hold on to the door like a lifeline and try not to think about the very real orgasm and very fake fantasy that played out last night between my own fingers and demented head. And that's saying something since I'm a doctor of the brain.

He moves closer, and since I'm not in heels today, towers over me in an angry rage. Being near him again makes me wish I could block fantasies as easily as I can phone numbers.

He lowers his voice and his words tease my face with a trail of spearmint. "I know people, Aria. I've got more contacts than you have hairs on that beautiful head of yours. Guess how much you cost me today by not answering my calls and texts?"

He advances again and I'm forced to let go of the door. An echo vibrates off my white walls when he kicks it shut and my tote holding my phone falls to the ground.

"Two fucking markers and two-thousand bucks. I now owe someone at the center a favor when they confirmed you weren't on duty today. I also have a new contact at your apartment complex. That cost me two grand to confirm you weren't sick or dead in that shithole you call a home."

"My apartment is not a shithole. It's nice."

He backs me up until my hamstrings hit the arm of the sofa. Finally, I put a hand to his abs, which will not help tame my fantasies. For the sake of my own sanity, the man seriously needs to back off.

"And the last marker to an asshole hacker who I fucking hate but he can break into systems that the Chinese government only has wet dreams about doing. He confirmed that you," he leans in closer, and I smell his body wash, as if the feel of his abs weren't doing enough damage to my resolve, "*blocked me.*"

I finally find my voice. "You toss around a lot of markers and money for a firefighter."

"I am not someone you want to fuck with, Aria. I don't dole out markers or money easily. In fact, when I woke up this morning hard as a rock thinking about you, no one had a marker on me, and I was two grand richer. How happy do I look right now?"

"Fine," I spit. "I blocked you. You seem like a man who follows through on a threat, and I'm a woman who means what she says. I don't have time for you." I give him a push and remove my hand from his body, hoping it will clear my head. "Or this."

It's true. I opened my eyes this morning from the best sleep I've had in a long time, floating around on my fantasy-orgasmic cloud. It was more delicious than my ten-ounce filet and the first beautiful thing I've experienced in a long time that has given me a break from reality.

But, like everything else good in life, I remembered the cloud of thunderstorms that continue to follow me, threatening to disintegrate from under me any moment.

And I know the landing won't be a soft one.

I should've ignored my curiosity and fantasies.

So I blocked him this morning before my feet hit the floor.

The two homicide detectives had nothing to do with it.

"You need to leave." I continue, ignoring his full lips flattening into an angry line, as I side-step him and grab my bag off the floor to dig for my cell.

I have the door halfway open when his palm flattens on the wood in front of me, closing it in my face. "You're not leaving."

My teeth find the tender skin inside my mouth I abused earlier during my session with Russ. It's everything I can do to control my tone. "It's been a long day. I want to go home."

He fits his front to my back, but it's different than last night. He's different than last night. He emanates the same power, but tonight his muscles are tense and heated—wired.

He presses me to the door.

Again.

I'm an athlete. I made it to the Olympic trials. I still swim countless laps a week and run at least two marathons a year.

But none of that has tested my heart as much as him. I can't catch my breath. I have office neighbors and could scream. There's a speech pathologist across the hall and a nail tech next door, but I doubt anyone is around at this time of night.

"Look at me," he demands.

With my cheek to the door, I angle my face to his. He easily slides my phone out of my sweaty palm and I hear its soft thud on my area rug.

"Brand," I whisper. "What are you doing?"

"I need your full attention." He twists and looks straight into my eyes. He has me anchored so snug I have to work for shallow breaths. "I know what happened this morning."

"I already admitted I blocked you." I rebound.

"After that." He narrows his eyes. "Did they question you or just warn you off?"

"Who?"

"Don't play stupid. The cops."

I say nothing.

In the short time I've been around him, Brand Vitale has been direct and says what he means. I talk to enough people in my line of work, I know the difference between a straight-talker, a bullshitter, and an ass-kisser. The man who has me glued to my office door is definitely the first in that list.

But he's even more. There's something about him...

And I wonder ... if I give him the truth, will he return the favor?

"Both."

He nods.

I keep talking. "They saw us together and asked what I knew about you. They told me your wife was found dead and you're the main suspect."

"That's what I hear."

"And they warned me."

"That's not why you blocked me." It's not a question, but a statement. His hips press into the small of my back, and I suck in a breath. "You blocked me at five-thirty this morning."

It's my turn to frown.

"You left the police department at nine-thirty-eight."

My frown deepens ... because ...

What. The. Fuck?

"You're following me?"

"I don't have time to follow anyone, but I have people who do." He shrugs. "My point is, you cut me out before the cops fed you lies about me and my dead wife. If you would've answered my calls, I was going to convince you to make time for me. Now I have to convince you of other shit too. So, again, why did you block me?"

"Because this can't happen. I knew if you called, I wouldn't be able to say no to you."

"I like that."

My teeth sink deeper into my flesh.

He lowers his voice. "I did not kill my wife."

My heart stutters. "You said you hadn't had sex with her in years. Why?"

He pauses, contemplating … something. If I had to guess, it's not why he hadn't had sex with her in years, but rather if he can trust me with the reason. "Marcia and I … we were complicated. She was a bitch from the get-go. We had more problems than a Jerry Springer episode."

I have to know. "Why would you marry someone if you didn't love them, let alone like them?"

He shakes his head. "You haven't earned that from me. Not yet. But I will say, if I were going to kill her, I would've done it years ago. Divorce is not an option in my world. I accepted her as the shitty life sentence she was. She made the last ten years a fucking pain in the ass, but I did not kill her."

"Yet you cheated on her."

He nods. "And she cheated on me. We had an unspoken understanding."

"This is not making me want to unblock you," I tell him the truth. "And the way you pin me to doors…" I take a deep breath. "You're stepping over boundaries, and I don't like it."

"I think you don't want to like it." Instead of shifting and allowing me space to move—or run away like any sane person would—a big hand feels its way over my hip and settles on my side next to my very sensitive breast. "And you're afraid of what will happen if you allow yourself to like it."

He couldn't be more right. The fact he has me figured out scares me even more.

He flips me around. We're face to face with my back to the door. "I think you're wondering what other boundaries I could shatter that you'd enjoy."

I exhale and try to erase the fantasies where he plays the starring role.

"Aria." He leans in and nudges the tip of my nose with his, lowering his voice. His dark eyes sear into mine. "I did not kill my wife."

I force my lungs to function and stay silent.

"Swear it." He places a hand on the side of my face—firm, steady. "Look at me. Really look at me and think that I did it. I dare you."

The taste of copper hits my tongue.

"Tell me you believe me." He's not asking.

Of all the things he's said to me so far, nothing has been as consequential as this.

Pleading.

Raw.

Desperate.

It's my nature to think things through to the ends of the earth and back, so when my next words slip through my lips, they couldn't be more out of character. "I believe you."

His grip on my face tightens, and his entire body goes taut. The next thing I know, his mouth hits mine.

How did this happen? How did I get here with Brand Vitale?

With one hand in my hair and the other possessing my ass like it's always been his, he devours me. His tongue forces its way into my mouth and the taste of us—mint mixed with the copper of my own blood—makes my head spin.

It's all it takes for me to tumble into his world.

Fantasies are shit. When it comes to him, reality wins—hands down.

He rips his mouth from mine and his fingers wrestle with my pants. "Fuck. Why can't I get you out of my head, Aria? I've tried. It's like you've seeped into my blood and became an addiction I can't quit."

I don't dare respond. Addiction is not nearly a strong enough word, but I won't allow myself to admit it. But the thought of being his addiction?

I've never felt so powerful.

"Tell me you don't feel the same," he goads. "I think you do. I felt it last night and it's even hotter now."

He forces a hand down the front of my slim-fit pants, straight into my panties, and I don't make a move to stop him. A remote part of my brain screams at me. Everything about him is mysterious and dangerous. It doesn't take a specialist to realize Brand Vitale is something much more than a hero—fighting fires and saving lives.

I want to know more.

I want to know *everything.*

I relish his kiss and his touch. I'm not sure I could say no to him if I wanted to.

Brand doesn't mess around. His big hand possesses me—fully and wholly—exactly the way he's taking over my body and psyche, the way no one ever has before.

"I knew you'd be wet," he taunts me with my own body's betrayal. "But this is more. You're drenched. Were you like this sitting across from me at dinner last night?"

He curls two fingers inside me and presses his palm into my clit.

When my head slumps in his hand, he fists my hair and my roots scream. "Tell me you went to bed last night thinking of me. Because the minute I got home, I jacked off harder than I have in years. All I could think about was this." His strong fingers pump inside me as his hand massages my clit. He's right. I'm soaked, just like last night when I came, fantasizing of him. "The thought of coming inside you was almost more than I could bear. It's a kind of pain I'll gladly wait on and I don't wait for anything."

I close my eyes and question everything about myself, because there's no way I can deny this man. I bite back a moan, but it comes out as a whimper.

"I'm not waiting on this." He gives my clit more pressure and I'm not sure how much more I can take. "I want to make you come. See you. Feel you. Fuck, I can even smell you."

I tilt my face to his and drag my hooded eyes open just enough so he's the only thing in my world. As much as I want to experience an orgasm induced by him in the flesh, I have to know. "Why me?"

He circles my clit again. "I could ask you the same question."

I lick my lips and shake my head. "Tell me."

He studies my features and hesitates a beat. "Don't ask for things you can't handle."

"I have to know." My eyes fall shut as a shudder runs up my spine and I have trouble standing. "Please."

"Please what?" He pulls my body flush to his to support my weight and his hand between my legs does things that should be illegal in all fifty states and Puerto Rico. "*Please* make you come or *please* tell you why my obsession with you is currently fucking with everything else in my life?"

I can't help it. I grip his biceps and grind on his hand for more. "*Please* ... both."

"I'll gladly give you one but you're going to have to work for the other, Doc."

His mouth takes mine and I willingly open for him. My mouth, my legs, and yes, even my life.

He doesn't make me wait long to guess which one he's going to make me work for. My orgasm creeps in and takes over, making me forget about my newfound debt, my patients, my new dog waiting for me at home. Hell, he makes me forget about my fucking life. I ride his hand as my jaw goes slack, wishing for this to never end. I'd do anything to stay forever in his alternate realm.

"Take as much as you can. I want to see you fall apart for me. Don't stop, Aria."

As if. I couldn't stop if I wanted to.

I gasp and bury my face in his chest. His black dress shirt is soft in contrast to the chain around his neck where a cross dangles and bites into my skin. I wonder if he ever takes it off.

His relentless fingers pump and his palm torments my needy clit. I cling to him as my lungs chase my speeding heart, but he doesn't let go of my sex. He holds firm and I'm not sure I ever want him to let go.

Neither of us says a word when reality returns to my brain like an unwanted, recurring nightmare.

And my reality hits me hard as I stand here in his arms with his hand firmly cupping my sex.

I just allowed Brand Vitale to have his way with me. And I did nothing but encourage it.

This is what I get for crossing something off my list.

"Next time, I'm coming too. Inside you. Your mouth, your pussy … we'll see where it takes us."

I tense, and I know he can feel it because his grip on my sex tightens. "What have I done?"

Letting me go, his hand slides out from between my legs. He forces me to look at him when that same hand comes to my chin and he traces my lips with my own juices before licking his fingers clean.

Then he kisses me, his tongue lapping my bottom lip before dipping into my mouth. My every sense is consumed with him and me and …

Us.

And there cannot be an *us*.

"You'll earn the rest." He teases me with the information I want, details about him that the doctor in me is curious about. The woman in me, on the other hand, is hungry for other parts of him.

He pushes me back against the door and bends to fetch my phone.

He holds it to my face and the damn thing unlocks immediately. Of course it recognizes the post-orgasmic me standing here a mess, but never unlocks if I'm yawning or brushing my teeth.

"I have some business to take care of tonight and a shift at the station first thing tomorrow morning." He flips through my phone, touching the screen at least twenty times before handing it back to me. "Don't block me again, Aria. If I have to search for you, I won't be happy."

He tosses my phone on top of my bag before turning back to me. I'm too overcome by what I just allowed to happen and him maneuvering his way through my private information, I haven't even bothered to zip my pants. His fingers come to my chin, tipping my face to his and he presses his lips to mine.

Ending his kiss with another swipe of my bottom lip, he demands, "Answer me when I call and text you."

I shake my head. "You can't leave until you tell me."

"Tell you what?"

"Why me?"

"I told you. That's something you have to earn. And you will."

"No. That's not good enough. I'm not like your late wife," I stress, shaking my head. "I refuse to be toyed with, be one of many, have some sort of sick, unspoken understanding. I know what that looks like. I grew up with that and want no part of it."

A small smile hits his lips. It falls somewhere on the scale between smug and sexy. It definitely does a job at chipping away at the weak resolve I cling to as if it's my last breath. If for no other reason, I need to appear as if I have some self-respect after what just happened.

He leans on the door next to my head and I gasp when he claims my sex again, this time over my wrinkled pants. "I like that."

I squeeze my thighs, causing his smile to lean on the side of smug. "What do you like?"

"That you're as possessive of me as I am of you."

"I'm not possessive of you," I lie. "This is about me protecting my dignity." And other things I don't want to admit to right now.

"I believe you even though you're also lying. Admit it—the thought of someone else touching me makes you jealous." He presses his hand into my still sensitive clit. "Because the thought of someone other than me touching you makes me crazy."

My eyes widen.

"And Aria." He leans to kiss me, gripping my sex in a way that would convince even the most skeptical of women. "I'm a scary man when something makes me crazy. Just because I didn't murder my wife doesn't mean I wouldn't go there for something I felt strongly about. And my feelings for you are pretty damn strong."

I bite into my flesh.

"Don't do that," he murmurs. "Tasted your blood when I kissed you. Stop hurting yourself."

I let go and lick my lips.

"Do we have an understanding? I don't touch anyone but you. You don't touch anyone but me. Stop hurting yourself and don't fucking block me again."

I nod. I can do that.

I mean, for now, I guess.

He squeezes my sex one more time. "We'll talk soon."

Like an idiot, I nod again.

Then he smiles and this time it's downright sexy. "I'm feeling a hell of a lot better than I did when I got here. For my first therapy session, I think that went pretty well."

My eyes fall shut and I exhale.

Then I slide to the side so he can open the door.

When I hear my lobby door close, my legs can't hold me any longer. I slide to my ass on the floor—exhausted, emotionally drained, and even sated.

I take a deep breath and admit to myself I'm a fraud.

I'm so far from getting my shit together, I have no business trying to help others.

Eleven

DOCTOR-PATIENT CONFIDENTIALITY

Brand

CROSS MY arms and look out the window onto downtown Redmond. It's no Seattle, thank fuck. Seattle is too big, too congested with too many people living on top of one another. I should know, I was raised there and hated it. I can't imagine what my cousins put up with across the country in New York City.

Redmond was my compromise with the west-coast family. I'm involved, but not. I work on the outskirts when absolutely needed, and manage contracts in my own way. I always wanted to be a firefighter. Doesn't hurt that it's a good cover and soothes my conscience for the other shit I agree to.

Knowing how to get rid of a body or cover up arson has come in handy a few times.

Or more than a few times.

But when I save someone from a burning house or a mangled car, I figure I'm atoning for it. A right for a wrong, all that shit. My own personal penance.

I've been working the job for over fifteen years. I've done my duty to the family in more ways than one during that time. I basically signed my life away ten years ago and was paid well for it. My gig at the station is a dream and hobby with a decent medical and dental plan. Life was trudging along, mundane and slightly miserable with no end in sight, until…

Six months ago.

Little did I know something I secretly dreamed of for years would have the cops on my ass twenty-four-seven.

"Brand. Your meeting is here."

I turn from the windows and look across the conference table big enough to seat at least twenty. I lift my chin to my attorney and friend. "Thanks for staying late, Art. Tell Tessa and the kids I'm sorry I kept you. I'll make it up to them the next time we get together."

"You spoil my family more than I do. What you pay me on retainer, I'm happy to share my conference room when you need it. Especially in these times, you need to be careful. I'm going to keep eyes on your new doctor for a few more days. If you didn't tell me she was a shrink, I'd think she was a librarian or some shit. Boring as hell other than being pulled in for questioning."

I shrug. "Boring might be what I need after the last decade."

"Whatever gets you off, man. I'll be in my office. We'll leave out the front together, take your time." Art opens the door, and his face immediately turns to stone. "Hey, asshole. I didn't say you could sit. My wife just redecorated the waiting room and that sofa cost me ten grand."

Art stalks out the door as Simon spits one apology after another when they pass in the hall.

"Close the door, Simon."

He looks around the darkened offices before settling his focus on me. "Is there anyone else here?"

"No. It's after midnight. I can't risk meeting you anywhere but my attorney's office with the cops on my ass."

"Oh, right. Sorry."

"Simon, we need to talk about the Realm project."

Simon isn't comfortable in his own skin and shakes his head too fast. "I don't know what happened, boss. They told me everything was a go. I checked with the inspector right before he showed. I—"

I hold my hand up. "Whoa."

"Sorry, boss. I just—"

"You just didn't do what you were supposed to do. You have one job. One job to make sure the inspector issues the permits on time. Do you know what happens when you don't do your one job?"

He shrugs.

He fucking shrugs.

"You bottleneck the process, Simon. I have workers I need to pay. If they don't work, I can't put them on the books. If I don't put them on the books, I can't move money." I take a step forward, put a hand to his shoulder. "Do you understand? We're behind schedule—and I don't mean on the Realm project. I'm talking behind on other things. Cash stacking up usually isn't an issue for most people, but, for me, it is."

"Sorry, boss."

"I'm sure you are, but sorry doesn't clean my money. I don't get my hands dirty, but my father has people who will. You were hired for a specific task. You were given money to line the pockets of the right people yet my building is at a standstill. You broke the chain. Now, what are we going to do about this?"

He pulls his cell out of his pocket and his fingers tremble as he looks through his contacts. "I'm on it."

"This is important, Simon."

"Yeah, boss."

I turn him and push him toward the door. "Take the stairs all the way to the basement. Slip out through the cargo bay between the dumpsters. Make sure you're not seen. The cops are out front and I know you have warrants. That would suck if you ran into them tonight."

He nods, texting at the speed of light, and barely glances at me. "I'll get this fixed. I will."

I pat him on the back. "I know you will. Next time make sure we don't have to have this conversation."

He's out the door and disappears into the stairwell without another word. He won't get caught. He's a sneaky fuck which is how he's gone this long with so many warrants.

I head to Art's corner office. "Done. Thanks for the office space. I can't afford an electronic trail with anyone like him right now."

Art looks from his laptop and leans back in his sleek office chair. "You can thank me by telling me about this Dillon chick."

Arthur Ramos and I were in school together. Between the two of us, we created havoc from preschool through our senior years at Saint Mary's in Seattle. Art knows everything there is to know about me, my family, and now, my legal battle that he's managing with a fine-tooth comb. I'm lucky my life-long friend turned out to be as cunning as he is book smart. I trust him with my life, and it's not just because I can afford the best defense attorney on the west coast.

He'd do it for free, but he knows there's no way I'd allow that. My dad has his own attorney who's older than dirt. I was Art's first client the day he passed the bar and the first person I spoke to after Marcia was found floating face down in Gray Mountain Lake behind my house.

I've yet to be officially charged despite being their only suspect. Art is fucking good at what he does and has painted me in the media as the devastated widower that I definitely am not.

I look at my watch and decide I need to kill at least another twenty minutes so it looks like I'm having an actual meeting with my attorney. "That's Dr. Dillon to you."

"Fine. What's with Dr. Dillon? Because six months might seem like a long time, but for someone who's been tried in the media for his wife's death, I can promise you it's not. Marcia might be six feet under, but you need to consider her lukewarm and not parade other women around in public."

I shrug. "She bid on me at the charity auction, which you knew I was doing. I owed her a date. I did it all in the name of charity. The cops can ask all they want—it's the truth."

Art leans back and rests one Gucci loafer on the edge of his desk before crossing his ankles. I know all too well he only had to work an hour and five minutes for those shoes. "While you were conducting business in my conference room, I got a call from my contact at the PD. Aria corroborated what you just told me. Should the cops pull you in again, feel free to tell the truth this time."

"I've told them the truth, Art. You think I'm a liar and a murderer?"

"I know you're the former and I don't give a shit about the latter. My job is to prove your alibis are solid—don't make me a fraud."

"I would never."

He drops his feet to the floor and his forearms go to the desk between us. "Don't fuck with me. You pay me too much and I don't want to see my lifelong friend go to prison. What am I supposed to tell my kids when they ask why their godfather isn't at their birthday parties? You need to give the good doctor a rest. Leave her be. You followed through on your part of the auction and took her to dinner. That makes sense when it comes to your public story. But I can't play you as the grieving widow in the media if you start something too soon. I know you know how to hide your affairs—"

"This isn't an affair," I growl.

"I don't give a shit what it is. I suggest if you want the doctor in any way, keep her a secret. Putting your lips to her neck after pressing her to her door with your hands all over her out in the open is not smart, Brand. And don't tell me that didn't happen. Not only are the cops following you, but so are the Riccis. Word is out and everyone knows."

I smile at the memory. And the very private one in her office tonight when she came on my hand. "Sorry, but I refuse to hide the doctor."

His face turns to stone. "You're going to fuck up everything I've worked hard to do for six very long months."

"I have confidence in you and your skills. It's why I'm paying for your shoe fetish and new waiting room furniture. You need to trust me."

He shakes his head. "This better not be a game."

I bring my hand that I've yet to wash to my face. Her scent brings me back to when she fell apart in my arms.

And now I'm hard while sitting across from my friend and attorney.

"You know I don't play games. I don't do anything that isn't completely deliberate and thought out."

He points to me. "You'd better not. Not only do I want you to remain a free man, but I don't need your family on my ass if you're charged." He takes that finger and stabs his mahogany desk. "I also don't need this mark on my firm when a jury finds you guilty of murder. I have a reputation and right now you're fucking with it by not walking the straight and narrow."

I adjust my hard-on before I stand to set him straight. "You know me, which means you know I'm not going to do anything to fuck up my life. I'll handle Dr. Dillon in my own way. If anyone asks about her, tell them I'm in need of therapy to deal with my wife's tragic demise."

He rolls his eyes.

"Doctor-patient confidentiality. Stick that up the District Attorney's ass and see how he likes it."

Art spins his chair around and looks out the floor-to-ceiling windows of his high-rent offices in one of the poshest buildings in Redmond.

I should know. My holdings corporation owns it.

He mutters, "Fuck me."

"No," I correct. "I plan on fucking my new psychologist. Eventually, that is."

He swings his chair around. "Is this someone I can tell Tessa about?"

"Yeah," I answer immediately.

"Really?"

He's surprised. He should be. I've never said that before about anyone. They know Marcia was a business arrangement and a joke.

And not a funny one either.

I say no more. "Walk me out. I've got a shift first thing in the morning and need to get a couple hours of sleep."

He shuts his MacBook and stalks past me. "You're the biggest pain in the ass friend I have."

I follow him out and hit the lights on my way. "I'm your only friend."

He punches a slew of keys on the security system before swinging the door open. "Which makes it even worse that you're putting me through this shit."

I hit the button to the elevator and cross my arms. When he finally joins me, I lift my chin. "As if I haven't been there for you and Tessa. I promise not to fuck this up. How about next month's rent is on me for your emotional sacrifice."

"It's the least you can do." The elevator dings. Art steps inside and punches the button for the lobby with too much force.

"Easy on my elevator. This thing is top of the line."

He stares at the numbers counting down from the top floor, because I don't fuck around when it comes to my friends. "Tessa's going to want to meet your doctor."

"I need a week. Maybe two."

"You're the cockiest son of a bitch I know."

"Don't talk shit about my mother. She'll whack you over the head with a wooden spoon."

Art stuffs his hands in his pockets and mutters, "It wouldn't be the first time."

Twelve

MASTER OF ALL THINGS

Aria

I PUT MY car in park and grab my phone that just vibrated.

Hero – Good morning, Doctor.

Muppet jumps over the console and lands on my lap, causing my phone to fall into no-man's land, where french fries go to shrivel up and die.

"Umph." I try to settle my dog who's too big to jump around the car when I jerk from a rap on my window.

Briar is standing there, her blue eyes—the only thing we have in common that remotely makes us look like sisters—are as tired as ever. One brow is cocked and she doesn't stop her slow, rhythmic knocking.

I hit the button to lower my window. "What the hell? You scared me."

"Boo." She reaches in and pulls Muppet through the window even though he's far too big for such things and wraps her arms around him. "There's my nephew. Are you here to spend the day with Auntie Briar? I bought you sweet potato treats. You're gonna love them almost as much as you love me."

"I love you, too, Briar," I drawl to get her attention while I dig for my phone.

She shifts my dog and holds him like a baby on her hip and he actually wraps his front legs around her neck. "I told you he was going to love me more."

"I let him sleep with me last night," I counter.

She leans in and snuggles his neck. "It's about time you let a man into your bed."

As if on cue, my phone vibrates again.

Hero – Now you're going to ignore me?

Yes. Yes, I might.

I'm also going to ignore Briar's comment about a man in my bed. "Please don't spoil him too much. Leave some of that for me to do. I really want to bond with him."

She takes his leash from me and hooks it to his collar. "I'll try, but there's really no such thing as spoiling a dog too much. Especially not one as cute and fluffy and smart as my nephew."

My phone vibrates again.

I sigh.

"You'd better go." She puts Muppet down, and he yanks on the leash so hard it pulls her petite frame to the side. "Someone is anxious for their doctor."

If she only knew.

"I'll be home early tonight." I did not tell her about my little visit with the police yesterday and don't plan to. "Well, maybe not early. But I won't be late again."

"Whatever time is fine."

"You're the best."

"You know me, nothing but easy-fucking-breezy." Something in her expression changes before she adds, "Just text when you're on your way." I don't have the time to dig deeper on what that means when she waves me off. "Go fix the world and be perfect."

"I love you!" I call as she walks away from me. "Love you, too, Muppet!"

I roll up the window. It's cool and gray and starting to mist. I crank the heat and grab my cell so a certain man won't send anyone to follow me again. The police are following him, he had someone follow me, and now the police have me pegged as the first woman he's been seen with since his wife was murdered.

This is not a radar anyone wants to be on.

They can focus on each other and forget about me.

Hero – I'd like to make an appointment.

Me – Sorry, I was driving. I don't text and drive. It's dangerous.

Me – And I'm not your doctor.

He responds instantly.

Hero – But I need someone to talk to and I want that someone to

be you.

Me – I need to go so I'm not late to the center.

Hero – I'm at the station 'til tomorrow morning. Schedule me for your earliest available tomorrow.

Me – You're making me late. And I'm booked all week.

Hero – Even better—afterhours. I'll settle for tomorrow night. I'll make you dinner and you can solve my problems.

I close my eyes and exhale. This is stupid and reckless and crazy.

My phone vibrates on my thigh, reminding me of other places he vibrated last night.

Hero – My place at seven.

Me – Wait. You cook?

Hero – I'm Italian and a firefighter. It's okay to be impressed. I'm that good.

It's hard not to bite the inside of my lip but I promised myself I'd stop. I'm sure I'll have a terrible case of TMJ by the end of the week from the vise-like clenching of my teeth.

Me – I don't know. I've already been questioned by the police once since I met you.

Hero – I'm not worried about the police and you shouldn't be either. They've been following me for months—they can't prove what they're trying to. I'm a single man who wants to make dinner for his psychologist.

I pause before typing the truth.

Me – Sorry if I'm leery. You're like Jekyll and Hyde, not to mention this isn't a good idea. And I'm not your doctor.

Hero – Seemed like a good idea last night in your office during our first session. If I need to come by and convince you some more, I'd be happy to.

Me – No! Dinner is good. I mean … I can't lie, you make me nervous. But okay, we'll stick with dinner. Only dinner. And I hate to cook.

Hero – Looking forward to our appointment tomorrow night, Doc. Bring the dog. But don't forget his leash. I'm not chasing him again.

Me – It's food, not an appointment. I have to go so I'm not late.

I toss my phone to the passenger seat, throw my car in reverse, and count all the ways I'm an idiot as I drive below the speed limit to the center.

Brand

THE WOMAN CAN eat.

I made her chicken marsala, salad, and bought bread and dessert at the bakery down the street from the station. I might cook, but I don't bake. And I'll eat some carbs, but I don't do sweets. I workout too much to fuck up my body with refined sugar.

I might not eat it, but I sure enjoy the fuck out of watching my new psychologist devour the éclair I bought her. And that was after she ate everything else I dished.

She refused the wine, though. Even after I offered to drive her home, or, if she preferred, to stay the night.

Needless to say, she's had nothing besides water since she arrived.

Her dog took over my house again, but finally crashed on the floor in front of the fire. Aria has been a silent statue since we finished eating, staring out my wall of windows into the black night.

I asked her every question in the book during dinner. I need to pretend to learn everything about her the old-fashioned way since I already know it all from my PI.

She talked about her sister but didn't have much to say about her parents other than her mother is deceased. I know everything there is to know about her career, and she made it sound like almost making the Olympic swim team wasn't a big deal, which it is. She swims at the gym and runs no fewer than forty miles a week. So far, nothing has made her more talkative than her passion to help people. She comes alive when she talks about her work.

In some demented way, we have that in common.

Some might consider our dinner an interrogation.

I asked.

She answered.

Either she's only here for a free meal and really doesn't give one shit about me, or she wasn't lying earlier when she said she was nervous.

She hasn't asked me one thing all night.

Still, she's here. And I know for a fact her body wasn't lying after what happened in her office.

She's into me.

I toss the towel on the marble and move through the great room. Her gaze jumps to my reflection as I close in. As much as I want to—because I haven't thought of anything else since I woke this morning—I stop short of touching her.

When it comes to her, I've done nothing but give in to my caveman instincts. Tonight, I promised myself I'd give her space to see what she'd do, but nothing's changed. She's as closed off as ever.

I stuff my hands in my pockets because, if I don't, I might rip her clothes off. The need to fuck her against my windows for all of nature to witness is eating away at my resolve.

She's watching me like a hawk, either waiting for me to pounce or, who knows, maybe kill her, since my name will forever be tainted because of my damned dead wife.

I have other things on the agenda tonight and I need to get those out of the way so we can move on from this awkward shit. The good doctor is so much more than she's letting on, and I'm sick of waiting. It's time, and she's going to hear it whether she wants to or not.

"You sure aren't curious about what happened to my dead wife."

Just like the night at the auction, not an ounce of emotion. In fact, she's this way most of the time.

That is, unless I have my hand down her pants.

She makes no move other than the smallest tip of her head, speaking to me through our muted reflections. "Maybe I don't want to know."

"That's very…" I let my thought hang in the balance between us. "Unhuman-like."

She shrugs. "If you think so."

"You're the expert. Isn't curiosity of the unknown a basic commonality of all beings? Look at your dog. He spent thirty minutes sniffing every corner of my house and he's already been here."

"One could say the lack of curiosity is a form of self-preservation."

"Now you sound like a shrink. Why do you feel the need to protect yourself when it comes to me? You know nothing about me."

"It's easier that way."

"What's easier?"

"The less I know, the easier it will be to keep you at an arm's length. And, eventually, walk away from you."

"Yet…" I can't fight it any longer. I reach out and hook my index finger into the waist of her tight-ass jeans and yank her the six inches separating us. She stumbles into me and her eyes widen. "You're here. If you insist you're not curious, I call bullshit."

She starts to pull her lip between her teeth before letting it go. Her body moves against mine when she pulls in a big breath, but she refuses to speak.

"I was twenty-seven when I married Marcia. She was twenty-two."

"I know."

"You do?"

She hikes a thick brow and leans into me. "Internet research. I found her obituary. You outed me—I am a curious creature, after all."

I wrap my hand around her hip and settle into the fact I enjoy touching her in any way possible. Despite her cool behavior, she rests against my chest. "What else did you learn on the internet?"

She shakes her head and remains tight-lipped while I fight my dick from stirring the way it does from being in the same room as her, let alone touching her.

I keep talking because the more she knows, the better. I never take unnecessary risks, but if there's ever a time to give up secrets about myself, it's now.

"My family is powerful in many ways, Aria. Nothing says power like control and money. About fifteen years ago, a man on the west coast challenged my dad. He pushed and pushed and pushed. People died on both sides—it went on for years. It was messy and dangerous. To a point, if they didn't do something to call a truce, both sides would be fucked. And by fucked, I mean dragged through the courts and lots of people would have been thrown in prison."

Her breathing becomes uneven. I feel it come quicker against my chest—it's her only tell that she gives two shits about what I'm saying. "Do you share this with everyone?"

"Fuck no. No one outside my circle knows any of it. But if I'm going to explain my marriage, you need to know this."

She crosses her arms and I don't need to be a shrink to know what that means. A defensive stance.

I push on because I know she can handle it. "I was young and didn't want to be my dad. I don't mind contributing to the family business, but I didn't want to follow in his footsteps."

She steps forward and turns. Her eyes widen, so blue and bright, they're a contrast to her dark hair. "Mafia?"

I shrug. "It's not what it looks like in the movies."

"But organized crime." Her tone is more condemning than her words.

"That's…" I close the distance again. "A technical term for it."

Her face falls. "I don't want to know any of this."

"But you need to know so you can understand. My marriage wasn't good—it never was. Even in the beginning."

She shakes her head and turns back to the windows, running her hands through her hair. Staring out at the darkness, she mutters, "I shouldn't have come. What am I doing?"

"Hey." I turn her, run my hand down to hers, and hold tight. "Marcia's father is my father's archenemy—the one who caused my dad hell years ago. When my dad asked for an agreement between the families, the only way old man Ricci would agree was if the families were joined by marriage—*for life*. Ricci said it was the only way both sides would have something so important at stake they'd quit fucking with each other. Until then, my dad was still trying to groom me to take over. I stepped up and made a deal with him."

Her curiosity finally comes out to play. "What kind of deal?"

"I agreed to marry Marcia if my dad let me off the hook for taking his place as head of the family. I was twenty-seven. I didn't want that life or the spotlight it comes with. All I ever wanted was to be a firefighter. I might be involved in a relatively innocent part of his businesses, but I love the department. If I took over the family, that would come to an end."

"You were in an arranged marriage? How does that even happen anymore?" She yanks her hand from mine and her back hits the glass. The surprise on her face is real and authentic. It's like I've ripped a curtain aside and am seeing the real Dr. Aria Dillon for the first time.

And I like it.

"I'm proof it happens. The deal was, if I married Marcia and took over my dad's holdings corporation, I'd profit from the family business and still be able to live my life without getting my hands dirty. You could say I got a dowry."

"You agreed to a loveless marriage for money." It's a statement, not a question. One filled with judgment and scorn.

"I never wanted anyone. Was never interested in settling down. And I really didn't want to be head of the family. Looking back, was it the best decision?" I shrug. "No. But I said '*til death do us part*. Which, lucky for me, happened sooner rather than later. Now I'm a free man. As in really fucking free."

Just when I was getting somewhere, her eyes fall shut. She turns her head away. "You talk about it like it's not a big deal. It's huge, Brand."

"Doc." I place a light finger under her chin, bringing her face back to mine. "I did not murder her. The police are grasping at straws because they have no other leads and the Riccis have a shitload of cops in their pockets. The PD is getting pressure from my former in-laws. But that's all it is. It's going to be okay."

Her tremble vibrates through the tips of my fingers and goes straight to my dick. Finally, I might have managed one crack into her thick resolve to keep me at bay. Her voice validates my theory—her tone is low and hoarse. "It was only one night out with some dogs. I thought it would be … safe. How did I get myself into this?"

"Aria, baby…" I stop myself and suck in a deep breath. Not only do I not eat sugar, I also don't do sweet. Pet names are for people like Art—pussy-whipped fools who allow a woman to lead them around by their dicks.

That's never been me, which was why I was okay with the business transaction that was my sham of a marriage. I was after the big, fat paycheck that came with it when I signed on the dotted line after muttering *I do*.

I never saw myself as one of those men.

But am I?

Aria is … fascinating. It's why I insisted on the date she paid for. I'm human and curious as fuck. I had to know why she shelled out fifteen K then told me to get lost. Especially after I found out her sister worked at the shelter and she could have her pick of any mutt she wanted.

But since then…

I push that thought away and slide my hand into her thick hair. "You're safe. Probably safer than you've ever been. I can give you that."

"Then why do I feel like I'm teetering on a ledge?"

"Because you are." I tell her the truth. "But you don't have to be. I'm right here. It's your choice, Aria. Grab hold or plummet. The decision is vital. But you have to know before choosing, I've never wanted anything in my grip more than I do right now."

"I'm scared," she breathes.

"You'd be stupid not to be." I lean in and barely drag my tongue over her bottom lip as her breath shudders. "You'll get past that. I can help you. But, baby." I nudge the tip of her nose with mine as something new settles into me that I've never felt. It's foreign and all-consuming and fucking heavy, but I don't hate it. "It's ultimately on you. If you grab hold, I won't let you go."

Her exhale is heavy. Her bright, blue eyes cloud.

"Ever," I stress.

A tear falls between us and her tenacity disintegrates into thin air.

It's been a long time since a woman has intrigued me. I can't remember when or if I've ever had the desire to be with anyone long term. And, sure as hell, no woman has ever stirred a desperation in me.

An eagerness that itches from the inside out makes me push her to make a decision, because if she doesn't choose correctly, I know I'll go crazy. "I won't let you regret it. I promise. Choose me, Aria."

Fisting my shirt so tight it might never be the same, she pushes herself up on bare toes.

Fucking finally.

A reaction.

I meet her—taking her mouth with mine, her ass in my hands, and everything else I can manage.

I take it all for my own.

She's mine.

Until I'm done.

For the first time in my thirty-seven years, I wonder if I'll ever get my fill. If I'll ever be done. And I haven't even had her yet.

I press her into the glass and allow her moan to bring my dick to full attention. For reasons that can only be described as self-inflicted pain, I did not jerk off to the thoughts of her today. I didn't want to release any pressure, to break up the storm brewing inside me. I wanted the tension and my need for her to burst my fucking seams. Being right here is all I've thought about.

I must be a newborn masochist because if I don't have her soon, I might explode.

I drag my lips from hers long enough to rip her sweater over her head. Her tits sit before me encased in lace that barely covers her nipples. Her bra is so thin and small, I wonder why she bothered to begin with.

I yank the lace down on one side and she slips free. I put a hand to the middle of her back and force her to arch.

I get my first taste of something other than her mouth or neck.

"Brand." She gasps as I suck her in deep while ripping at the button on her jeans.

Jeans that look great on her ass, but will be a work of art when they hit my floor.

I pull her nipple between my teeth. Her head hits the glass with a thud. She grips my hair with the same intensity she did my shirt.

All of it—fucking perfect.

"That shouldn't feel so good, but it does," she breathes.

I bend to drag her jeans down and I'm not upset when her panties don't wait for an invitation. She stumbles, stepping out of them. I stand, letting her do the rest of the work until she kicks them to the side.

I don't move. I can't. I take her in standing before me—naked, except for her bra.

Going from sixty to nothing makes her uncomfortable and she starts to cover herself, but I shake my head and grab her hand. "Don't."

"I thought…" She sucks in a breath and I wonder what's going through her head. "What are you doing?"

She's a masterpiece. Athletic with curves. Fair skin, eyes like ice, and her thick dark hair. An equation that has me doing things I should not be doing, for more reasons than I can count.

I shake my head. "Got to be honest. I want this but I didn't think we'd be here. Not tonight."

Her face falls and she tries to rip her hand from mine but I'm enjoying my view too much, so I hold tight. "What are you saying?"

I don't know if this is going to fuck it up or put me in the record books for being the true master of all things.

But since we're skating the line of honesty, I guess we'll see where it goes.

"I'm saying, I'm trying to figure you out. Could've sworn when I had you in your office the other night, you needed a Dom."

Thirteen

FUCKING WITH MY HEAD

Aria

*E*VERY TIME WITH this man…

For once in my life I think, *go for it, Aria. Do something that moves you. Go with your gut instead of what's smart.*

Boring.

Predictable.

Then I prove to myself how I'm capable of one bad decision after another.

"Fuck you," I mutter and bend to pick up my jeans I just allowed him to drag off my dumb ass.

He stops me and pulls me to him, which at least offers me some modesty. "Don't do that."

"I don't need a Dom," I bite. "My father ruled every faction of my life with a heavy hand. Tell me what to do, Brand, I dare you. I'll be out of here so fast, your big, fat head will spin."

He holds me to his large frame and his dark hair falls to his forehead. I try not to think about how thick and soft it was just a minute ago when I had my hands buried in it.

"Shh." His big hand cups my bare ass. "We're just talking. That's it. You're not going anywhere, Aria. But you're finally opening up and I might actually make some progress with you. I want to figure out what you need."

"Why?" I snap. "Because you're a Dom? If so, then you've got the wrong woman standing naked in your family room."

His other arm angles up my back, strong and possessive as his other hand makes its way to my hair. Unlike the other night, now he's gentle, dragging his fingers methodically through to the ends. I don't know if it's meant to be comforting. Maybe done by anyone else while I was fully dressed, it might be.

But right now, it's not doing my frayed nerves any good.

He leans in and presses his lips to mine in a soft kiss I didn't know he was capable of. "I'll be whatever you need me to be. But I can't figure you out because you're so guarded. All I can do is take what little clues you're giving me and guess. But I got it now—you don't need a Dom."

I take a breath and try to relax a fraction, but don't let go of him. How am I going to get myself out of this now that he has me stripped naked?

"Not gonna lie." He squeezes my ass. "I've never had to win over a woman. This is not in my wheelhouse."

"That's crazy."

He looks over my head and his eyes heat, no doubt taking in the reflection of me, naked, in his arms. When he finally looks down, I get his rare smile, even if it is small. "Not sure how I feel about my psychologist calling me *crazy*."

"The last thing I am is your doctor, Brand."

He leans to kiss me again at the same moment my bra goes slack. I tense but he deepens his kiss and his hands start to roam.

"I fucked up the mood," he mutters against my lips, his fingers brush my sides and tease my breasts. "I need to fix that."

I press my face into his chest. His shirt is soft and fresh and I wonder if he does his own laundry. I mean, now that I know he married for money, I understand how he throws cash around so easily and lives in a place like this while working as a firefighter. His house is amazing and not only belongs on Pinterest boards, but also in *Architectural Digest*.

And I can vouch for that because my parents' estate in Miami was featured on the cover. It was the highlight of my mother's year.

"Do you know how fucking complex you are? From the first moment I laid eyes on you, I wanted to know you. Not long after that, I thought about you being right here." He slides a finger through my ass cheeks and I shiver as wetness pools between my legs. His lips come to my ear. "I hope you know that your body is a work of art and your mind is just as fascinating. Every bit of you is riveting—I can't get enough. Turn around."

The man is giving me whiplash—making me hot, angry, and then hot again. And now talking to me the way no one ever has.

"Aria." His tone is firm as he breaks into my thoughts. "Turn around."

I peek over my shoulder. The windows go from the floor to the vaulted second story. They've got to be over twenty-five feet high with no blinds or curtains. I look back at him. "No."

"I live on thirty acres. My neighbors have even more. The lake is private and it's fucking cold outside. No one is out besides some rabbits, squirrels, and maybe deer. You can do it—turn around. I want to show you something."

I exhale and wonder how Brand Vitale has made me into someone I don't recognize.

His breath fans my face. "*Now*."

I let go of his shirt and do something that took me years to get over—allow someone to tell me what to do.

He pries my fingers from his mangled shirt and guides me in a half-circle.

"Baby." The way he says that… "Open your eyes."

I do.

The windows are opaque. There's no problem seeing every detail of his house behind us. The steep ceilings, black metal industrial beams that contrast with the raw wood. His huge kitchen makes me want to learn how to cook and I've never, ever cooked for myself. His stone fireplace climbs to the ceiling, and even my sweet Muppet is completely oblivious to what's going on as he snores away on the blanket Brand put out for him in front of the fire.

And I see us.

Me, naked as the day I was born.

And him, in his Station Six T-shirt and jeans that fit so perfectly, any male model would kill for his *I don't give a fuck* look.

His intense stare meets mine in the reflection. "See? Pretty fucking perfect. I'd go so far as to say *completely perfect* if you'd tell me your secrets."

My lids fall, closing him out, because there's no way. That will never happen.

Despite the crackle of the enormous fireplace warming the massive space, I shiver. A touch, light on my breast, demands my attention and I force myself to focus on the display he's orchestrating. This is like nothing I've ever done before. Nothing I've ever imagined myself doing.

His eyes are laser focused on his ministrations as my nipples betray me, hardening into devious pebbles as he circles one. "I'm pleased you've had to work yourself to the bone and no one has pressed you for your time before now. I'd ask why no man has pinned you down yet, but I have no desire to know who might have touched you in the past."

Hyperaware of everything around me, my swallow echoes in my ears before I croak, "I've had men in my life, but I can promise you, I've never been *here* with anyone. You're definitely … one of a kind."

His hot stare shifts from my body to my eyes in the windows. "You're brave."

"Hardly," I argue. "You'd be surprised how timid I am."

I try not to shift when I lose his touch altogether.

His T-shirt is no more and lands on top of my clothes in a heap on the floor. I'm teased with his bare shoulders, olive in contrast with my fair skin, as his body frames mine in the dark windows.

The rip of his zipper screams in the quiet room and I can see him arranging himself before his arm moves.

The need to shift and turn to see him, watch him stroke himself, is an itch I want to scratch. But I can't look away from his reflection as his tongue sneaks out to taste his full lips.

He takes a step forward, pressing every inch of his cock—hard and long and bare—against the small of my back. Skin-to-skin—hot, heavy, and heady—from his pelvis to his shoulders.

His arms circle me, pulling me in tight like magnetic forces, one hand goes to my breast and the other to my sex.

I groan and lift my hands to his arm.

He stares at what he's doing in the windows and demands, "Give me some space and hold on."

My grip on him tightens as I shift my legs. I get his fingers back and it's better than it was the other night in my office with the added bonus of his cock pressed against me. The moment I rest my head on his chest, he immediately twists my nipple so hard, it shoots straight to my clit.

I gasp and raise my head to look at him.

"Watch," he demands.

It's not lost on me that I told him there was no way I wanted or needed a Dom, yet he's done nothing but tell me what to do.

And I've done nothing but obey, dammit.

But it's just too good. I can't stop. Not only do I allow him to push me, I can't wait to see where he'll take me next.

This is me at my most vulnerable. He was right to question my lack of curiosity—the novelty of him is what's driving my next breath. I'm not only physically hanging to him, I'm hanging on his every word and want to know his every thought.

If this makes me desperate, I don't care. I'm tired of wondering. I need to know everything about him.

Mesmerized by his touch, his expression, and how his every move is causing my insides to burn for him, I'm completely entranced. The fire has nothing to do with the temperature of my body.

"I want you to see what I see. What I've been thinking about nonstop. No one has fucked with my mind like you have. Ever."

My breath shallows. "You say that like it's a bad thing."

"It would be if I didn't have you here." He twists my nipple again and circles my clit harder. It doesn't matter how many miles a week I run or how strong my legs are—they might give out. He grinds his cock into my back as he works my clit, both of us watching the live feed playing out in our reflection. "But I don't see how this is going to help. The way I see it, you'll be deeper in my head. And do you know what, baby?"

I'm so close—I can't utter a word. I shake my head and watch him do whatever he wants to with my body. If I were able to string two words together, I'd beg for more.

His arms constrict, his fingers move, he pinches, and his lips hit my ear. "Bring it on. I think I'm going to like it. I'm already consumed by the thought of you. To have you here like this—the real deal instead of my fictionalized thoughts—has me shackled and bound."

I turn my face and he gives me what I want. He takes my mouth the moment my orgasm washes over every inch of me. Strong and steadfast, he holds my weight and doesn't let up when I squeeze my thighs. He's doing to my body what he's done to my mind—consuming me completely and wholly without any reprieve.

Before I have a chance to recover, he twists me in his arms. The cold windows are a shock to my system when he presses my back to the glass. He grabs a condom from his back pocket and rips it open between his teeth.

"We'll talk about these later." He spits the wrapper to the floor. Another shiver travels my spine that has nothing to do with the cool glass supporting my weight. I watch as he slides a condom over his cock, inch after delicious inch.

He lifts me, one hand under my ass and the other supporting my knee. "Never been desperate for anyone. When you're with me, you don't have to pretend to be anything you're not, and you don't have to fucking hide who you are. Do you understand?"

I bring a hand to the side of his face and drag my thumb over his bottom lip. The tip of his cock is teasing my sex as he moves his hips, waiting on my answer.

I don't give him one. "Please, Brand. This has been a whirlwind, but I want you."

"Eventually, you'll understand. I'll make sure of it." He leans in and takes my mouth. I thread my fingers through his hair, holding him to me, allowing my heart to realize this is no fantasy.

This is very, very real.

No more dreaming when it comes to Brand Vitale. I'm here. Wrapped around him. Encased in his arms.

For now, he's mine. Mine to take.

And I'm his.

He surges into me in one go. Like everything else when it comes to him, there's no easing into it or allowing me to slowly get used to him.

All of him.

And there's a lot.

And he doesn't take me gently.

"Oh," I moan into his mouth.

"Not holding back, Aria. I gave you a piece of me tonight and I'm gonna keep doing it. I'm all in. I need you to be okay with that because there's no other option."

He's not speaking metaphorically, because he's really not holding back. Pounding into me, his nose rests aside mine. Our lips are so close, I'm not sure where one breath ends and another begins.

He takes me with everything he has, over and over and over. Each thrust pounds my clit and it's all I can do to hold on.

When I come for a second time, his fingers bite into my flesh where he's supporting me. This orgasm is different, and better with him inside me and I realize Brand Vitale is like the most addictive of drugs.

I never want this to end.

I lose his dark eyes when he squeezes them shut and stuffs his face in the side of my hair. His groan vibrates through every part of me.

He pounds into me once more and pulls me onto him. I'm full and sore and...

I don't know.

But I'm definitely something. I'll decide later when I can think straight and psychoanalyze all my mistakes.

Until then, I want this moment to last forever.

I turn my head and press my lips to the corner of his mouth as he continues to catch his breath. He rests a forearm over my head on the glass, and now that we're returning to earth, I really hope he was right about no one being outside. I'm not into voyeurism.

When he finally opens his eyes, they're dark in the dim space and his hair is a mess, thanks to me. His sharp, defined jawline is covered in stubble and his lips are parted.

This frightening and complicated man has never been more beautiful.

I did this to him.

He speaks on a heavy exhale. "You're not leaving tonight."

When I move, I feel it on the skin of my abused back, but I ignore it and everything else but him.

I nod.

And then I pull his lips to mine.

Fourteen

PAY FOR SEX

Aria

"I WAS AT work today and I thought my boss was going to wet herself. I was already her favorite, but after the sizable donation you made to the shelter, I'm worried she'll name a litter of kittens after me. All of them Briar, Jr."

I freeze, not because of what she said, but because I have no clue what to do now that I burned the garlic and onions.

I had twenty minutes to spare before Briar was going to drop Muppet off on her way home from work, so I swung by the store and bought ingredients for enchiladas from a recipe I found on Pinterest.

Briar loves Mexican and I love Briar, so I'm stepping into an unknown world—my kitchen. Now I'm kicking myself for not going through a drive-thru for greasy tacos. We both would've been happier.

For some reason—that I do not want to think about or admit to—I was inspired to cook for her because it felt really good when someone cooked for me. I can't remember the last time anyone cooked for me who wasn't hired to do the job.

And it had nothing to do with what happened after dinner, though that was even better.

It was mind-blowing, naughty, and made even my fantasies jealous. I don't dream big enough.

I didn't want to leave him or the sanctuary of his lake house this morning. I actually dreaded going to work and I love my job.

Briar does not like schedules and making plans gives her anxiety. I'd travel to the ends of the earth to not add to her unease. She's had more of that in her short life than anyone deserves.

So when I thought I could do something for her, like cook her dinner, it sounded like the best idea ever.

But now the onions and garlic are black and I don't think that's what the recipe meant when it said sauté. My kitchen is a wreck, my apartment stinks, and we're both starving.

Now she's talking about the donation, or what I have started referring to as my newfound, brazen debt.

I pick up the pan and dump it in the sink. "It wasn't a big deal."

"It's a big fucking deal and you know it."

Opening the freezer, I don't turn to her. "Pick your carbs—frozen pizza or frozen rice bowl? That's all I have to offer at this point. I somehow managed to get my doctorate, yet I can't follow a simple recipe."

"Pizza." I always push Briar for information since she's locked tighter than a clam, but tonight she's turning the tables on me. "Worthy cause or not, you'd never throw around that kind of money unless there was something else going on. So why did you?"

I toss the frozen disc on the counter and preheat the oven before I turn to her and cross my arms. Explaining what happened the night of the auction is complicated. I'm not sure I have the answer myself. "I don't know."

"You don't know?"

I shrug before allowing my shoulders to sag. When I agreed to stay with Brand last night, I knew what I was getting myself into, I just thought it would include a little more sleep. I'm accustomed to not getting a full eight hours, but the mental exhaustion is setting in.

I look over at Muppet, jealous of him sprawled and snoring on my sofa after a day playing at the shelter. "I got a dog out of it."

"I tried to tempt you into adopting one of those puppies and you said you were too busy. Now suddenly you're the proud doggy mom of a pup you could've gotten for free. And my furry nephew may be cute and a genius," she lowers her voice as if she doesn't want him to hear, "but he's not worth fifteen fucking grand."

I decide to give her a sliver of truth because her pushing me shows how worried she is. "Before the bidding, I met Muppet with the firefighter he was paired with. It was easy to fall for Muppet, even though I knew I'd need your help with him so he wasn't alone too much. But the man

… he was a different story."

Her eyes widen. "What about the man?"

I sigh. "I found him interesting."

"Oh, shit," she mutters.

"He didn't want to be there, Briar. As in, really didn't want to be there. He was angry and irritable and downright mean at moments."

"Well, he sounds like a catch totally worth fifteen K." Her lips tip in a barely there smile. "Which must mean he's majorly hot."

I put the pizza in the oven before it preheats completely because I'm starving. Then I sit at the tiny table where Briar and I have shared countless frozen dinners. "I didn't plan on bidding, but things got out of hand. He was standing on that stage holding Muppet and I had to do something. It happened so fast my head was spinning when it was all said and done."

"That's not like you, yet it's so you." She picks up her glass and takes a big drink. "Tell me what happened at your fifteen-thousand-dollar dinner."

"Nothing." Briar frowns and I pull in a deep breath. "Everything. It was bizarre. Full of sexual tension, yet he still scares me. But in a way I want more."

"Who wouldn't want more sexual tension?"

I nudge her foot with mine and smile. "I've seen him a few times since. He's complicated, Briar. So much so, he's intricate and that fascinates me. *He* fascinates me."

"Everyone fascinates you. It's why you're a psychologist."

I reach across the table and grab her hand. "I agree, that's what I'm normally like. But this is different."

She narrows her eyes and pins me in my spot before her mouth curves into a rare grin. "You slept with him, didn't you?"

I cross my legs at the thought of last night. Brand took me to his room, which was just as beautiful as the rest of his house, for round two. Then we took a shower before he wrung my last orgasm of the night out of me. We passed out for a few hours in his big bed. I was up before the sun and he made me promise I'd see him again before his next shift.

I was hungover on sex and éclairs, so, of course, I said yes.

As if I could say no at this point.

"This is the best news. *Ever*." She tilts her head. "Please tell me it was good."

I sit back in my chair and decide it should be illegal to use the word good in the same sentence as Brando Vitale, Jr. "It was … life-altering."

Briar doesn't smile much, so when she continues giving me a genuine grin, I don't take it for granted. "So you're saying this man has ruined your self-imposed celibacy?"

"It scares me." I tell her the truth. "There are circumstances that I can't explain, but they're so extreme, I can't believe I'm in the middle of it. And I'm in the middle of it by my own doing. I look at myself from afar and want to scream and shake the fool who's going down a dead-end road. Because there's no doubt in my mind this will not end well."

Briar hikes a foot on her chair and rests her chin on her knee. "Self-destruction—it's what all the cool kids are doing. Welcome to the party."

Usually a comment like that from her would worry me, but there's no malice in her voice. Actually, now that her worry about me has faded, she seems almost … happy.

I'm trying to decide if I should risk pushing her on it when my phone dings from the counter—rapid fire, one text after another. I realize it's been a quiet night so far. Demons come out to play at night, making it the busy time for doctors like me.

Hero – Come over.

Hero – You can bring the dog.

Hero – I need a session with my doctor.

Hero – I think I have an addiction but I don't want to cure it. I want to feed it. I need your professional opinion, preferably while you're naked.

Hero – Where the fuck are you?

My skin tightens and the hair on my arms stand.

"What's the emergency?"

I look at Briar and bite back my smile. "No emergency."

Me – I'm having dinner with my sister. Maybe you should work on your patience.

Hero – If you only knew how patient I really am, Doc, you would eat those words with as much enthusiasm as I ate you in bed last night.

"What's that smell?"

"Shit. I forgot to set the timer."

I ignore all thoughts of Brand's mouth between my legs after our shower last night and open the oven.

Smoke hits my face and cheese sizzles on the coils. "Dammit."

I grab a spatula and cutting board, and scrape the second meal I've ruined tonight off the racks before slamming the oven shut.

Briar and I stare at the mutilated pizza. She leans into my arm. "We've eaten worse in the last year."

"True."

I put my arm around her and tip my brunette head to her blond one, not looking away from the mess I've made. "I promise I'm going to learn how to cook—I want to make you a home-cooked meal. I was distracted tonight."

"Were you thinking about the life-altering sex or the man giving it to you?"

I sigh. "Both. But really the latter."

She turns to me. "Will I get to meet him?"

I shrug and don't answer. The battle between what I should do and what I am doing is raging strong. I'm not sure a winner will emerge for some time.

She reaches for plates. "Next time you want to surprise me with dinner, I'm good with chips and salsa."

"Perfect. It's cheaper since I'm knee-deep in credit card debt."

She starts to cut our burned dinner. "If you're going to pay for sex, at least it's good sex."

My phone dings.

Hero – I'm coming over. Be there in an hour.

Fifteen

CONVOLUTED WEB

Brand

"JUST HAD A meeting. Permits will be issued first thing in the morning. Our guy said everything is in order. He apologized. Said he doesn't want it to reflect poorly on him," Art says.

"As long as it's fixed." I pull into Aria's apartment complex and throw my Tahoe in park. "We can be back to work before sunup. We're behind schedule. My contractors will be anxious to get back to work."

"He said he'd touch base. I'll keep you in the loop."

"I appreciate it. I've got to go, I just arrived at my therapy appointment. Call you later."

Art sighs. "Fuck me."

I ignore that, hang up, and hit go on my dad's number.

It's late but not late for my dad. When he answers, music and voices fill the background. "Brand, tell me you have good news."

"I'll confirm in the morning, but my guy says permits will be posted first thing. I'll be able to pay contractors tomorrow."

"Good." He pauses and the background noise fades. "I was about to call. We have another issue we need to discuss."

I watch Aria climb out of her Merc across the parking lot. "Make it quick. I'm busy."

"I hear you've been busy." His tone is a sharp whip through the phone. "Lonnie got a visit today from Saul Ricci's right hand. This is not the time to be tempting your dead wife's family. If you're going to fuck around, be careful. I do not need this kind of heat from them. We have enough attention with the police tailing you. Get your shit together."

I don't mince words. "I have my shit together."

"The hell you do," he hisses. "People are talking and it's not good. I have a feeling it's gonna get uglier than it was before the families were tied by marriage. And this has nothing to do with the investigation. This is worse."

"I met someone." I watch Aria as she jogs the stairs and wonder what it's gonna take to get to the bottom of her. "I'm not an eighty-year-old widower—it's been six months. I was held prisoner in my marriage from hell long enough. I'm done."

"This isn't good—"

"I can handle it," I assure him.

And also, I don't give a shit anymore.

"It's hard to give you the protection of the family when you don't work in an official role. It will draw the kind of attention you don't want. Even so, let me send someone. I don't like this."

I climb out of my SUV and scan the parking lot. "I'm not stupid. They were my in-laws. I fucking hate them but I know them. Before they completely hated me, I got to know their organization. I know how they operate and can take care of myself."

Aria unlocks her apartment, but turns and catches my eye from where she stands at the balcony. She pulls that damn lip between her teeth again.

"If I hear anything else, I'm putting a man on you. If you don't want to run this family, you don't get a say in the matter."

"Whatever," I mutter as I climb the steps. "He'll be bored, and it's a waste of money."

"They're on my payroll no matter what." He sighs and I wonder how much longer he's going to draw this out. "God forbid anything happens to you. Your mother would kill me and I'd never forgive myself."

I can practically hear him crossing himself when I clear the third set of stairs. Aria is leaning on the door jamb waiting on me in a pair of leggings, a sports bra, and running shoes. Every curve is taunting me. She looks like she just worked out or is about to. I wonder if I can talk her into working out in a whole different way. Her hair is pulled back and her blue eyes are prying, curious, and trying to penetrate me.

Yes, my psychologist wants to know everything.

At this point, all she has to do is ask. I'll tell her whatever she wants because I have her exactly where I want her. Which is interesting, because a week ago I had no idea I'd be standing right here thinking the things I am.

"Gotta go, Dad. I'll call tomorrow when Realm is up and running."

He sighs. "Love you, son. Watch your back."

"Love you, too." I disconnect and slide my phone into my back pocket.

"Do you?" she asks, giving more of her weight to the door frame.

I lean in closer. "Do I what?"

"Love him. That was your father, right?"

It is not lost on me this is one of the only questions she asked that hasn't been instigated by my getting her naked and saying the wrong things.

"Yeah. He's my dad. Of course, I love him."

She nods once and bites that lip again.

I drag my thumb across it and pull it from between her teeth before leaning to kiss her. "Don't do that. I tasted blood the first time I kissed you."

She pulls in a swift breath.

"Why do you ask about my dad? You don't love yours?"

She licks her lips and her answer couldn't be more clear. "No."

I shift my body closer to hers. "That's odd."

"It wouldn't be if you knew him."

Interesting. "What about your mom before she died?"

"Absolutely not. Yours?"

I frown. "Yes. I have good parents despite their fucked-up marriage. It seems to work for them, so who's to judge."

"One might say you had a fucked-up marriage."

I shake my head and grab her hand, pulling her into her apartment before kicking the door shut. The dog jumps on my legs, but I can't focus on anything but her. "You're full of questions tonight, Doc. Why is that?" I look around. "And what is that God-awful smell?"

She pulls her hand out of mine and goes to the kitchen sink. "I burned dinner. I actually burned two dinners. I am not Italian or a firefighter, so apparently cooking is not in my blood." She flips on the water and starts scrubbing on something. "I'm just pointing out that you told me yourself you had a bad marriage. I find it interesting."

I move to the mouth of the small galley kitchen and cross my arms. "Can't lie. When a shrink tells me they find something interesting, I find that even more interesting. Tell me why you don't love your dad?"

She doesn't look up and isn't fazed by my question. "Because he's horrible."

Huh. Made-man horrible or I-missed-all-your-soccer-games horrible? Because this is something I didn't learn from the PI report. "How?"

She might need a jackhammer as hard as she's scrubbing. "Because he's mean. He's demeaning. He cut me off from friends. He yelled. He demanded perfection. How many reasons do you want?"

I walk over to stand next to her and she's scrubbing black shit off the inside of a pan. "That's fucked up."

She flips the water off and drops the pan into the sink before turning to me. "I could never make him happy. And it wasn't for a lack of trying. All I did my entire childhood was try to please him. Do you know why I started swimming as a child?"

"Because you found something you were good at and you loved it?"

She dries her hands and tosses the towel on the counter. "I hated swimming when I started. And I really didn't want to swim competitively. I didn't like sports."

I barely hike a brow, almost fearful to move a muscle and I don't fear anything. She's in a talkative mood and I don't want her to stop.

"Do you swim, Brand?"

"Sure."

"No," she shakes her head and fists my shirt at my abs, pulling herself closer to me. "I mean, have you ever swam competitively? Or for exercise?"

"I lift, run, and bike. I run stairs for work. I ski in the winter and in the summer we swim off the boat."

She lowers her voice and her intense stare penetrates me. "Then you don't know. Being under water is beautiful. Poetic. You can have a lion roaring in your ears, but when you go under…" She shrugs. "It all goes away. It's a peaceful silence—tranquil and solitary."

I steady my breaths even though I have to work for it. And I'm a firefighter—I could be in a four-alarm emergency with full gear and tanks, and my breaths are as steady as the second hand.

"Being under drowns out everything. It was the only way I could block *him* from my mind. I used to wish there was a way for me to never surface for air."

I slide my hand around her neck and tilt her face to mine. "You don't mean that."

She nods. "If you knew my father, you'd understand."

"Your mom didn't protect you from that?"

"Bette Dillon was too busy ruining Briar's life. I was the smart, athletic one. Briar was the beauty queen."

One could argue that, but I'll save it for another day. "You almost made it to the Olympics doing something you hated?"

A smile takes over her beautiful lips, one I've never seen.

It's secretive and shrewd and something inside her comes to life.

It also makes me hard.

"What?" I ask. She leans into my palm when I slide my hand to the side of her face.

"If I made the Olympic team, that would've meant months of training and then the event itself. That would have put my master's and doctorate program behind at least a year, maybe more. I'd been accepted to Harvard. You'd think a parent might be proud of that. But my father wanted me to go to med school and work for him in his practice. Not to be a *fake doctor* who didn't go to medical school, only to work in one of the lowest paying medical professions. Psychologists aren't exactly rolling in it."

"Are you saying you threw the Olympic trials to piss off your father?"

That smile gets bigger, and I feel her shrug. "It was one of the last times I've spoken to him outside of my mother dying. I haven't seen him in over a year. I hope I never see him again."

"You're alone."

She shakes her head. "I have Briar. And now I have a dog."

"That's fucked. Your father, not your sister. The dog is still a toss-up."

"Don't talk shit about my dog. We're bonding and I need him to love me."

"I don't think that'll be an issue."

I want to dig deeper, make her tell me things I know she's hiding. But that time will come. She pushes onto her toes and presses her mouth to mine. I'm about to deepen her kiss when she cuts me off and shakes her head, pushing me away. "I need to run or else I won't be able to sleep, no matter how long you kept me awake last night."

I pull her back to me. "I'll wear you out again."

"Sorry. Make yourself at home, Brand. Play with my dog, but don't bond too much." She points at me. "He has to love me more than anyone else."

I cross my arms and watch her walk down the hall. "Where are you going?"

"Treadmill."

The next thing I know, shoes are pounding at a quick clip.

I look at the dog who's shit at reading humans because he wags his tail as if I'm someone who wants to spend time with him.

"What?"

"Ruff!"

He runs in circles to the door. I grab his leash and wish I'd made her come to my house. My home gym is the shit, and once she sees it, she'll never leave. Who knew that's what it would take to make her come to me.

"You're still a shithead. Let's go."

As I'm walking an uncontrollable dog while at a woman's crap apartment complex instead of my modern lake house, I realize, for the first time in my life, I'm doing shit that is not like me.

And the longer she weaves me into her convoluted web, the more open I am to being tangled in every way she'll have me.

Sixteen

DOPAMINE LIMBO

Aria

WITH OVER ONE hundred million neurons, the brain is the body's most complex organ.

Some say it's the most complex thing in the universe.

It controls our actions, reactions, thoughts, emotions, memories.

It's what sets us apart from other species.

Our brains make us human.

There's a reason why humans feel less inhibited, bold, and, yes, even brave during sex. The part of the brain responsible for reason, decision making, and value judgments shuts down when the body is aroused. It's how the organ is wired. Orgasm cannot be achieved if fear and apprehension block it.

That's called performance anxiety.

To put it simply, the lateral orbitofrontal cortex takes a beach vacation to the Maldives so the rest of the brain can produce a slew of hormones and neurochemicals so our bodies are able to achieve the big O.

It's the beautiful and natural drug-like chemical called dopamine.

The brain is a magical organ, studied for centuries. Even with a Harvard doctorate, I'd be a liar to declare myself a master of the most complex thing in the universe. I've barely scratched the surface.

But what I do know, without a shadow of a doubt, is no one has spiked my dopamine like the part-time mobster and fulltime firefighter, Brando Gian Vitale, Jr.

Yes, despite jumping straight to hot sex, we've moved to the middle-name stage of our fucked-up relationship. And I know it's fucked because, unless dopamine is taking over my brain, I have a clear and concise grasp on my poor decision-making skills.

One after another after another.

But, the dopamine.

Sometimes he only has to look at me, and it spikes. As I check the days off on the calendar, counting my time with Brand, I'm finding it easier and easier to ignore intellectual reasoning and values and…

Morals.

Hell, my rational judgment took a flying leap off the top of the Space Needle the night I bid thousands of dollars I don't have.

"Please."

He doesn't answer since his mouth is occupied between my legs, but I do get a squeeze. His big hands cup my ass, determined to keep me on the edge, teetering and swaying, leaving me treading water in dopamine limbo.

If I get close, he backs off. When I start to come down, he gives me a push.

This has been going on far too long.

Which is why I'm acting out of character—bold, brave, desperate.

Begging.

"Brand." I reach for his head and hold him to my sex, pressing my clit to his mouth.

His teeth sink into my sensitive skin just enough to warn me. But even that feels good.

I lose his hands as he tears his mouth away from my desperate clit. My eyes fly open and he drags his forearm across his mouth. His stare is hungry, travels my bare body. I barely have a chance to maintain eye contact before he flips me to my stomach. His lips come to my neck in a kiss and a vise, pressing my face to the mattress as his hand dips between my legs.

Cupping me in the most basic and carnal way, he lifts me to my knees and forces me to arch.

"I figured out what you need." His words drip like honey, thicker and heavier than the English language intended.

I open my eyes and take him in. He uses his chin with his three-day whiskers to pull at my messy hair fanning my face. Now I can see him clear as day since he turned on the bright lights in my bedroom.

Fingers easily sink into me and I press into his hand, trying to find relief from his perpetual torment. "What?"

"You don't need a Dom."

My eyes widen as I lose his fingers.

His stare penetrates me when the flat of his hand connects with my ass. It's sharp and backed with muscle. I'll never forget the crack of his skin connecting to mine as it echoes around the room.

A spank.

A yelp escapes my lips.

"You need to escape reality," he finishes as he delivers another— harder this time.

A shock to my system.

I get a third, this time on my sex.

So hard it hurts. At least, I think it does.

Pain dances with pleasure in a complicated choreography coursing through my veins.

In a good way. The best way. A way I've only read about, but doubted it existed in real life.

He delivers a fourth.

I moan.

Lips touch my ear, arrogant and satisfied. "Told you."

When he barely brushes my clit with the tips of his thick fingers, I fall.

Kill me now. I'm sure to overdose on dopamine, otherwise.

When I come, it's different. I escape to a place I've never been and never want to leave. I wonder if this is how addicts feel—the high, the want, the need. Leaving them obsessed and willing to overlook everything else in life for their next fix.

With my hips tight in his grip, he fills me from behind, and not with his fingers. My sex conforms to his size and length, molding to him, making me wonder if this was meant to be.

If I was made for him and the universe has some morbid sense of humor to bring me to this spot.

Wishful thinking.

There's no way this is meant to be.

"Tell me this is happening." He uses all his power, his breaths coming hard and quick. "I can't get my fill of you."

I fist the covers beneath me and press into him. I can't find my voice to answer.

"Aria."

I meet his every thrust as best I can.

"Fuck," he hisses and slams into me two last times before planting himself deep.

My lungs race to catch up with my heart. Brand bends at the waist and cages me in before giving me his weight. I fall flat to the bed and he follows. I'm crushed, and nothing has ever felt so good.

I want to stay here forever, but I have appointments and he has a shift at the station. He woke me with a hand between my legs, which was easy for him since we passed out naked.

I never thought insatiable was a real thing until I met him.

He's still hard inside me, unmoving besides his head that twists to take my mouth. "Your bed is shit."

I manage a small smile. "It's fine."

"Fine is not okay." He presses into me. "Your bed is shit. My bed feels like a cloud. From now on we're in my bed."

"Ruff!"

I try to shift under him. "I need to walk Muppet."

Brand shakes his head. "You never answered me."

"Yes, I did."

"No, you didn't."

"Brand, Muppet needs out. He's doing so well, I don't want him to have an accident. Walk with me and you can ask whatever you want."

"I've figured you out, Doc."

I push up as hard as I can and he proves he wasn't giving me all his weight before, because now I really can't move. "There's nothing to figure out. Please, you're heavy."

"You're fine. Eventually you're going to have to answer me."

"Ruff!"

"Brand," I whisper.

Before he pulls out and rolls to the side, he nudges the tip of my nose with his. I'm becoming obsessed with that minute gesture.

He wasn't lying, my mattress is shit and complains as our weight shifts. While he takes care of the condom, I climb over him and head straight to my bathroom with Muppet on my heels.

"Hang on, buddy. I'll hurry."

I throw on a pair of sweatpants and a hoodie that are laying on the floor from yesterday and pile my hair high on my head. I open the door, and on my way out of the bathroom, I find Brand standing there, buck naked and beautiful, blocking my way to Muppet.

I take him in. His cock is still at half-mast. I can't resist and drag my index finger down every chiseled ab until I get so low, I outline the V above his pelvis.

"Stay at my house tonight."

I look up. "But you have a shift."

"I do. But I have security, inside and out. You don't have to walk the dog on a busy street. It's quiet. You can hang out and do whatever you want."

I shake my head and tell him the truth. "I'm not ready to be there without you."

He steps forward and cups my face in his hands. "You haven't seen my home gym. Every almost-Olympian would be impressed. Promise me you'll come. I'll give you a key and the code to the security system."

"That's sweet. And if the rest of your house is any indicator, I'm sure your gym is amazing. But I think it will be weird to be there without you." I pause and my gaze drifts to his chest. "You know, your wife and everything."

He tips my face to his, and I can't keep myself from biting my lip.

His thumb immediately pulls it from between my teeth and he leans in close. "I owe you more. About her and my marriage. I'll tell you whatever you want to know, but you can be certain of this—that is my house. I designed it and had it built five years ago for the sheer purpose of living separately from her. I had it decorated and she had no input. I chose every last thing down to the espresso maker. She lived there because she was dead set on making my life miserable, which is exactly what she did. Don't make more of it than it is. We had separate rooms. We did not live there as husband and wife."

He doesn't give me a chance to refute him and leans in to kiss me.

Against my lips, he hesitates before admitting, "Not sure how I'm going to make it twenty-four hours at the station knowing you're sleeping in my bed. Just don't burn my house down trying to cook. You'll start a forest fire."

I let out a breath and smile. Why am I being such a freak?

"Promise me you'll stay. It's Friday. You can sleep in tomorrow, if that's your thing."

How can it only be Friday? The past week feels like a lifetime.

With my face held tight in his hands and only him in my sight, I can't refuse him. He's captured me in so many more ways than this. "Okay. I'll stay."

He stands straight and moves around me. "Give me two minutes and I'll walk with you."

Muppet is sitting at the threshold of the bedroom door, his tail banging against the baseboards. "Are you the happiest puppy ever?"

He jumps to his feet and escapes down my short hall to the front door. I grab his leash and bend to give him a rub. "Tonight I'll take you to Brand's and you can play by the lake."

He starts turning in circles.

"See, you'll love me most. I promise."

I feel a hand at my back before it slides to my ass. "Will you feel this all day?"

It's everything I can do to bite back my smile when I turn to him. "Was that your intention?"

"Hell, yes. And tonight when I can't be with you."

I hike a brow before turning to my front door. "Maybe I'll touch myself in your bed and you'll be left wondering how it went without you."

I turn the knob and Muppet leads the way to the stairs. "I want a detailed report, Doc. Every single detail."

Seventeen

THINGS

Aria

MATERIALISM.
Stuff.
Things.

Possessions don't impress me. My father is the top plastic surgeon in the state of Florida, and, if you run the numbers, beyond. People come from far and wide to dump money at his feet because the price for youth and beauty is steep. Even steeper the older you get.

Possessions were plentiful in the Dillon home. My dad paid a pretty penny to make sure I was the best at everything. And when that didn't work, he put the pressure on to ensure I was. I had every tool money could buy at my fingertips to achieve perfection.

My mom also paid a pretty penny to make sure Briar was a child beauty queen and the envy of every other ostentatious parent in a five-hundred-mile vicinity.

Growing up, the Dillon home did not consist of happy-go-lucky unicorns, even though my parents sure made it appear that way to every acquaintance they could get to pay attention.

When one is raised with anything and everything, the most impressive things are merely ordinary.

However, things that *others* choose to surround themselves with?

Those, I find utterly fascinating.

Tangible objects help define us. Whether it be a plethora of them or a lack thereof.

The day drags on like an eighth day of the week. Focusing is hard while listening to my patients secrets and problems—all I can think about is spending the night at Brand's house again.

Alone this time.

I'm anxious to be in the space he lived in with his late wife, even though he insists they cohabitated at best. I have no choice right now but to take him at his word. If I didn't, I'd be running the other way as fast as my marathon feet would take me. And the thought of that is more painful than the consequences I could face from staying.

I picked up Muppet from Briar's to get here as fast as I can, not wanting to waste one moment to be among his things.

And learn.

Brand Vitale has elicited every possible emotion within me. He scares me and angers me. He turns me on and comforts me without trying or knowing he's doing it.

He's dangerous. And still, he's a hero.

The man excites every part of me for reasons that are very, very wrong.

I turn the key he gave me to get into his house. When the lock slides open, my heart skips a beat. Muppet and I cross the threshold, and I disarm his security system with a set of numbers so long, I'm afraid I won't get them entered before a mob descends on me for breaking and entering. My fingers tremble at the thought. But the musical tone confirms I'm in—smoother than water on a calm night.

Muppet immediately disappears quicker than lightning to reacquaint himself with every square foot of Brand's monstrous house.

I, on the other hand, zero in on a piece of paper tented next to a bottle of wine sitting on his exquisite, veined marble island. On the front, the nickname he's given me is spelled out in a heavy, masculine scrawl.

Doc

Relax and drink wine. There's food in the fridge. The house is yours, just be gentle with my pots and pans. Text me later when you're naked in my bed.

And yes, that means when you're in my bed, I want you naked, regardless if I'm in it with you or not.

B

I read it again.

And again.

I study his handwriting and find it odd that I'm more turned on by the strong slant of the letters than I am the meaning of the words themselves. Formed by the same fingers that have done all kinds of things to me.

That should not make me wet, but it does.

I slide the note into my purse before dropping my bags to the floor. I look around. Just like the other night, his home is pristine—clean and tidy, but it smells of citrus instead of chicken marsala.

I look to the wall of windows with the lake beyond, surrounded by a vast green forest that goes on for miles. A tingle low in my belly teases me with the moment we shared there when I was naked.

I turn away from the lake and round the island to the wide refrigerator. It's not lost on me that during the few meals I've shared with Brand, he skipped dessert, which is crazy. I never skip dessert when it's offered.

My mother had a closet eating disorder. Everyone knew but to talk about it was taboo. She did all she could to transfer that to Briar, because beauty queens, no matter their age, are rail thin. My father had me on a high-protein diet that only included the cleanest of carbs with no processed sugar. I was an athlete and needed to treat my body like a machine, which meant I had to feed it only the best to be at its top performance.

Our parents cursed us in so many ways. Briar has trouble enjoying food in general, and I eat fast food regularly and never say no to sweets.

Brand's refrigerator is … interesting. Hummus, containers of cut vegetables, and fruits. There are more cups of Greek yogurt than I can count, and just as much beer. Packages of raw, organic chicken breasts, filets, and pork tenderloins are stacked neatly on one side.

So much meat, I wonder if he plans on hosting a dinner party soon.

Sugar free almond milk, water in reusable glass bottles, and green juice.

Yuck. At least he's environmentally conscious.

And so many eggs.

But front and center is a plastic container with a sticky note attached. I reach forward and pluck it off.

Dessert.
I'm pissed I won't be here to watch you eat it.
B

I grab the plastic container holding the biggest cupcake I've ever seen. Its chocolate frosting is as tall as the cake itself, layered with more chocolate shavings, and topped with a fanned strawberry that looks like a work of art.

Wow.

I take the cupcake and shut the refrigerator on the rest of my healthy options. Plucking the strawberry off the top, I bite into the luscious fruit and dip my index finger into the icing.

If Brand hadn't given me so many orgasms the last few days, this chocolate buttercream might get me there.

I don't look for anything else to eat. This will be dinner and the wine will be dessert.

I kick off my shoes and dig in. My plan can wait a few minutes.

Life is too short to put off dessert. If I've learned anything, it's to eat the fucking cake first, because you never know what might happen next.

BRAND

THIS COULDN'T HAVE gone better—kudos to me. I'm fucking brilliant.

My only mistake was not installing closed-circuit cameras in my bedroom like I have in the rest of the house. I don't have them there for obvious reasons. Who does?

Freaks, probably. That's who.

I ignore that little piece of self-reflection as I watch her.

She has to know with the security in my house that I'd at least have cameras in the living areas, especially on every door. If she knows, she sure doesn't give a fuck, which is also interesting.

Today hasn't been busy. No fires, a few minor medical emergencies, and two accidents. Since she and the dog arrived, I've been able to keep an eye on her without my brothers knowing what I'm watching on my phone as the game plays on the main TV.

She inhaled the dessert I left for her before losing her jacket. If there were a way for me to lock myself in the broom closet to jack off, I would have. Watching the woman consume sugar is like nothing I've ever seen. I regret not buying her a three-tiered cake.

When she finished every last crumb and licked her fingers clean, she uncorked the wine, poured herself a glass, and got to work.

Just as I expected.

That's when things got interesting.

She's opened every cabinet in my kitchen, and not because she was looking for the perfect pan to burn dinner. She disappeared inside my pantry for at least ten minutes.

Then my laundry room. She rummaged through the closet by the front door and even tried on three of my coats.

132

Then she inspected every title on the bookshelves of my study. She ran her fingers over a picture of Art and me fishing in Alaska two years ago. She sat behind my desk and went through every drawer. Then she spun in circles for at least three minutes in my office chair. Most people keep their skeletons filed away in a home office, but not me. I knew that room, more than the rest, would bore her to tears.

She disappeared to the basement for thirty minutes and I hope she liked what she saw. There's no reason for her not to stay with me when she can workout with my top-of-the-line equipment as opposed to the cheap treadmill she keeps in the corner of her bedroom in her miniscule apartment.

I had to switch cameras when she went upstairs. I only have one in the main hallway so I have no idea what was so interesting in the spare rooms. I cleared Marcia's shit out of the house the day her body washed ashore. It was no skin off my back. Hell, I might've enjoyed it more than I should have. Her family wanted in the house to get her things, but there was no way I was allowing any Ricci on my property after that day. The police have come by many times but they've never managed to secure a warrant.

If the Riccis weren't welcome, there's no fucking way the police are stepping through my door. My dad made sure no judge in the state of Washington would issue a warrant.

Art has handled the media, since her death sparked national attention. It's died down—pun intended—and my mug isn't plastered all over the tabloids every other day. The longer Marcia's death frosts over, the better. Six months have made all the difference.

Which makes moving on sweeter than the cupcake my psychologist just inhaled. I might buy the damn bakery, because Aria consuming sugar is a more erotic sight than any porn on the planet.

Tomorrow I'm installing cameras pointing at every corner of my place, because wondering what she's doing is torture. Watching her touch every inch she inspects is everything I thought it would be and more.

I'm able to watch when she flips on the light in my four-car garage since I have cameras surveilling every square inch of that sanctuary. She sits in my Jeep and goes through the glove box and console. She pokes through my work bench and even the storage cabinets. As she works her way to the far side of the space—dragging her fingertips over my mountain bike, snow board, riding lawn mower, and snow blower—she comes to a stop in the corner.

When I insisted she spend the night without me there, I knew she'd snoop. Who wouldn't? I would if I were in her shoes.

But I hadn't thought it would go this far.

This should be interesting.

ARIA

IF I DIDN'T KNOW better, I'd think Brand was in the military as neat as he keeps his shit. Even his garage is organized and clean. No clutter, no mess, and certainly no trash.

So the four black, waste bags tossed in the corner of his garage is odd. I pull the first one open and peek inside.

Shit.

Clothes.

Women's clothes.

I stumble back as if it's a sack full of snakes instead of sweaters. My heart speeds as I stare at the red cashmere tossed on top—unfolded and stuffed in like whoever did it was in a hurry.

No wonder I haven't found one thread of evidence Brand was ever married, let alone lived with his wife just six short months ago. Not an old tube of mascara stuffed in the back of a drawer. Not one picture. Not even a hair tie—and those things are everywhere.

It's like he wiped her from the face of the earth.

I force myself to step forward and wrap my hand around the red material. Perfume hits my senses, thick and heavy, and I wonder how long it's been here. I hold it in front of me—it's a medium. Lots of people are a medium, by the law of averages, anyway.

Holy shit, Aria. Why does it matter?

I dig deeper. Pants. Jeans. Blouses. Silk.

Marcia Vitale was a label snob. It takes one to know one. Not that I'm a label snob now. I couldn't be one before I had a fifteen-thousand-dollar dog and date to pay off and definitely can't now. But I was raised in a home with parents who were snobs about everything.

Before I know it, I'm sitting on Brand's garage floor—clean enough to lick icing off of—surrounded by his dead wife's clothes. For the most part, I've pushed the thought of her out of my mind.

Until now.

The fact he was married. Learning it was arranged. How he wasn't happy. And how his late wife took her last breath right here, on this property, where I'm now spending the night.

By myself.

The weight of it all hits me.

"Ruff!"

My head jerks to the garage door. Muppet is losing patience. I left him in the house by himself.

I grab everything and stuff it back into the bags, just as haphazardly as it came out. Before I throw the red sweater in, I bring it to my face and inhale.

"Fuck," I mutter. "I need more wine. And then I need to make an appointment with Russ. I don't even recognize myself."

I toss the red sweater in the last trash bag, pile them back in the corner, and hurry back into the house where Muppet attacks me.

I lean down and let him lick me all over the face. It's gross, but I'm getting used to it. It seems this is what good dog owners do. "Sorry, buddy. Come on, it's a good thing I brought your treats because Brand has shit food in his house. And I need more wine. A lot more wine."

BRAND

SHE'S BEEN AT it for over an hour. If I hadn't had my PI run her complete history, I'd think she was an undercover officer for the homicide unit. Her every move through my house is thorough and methodical. It's certain her fingerprints will remain for a very long time.

After she finished snooping through Marcia's shit—that I'm only hanging onto in case I need to look like the grieving widower instead of a chipper one—the doctor has done nothing but drink.

And dance.

I've moved to my bed in the bunkroom because I can't pretend to watch the game any longer.

She pours the last drop of wine into her glass and I'd like to kick my own ass right now for not putting cameras with audio in my house. She spins, hops, and plays with her dog. I've never seen anything like it, but I'm also not in the business of giving a shit what other people do unless they're trying to cross my family.

Another gulp of wine. She's going to have one massive headache tomorrow if she doesn't eat some protein before she goes to bed.

Naked.

Her lip disappears between her teeth, and I wish I were there to suck on it.

She sways into the island, stumbling as she grabs her bag, and looks across the great room. Past my two-story stone fireplace, beyond the entryway, and toward the short hall leading to my bedroom.

Her bare foot taps and she starts to chew on the tip of her thumb.

She tags her wine and I wonder if she realizes she's inhaled an eighty-dollar bottle of finely-aged cab. She turns to call the dog and he scampers after her.

Finally, she disappears into my bedroom.

And my cock swells.

Eighteen

PLAYING

Aria

I'M PAST FEELING guilty.

Anyway, who feels guilty when they're drunk?

Not me. That's who's not.

Doesn't.

Or isn't.

Whatever.

I mean, what did he expect? He's the genius hero who said curiosity was a basic instinct of human nature—or some shit like that. Whatever he said sounded as philosophical as something I would spew to my patients.

When I'm sober.

He had to know I'd at least look around. What does he think people do when they go to the bathroom during a dinner party?

I've taken more than a peek. I'm a class-A, hella-stealth snoop. If snooping were an Olympic sport, I wouldn't have thrown those trials, and my dad would have been happier than a woman having a midlife-crisis facelift while getting a new set of boobs.

Because everyone throws in the boobs when having something else done. Why wouldn't they?

I've learned a great deal during my snoop-a-rama.

First, Brando Vitale, Jr. is a health freak. No wonder his body is a lean, mean, firefighting machine. His pantry is practically a GNC pop-up kiosk from the mall. His only saving grace in this department is he hasn't tried to push his clean-eating agenda on me. The wine is smooth and the cupcake was decadent. I need to do something nice for him.

Maybe the next time he takes me to dinner, I'll give him my salad.

I figured out what magical detergent he uses to produce the softest and sweetest smelling T-shirts. I also relished the way his coats swim on me. They smelled like his aftershave, and I know for a fact if I were this drunk at that stage of my snooping, I would've licked the collar.

When it comes to health and wellbeing, Brand not only keeps a fully-stocked GNC at his disposal, but his workout equipment is top of the line. I might've jogged a quarter of a mile barefoot on his treadmill. It was like running on a cloud compared to the one I bought off Craigslist when we moved here. I can't wait to run on it again.

Like, when I'm not drunk.

Tonight, I have other priorities and they do not include exhausting myself to a point that I can sleep. I hate running, but it's the only way I can be a functioning member of society without taking meds. My mind doesn't shut down unless my body is physically drained and my brain has no choice but to follow.

Since I'm brazen and bold tonight—the sugar and fermented grapes coursing through my system have certainly helped—I finally mustered the confidence to enter the one place I'm most anxious to check out.

Brand's bedroom.

The place where he fucked me until the wee hours of the morning a few nights ago after he fucked me in front of the windows.

So much fucking.

I drop my bag at the foot of his bed as Muppet jumps up and circles so fast, he's sure to pass out. I have to look away from him so I don't tip over dizzy. I move to his bathroom—a place he had his way with me in his enormous shower—and focus on the unknown.

His closet.

I flip on the light.

What the hell? It's empty.

It's also huge.

But empty.

I turn the light off and stand in the middle of the big-ass bathroom. On the other side of the room is a closed door, begging me to bulldoze through it.

I take another sip of my wine, set the stemmed glass on the bathroom vanity, and go for it.

When light fills the space, the wine kicks in, and I'm forced to lean into the doorjamb for support.

Wow.

I steady my legs and move forward. I hardly ever see Brand in anything but jeans and a T-shirt, or his fire gear and uniform.

Well, I guess he did wear trousers and a button down when he took me to dinner.

He doesn't seem like a clothes horse, but I stand corrected.

Suits, sport coats, and dress shirts line one wall. The colors are conservative but when I hold up a jacket, the cut is definitely modern. What they all are is custom, his initials are even monogrammed on a silk label.

On the other side are stacks of denim. A bank of dressers hold socks, boxers, and a shitload of T-shirts. More fire uniforms hang opposite his suits and I'm tempted to ask him what it is he loves so much about that job when he seems to do well with his organized-crime side hustle.

The room smells like him—a mix of soap and aftershave and masculinity, to the power of ... whatever.

Infinity.

Something comes over me. I rip my sweater off and kick my pencil pants to the floor. My bra barely has a chance to settle with the rest of my mess as I'm yanking a dress shirt off a wooden hanger. I pull it up both arms and secure just one button below my breasts. Then I turn to his full-length mirror.

My hair is a mess from snooping, dancing, and playing with Muppet. My face is flushed from the wine, and I can't lie, the sight of me in his dress shirt with my black lace panties barely peeking out turns me on.

I wonder what he'd do if he were here?

That thought hardens my nipples against the crisp white of his dress shirt.

I wonder if his dead wife ever did this. If she secretly wanted to be right where I am—in his room and in his bed. Or if she was ever as desperate as I feel right now, afraid this might end at any moment.

My pants buzz at my feet and I dig my phone out of my pocket.

Hero – *What are you doing?*

I look at myself in the mirror. This time I know the flush on my skin is not from the wine. It's from the wetness between my legs.

Instead of texting him back, I point the camera on my phone at the mirror. The one button clasped on his dress shirt will allow him to see everything ... yet nothing.

Click and *send.*

Then I let my fingers fly.

Me – I'm playing.

So many bubbles.

Hero – Fuck. I like the way you play.

Hero – Do you know how many people want me dead? And you're going to be the one to finish me off with a heart attack by doing shit like this. I'll happily die at the hands of my psychologist if it means you sending me pics like this.

I hiccup and turn back to the bathroom to get my wine. I tip the glass back to finish the last drop of the entire bottle and return to his room to fall into bed.

Muppet snuggles next to me and I roll into him, dropping a kiss on his curly-haired head, and decide this is dog bonding.

Me – I'm drunk.

Hero – I'd call but I have no privacy. Tell me you locked the door and set the alarm.

Me – Always the hero, huh? It's locked but the alarm isn't set. I've been busy.

Hero – Busy trying on my clothes? Because seeing you in my shirt makes me almost okay about you not being naked yet.

My head feels like a hula hoop at recess.

Me – I have a confession. And thank you for the cupcake.

Hero – Confess all your sins to me, Doc. And you're welcome.

Me - I've been snooping.

Hero – You don't say.

Me – You were right about curiosity. Turns out I'm basic as hell. Basic and drunk.

Hero – I have a confession.

Me – What would you have to confess?

Hero – I have closed circuit cameras in my house. I've been snooping too.

I smile.

Me – That's creepy.

Hero – And you snooping isn't?

I ignore that.

Me – I need to ask you a question.

Hero – Yes. I'm hard thinking about you in my bedroom, wearing my shirt.

My smile swells.

Me – I hope there's no fire then. That would be awkward.

Hero – Get up and go to my sofa.

Me – Why?

Hero – Why do you think? I don't have cameras in my bedroom but you can bet your sweet ass I'm going to install them there before my next shift.

Me – I'm tired.

Hero – You can do it.

I pull myself out of bed. Muppet whines and decides he's too tired to move, staying snuggled warm in the middle of Brand's pillows.

I fall into the corner of his big sofa.

Me – Happy?

Hero – You don't even know. What's your question?

Me – Why me?

Hero – This again?

I yawn.

Me – Yes. I have to know. Why me?

Hero – Maybe I should ask you—why me?

Me – Brand.

Hero – Slide your hand into your panties and I'll tell you.

Me – Can you see me?

Hero – Look above the fireplace in the corner by the windows.

I look over my shoulder. Sure enough, there it is. Hidden in one of the beams. I smile and look back at my phone.

Me – Creepy.

Hero – Unbutton the shirt and touch yourself.

Texting with one thumb is hard when I haven't been drinking, but knowing he's watching sends a tremble through me—and not a bad one. I shift my cell to one hand and do what he says with the other.

Me – Okay.

Hero – You wet?

I run my fingers through my folds.

Me – Very.

Hero – Play with your clit. But don't come.

Being in his house and going through his things—completely enveloping myself with everything *Brand* has been enthralling.

But this?

My breaths turn to pants and my eyes close, remembering the first time I did this while fantasizing about him. And now he's watching.

My phone vibrates.

Hero – Aria?

Me – Yes. I'm close.

Hero – Fucking jealous of your fingers. Don't stop.

Me - Why me?

His bubbles tease me, and it's all I can do to hold off my impending orgasm.

Hero – Because from the first time I laid eyes on you, you intrigued me. When I saw you again, I knew you weren't a good idea. The timing was bad, but I knew I had to figure you out. I couldn't stop myself and I was right to be intrigued. I want you but I want you on my terms. We'll get to that eventually.

I swallow hard and try to focus on his text while at the same time, I'm scared to death of what he means.

I've never felt desperation in my life.

Not while growing up with the burden of perfection weighing on me. Not when I was alone and poorer than I am now. Not when I was putting myself through school, knowing I could only rely on myself. And not when failure wasn't an option because Briar was counting on me. There was no one to rescue her from that hell but me.

But being with Brand on his terms? That scares me more than anything.

As the days click by, I'm growing more and more desperate the farther I fall.

Oh, God. I'm close.

Me – Brand. Please.

Hero – Tell me it'll be on my terms, Doc. Tell me you'll be mine.

I'm either brilliant or the most idiotic woman in history. Because right now, the thought of not being right here is devastating.

Me – Yes. Anything.

Hero – That's my doctor. Drop your knees to the sides and make yourself come.

I squeeze my thighs together.

Hero– Knees, Aria. Now.

My knees fall and I almost can't take it.

Hero – Show me how much you want me.

My phone falls from my hand, disappearing into the sofa cushions. I close my eyes. It's not as good as the real thing but knowing he can see me sends a rush of excitement through my veins.

Erotic. Naughty. Powerful.

And all Brand.

I feel my phone vibrate next to me but I can't focus on anything else. My mind clears as his demanded orgasm takes over. It tickles the tips of my nerves and travels through every inch of my body.

Not even an overbearing man or the ghost of his dead wife can break through my euphoria.

Spent, my shoulders slump and I wrap his shirt around my mostly bare body. I cross my legs and roll to my side on his deep sofa. When I finally recover, I dig my phone from the cushions to find a slew of words.

Hero – Fuck.

Hero – Don't stop.

Hero – You'd better be there when I get home in the morning. You're mine the minute I walk through the door.

Hero – Shit, we have a call.

Hero – Lock up, eat something healthy, and drink a bottle of water before bed. You're going to have a hangover.

Hero – Gotta go, but have to say, baby, that was fucking magnificent. I'm off at eight in the morning. Be ready.

My head is really spinning and it's not only from the wine.

I'm tired, but really, I'm emotionally exhausted from snooping. Brand stuffed what was left of his dead wife into four trash bags, but Marcia Vitale lurks in the dark corners of my mind.

I'm mortified by my own behavior as her unsolved murder lingers in the shadows.

I pull myself to my feet and stumble into the kitchen to get one of his fancy bottles of water. It doesn't take a paramedic to tell me I'm going to have one hell of a hangover in the morning.

Hero – Good girl.

I crack the bottle open and take a big drink.

Me – I thought you had to go play hero.

Hero – We're on our way.

I take another drink before screwing the cap back on and making my way to Muppet. Before I get to the hall, I look at his camera and shrug off his shirt, tossing it to the floor of the entryway.

Then, forgetting all about his dead wife, I send him a small smile.

I've dropped my panties, climbed in bed, and pulled a pillow to my bare chest as Muppet snuggles in at my back when my phone vibrates again.

Hero – Yeah. You're getting fucked hard when I get home.

Ninteen

RESTRAINING ORDER

Aria

"**R**UFF!"

My head is pounding. I hardly ever have more than two glasses of anything.

I roll over and groan as my stomach churns. Muppet jumps off the bed and it's not because he's an early riser. Someone is pounding on the front door.

I pull the covers over my bare breasts and push my hair out of my face. I look to his nightstand and it's not quite eight. Brand said he'd be here right when he gets off, and his station is at least a twenty-minute drive. Plus, he wouldn't knock at his own house.

Whoever they are, they're persistent.

I roll out of Brand's warm, soft bed and head to his closet. Whoever is at the door won't stop banging, which means Muppet won't stop barking, and until everything loud stops, there's no way my head will stop pounding.

I haven't opened my bag since I got here last night and the need to brush my teeth is right up there with the demand for world peace. But whoever is at the door is having none of it, so I yank one of Brand's sweatshirts over my head and pull on a pair of his joggers, commando.

I'm cinching them at the waist and rolling them over twice on my way out of his room when the angry guest yells, "Vitale! Answer the fucking door!"

I round the corner from the hallway and a man is standing on the other side of the glass. Damn his house for having so many windows. The moment he sees me, he freezes. Shock, followed by contempt, washes over him. His growl is muffled through the thick glass. "Who the fuck are you?"

I don't answer and I regret being so drunk, tired, and stupid that I never bothered to set the alarm. I live in an apartment that wouldn't withstand a tropical storm in Florida and I've made it just fine without a security system. I felt safe locked in Brand's house.

Until now.

Muppet is running between me and the door.

The man's face falls and he takes me in from the dark bags under my eyes to my bare feet sticking out from under Brand's baggy joggers.

"Who are you?" I ask.

I don't move, contemplating grabbing Muppet and locking us in Brand's room.

He doesn't tell me his name and keeps on. "Where's Vitale?"

I roll the cuffs of the sweatshirt and push them up my arms. "He's at work. Can I help you?"

"I know he's getting off a shift. Open the fucking door."

"I'm sorry. What's your name?" I counter. He's wearing a ballcap and his own Saturday morning uniform of sweats, but unlike mine, his fit. It's hard to tell but he could be around Brand's age, but not nearly as tall or wide.

"Cory."

The first thing that comes to mind is Brand telling me there are people who want him dead. The second, I have no desire to be one of those stupid women who know they shouldn't open the door, yet still, they open the door.

Why do they do that?

"I'm sure he'll be here anytime." I grab Muppet by the collar. "Calm down, buddy."

"You're the bitch hooking up with my brother-in-law."

It's not a question and I look from my dog to Cory.

Brother-in-law.

Shit.

Brand told me he has sisters, but every instinct in me screams this guy is not from the Vitale side of his family.

I look him in the eyes, and my insides tighten.

"Open the door!"

I'm about to return to plan A—drag Muppet into Brand's room and lock us away when another car tears down the long, wooded lane. A black Tesla comes to a screeching halt in the circle drive behind a Cadillac.

"Ricci!" My new visitor has a cellphone to his ear as he jogs up the walk with a look on his face that threatens war. His focus lands on me. "Stay in the house and get your phone. Brand is trying to get hold of you." He turns back to Cory. "What the fuck? Have you forgotten the restraining order Brand slapped on you? I would know, I drew the fucker up myself. You've got one minute to get off this property."

Cory throws his arms out to his sides. "Oh, so today the cameras work? That's fucking convenient. Good to know Brand's security system works when he needs it to and not when he's *drowning my sister!"*

Muppet is whining, and my breath catches as I back up from the glass. Brand wasn't kidding about a list of people who want him dead if he has restraining orders against others.

Cory points to me and yells at the other guy. "Word is out, and she's proof. He's parading this bitch around just six months after he killed my sister, Ramos! I don't give a fuck about your restraining order!"

The blood drains from my head.

Ramos looks at me and raises his voice. "Make yourself scarce and call Brand."

Cory turns to me and yells through the glass, "Better not piss him off, you might be next!"

My stomach churns from the thought of … everything. Or the wine. Either way, it's all bad, bad, bad.

I bend and scoop up my wiggling dog who only wants outside to greet our angry visitors. I slam the bedroom door, lock it for good measure, and go straight to my phone.

Three missed calls and a slew of texts—all from Brand. I never would have missed these in the good old days when leaving your ringer on wasn't taboo.

I ignore them all and hit go to call the man whose bed I slept naked in last night for the sole reason that he told me to.

He answers instantly. "You okay?"

I barely hear World War III from the sanctuary of his bedroom. "I didn't let anyone in. Who are they and what's going on?"

"Seems word travels fast and Marcia's family isn't happy. But then again, they're never happy. I was on the phone with Art—he's the one who told you to call me."

"Brand—"

"Art will take care of it 'til I get there. He lives on the other side of the lake—I called him when I saw Cory drive up on the cameras. Stay put. I'm a few minutes out."

I look to the locked door. "You have a restraining order on him?"

"I have one on all the Riccis. They're fucking relentless. Have been since Marcia died. Became the biggest pains in my ass, so Art took care of it."

I sit on the edge of the bed as Muppet barks. "I should leave."

"You're not going anywhere. I'm pulling off the main road now."

He hangs up on me, and I drop my phone to the floor, following it down to my ass. I lean against the side of the bed and drop my pounding head into my hands.

Muppet licks my face between turning circles. He needs to go out but there's no way we're leaving this room until Brand gets here. I don't want to be anywhere near his dead wife's family.

I need to get my shit together. I don't know why I thought I could handle this—handle him. He's too much. The longer I'm here, the closer I fly to the flame, and there's no way I'll make it out unscathed. The consequences are too high.

I give Muppet one more scratch before laying a kiss on his head and crawl over to my bag.

My teeth are brushed and my face is washed when voices enter the house. I'm popping a couple Motrin I found last night while snooping when more knocking ensues, this time on Brand's bedroom door. "Doc, open up."

Muppet attacks the door. I twist the lock and swing it open. Brand is filling the doorway, wearing an outfit similar to my own. His hair is a mess and his face is smudged with black. This is the first time I've seen him shaved in days.

"He's gone." He narrows his eyes as they move to the overnight bag I'm clutching as Muppet escapes. "Where are you going?"

"I need to find Muppet's leash and walk him. My head is killing me and I don't have the energy to chase him if he runs."

He frowns and rips the bag out of my hand. "I'll walk him and then I'll make you some eggs. Go sit at the island."

He turns and disappears with my bag before I can argue or wrestle it from him. His voice is deep and irritated as he calls for Muppet, mingling with another male voice that's equally as aggravated.

Not anxious to rejoin the fray of the morning's drama, I move quietly into the great room, now vibrating with energy.

Art still has his cell glued to his ear, pacing in front of the stone fireplace. When I walk by the front door, there is no sign of the Cadillac.

"Why are we just now finding out about this?" He scrutinizes me, looking me up and down before turning away, shaking his head. "Brand was at the station, but she was here. Yeah? Well, figure out what happened. One is dead, two are in the hospital, and one of them is ours. It's too fucking coincidental—the feds are not stupid. Senior is flipping his shit and I want to know how it started. It's your job to keep an ear to the ground. Think about that as you dig deeper." He turns back to me as he punches at his screen. "I don't know who you are, but you sure have stirred up a shitstorm. My boy is out there walking a fucking dog, of all things, while the Riccis have declared war. You must be a four-leaf clover who shits glitter, because I've known him since we were five, and I've never seen him like this."

His words stop me in place.

All I can focus on is one is dead and two in the hospital.

I look out to the lake and Brand is talking into his cell as Muppet takes advantage of every inch of radius to sniff. Brand's gaze meets mine as he gives Muppet a little tug, making his way back to the house.

He's still talking on the phone when he returns. "Don't put this on me. This was your war long before I married that bitch. I stepped up when you asked me to. I know my place in the family, but if this is going to be thrown at me, I have no problem stepping in. The Riccis will not hold me hostage another day."

He doesn't bother saying goodbye as he stalks to the kitchen and starts to dig through the refrigerator. Eggs and a white butcher package land on the counter next to his huge range before he produces two frying pans.

Art goes to the island. "Breakfast? You don't think we have bigger problems than making sure your overnight guest is fed? First, you parade her into Vinnie's, knowing that's the quickest way to spread word all over Seattle. From what I'm hearing, you two have spent every available night together, here or at her apartment. You know people are following you. The least you could do is park her car in the fucking garage. It's like you're poking the bear on purpose."

Brand fires up the range, unwraps the package, and peels off piece after piece of thick-cut bacon, tossing them in a skillet. "Don't start with me, Art. And what if I am?"

"Don't start?" he bellows. "Do you understand the ramifications of what happened last night?"

Brand turns and spears him with a glare before turning it on me. He points to a barstool. "Take a seat. You look like shit."

My eyes widen, and I cross my arms. I know I look like shit—I feel like it, too. But it never feels good to have it pointed out. "Where's my bag?"

He doesn't answer. "Doc, this is Arthur Ramos. He's my attorney, whom I pay a fuck-of-a-lot of money, so he needs to start doing his job instead of questioning me."

"Fuck you," Art snaps and turns to me. "If you call me Arthur, we really will have problems."

"Talk to her like that one more time and you're fired. I don't give a shit how long we've known each other." Brand looks back to me as the bacon starts to sizzle. "Sit down. I'll make you coffee."

My stomach growls and churns at the same time from the scent of frying bacon. I move to the island and pull out a barstool because I'm starving, tired, and hungover. It basically hurts to stand. "Who died?"

"One of Ricci's soldiers," Brand explains. "He and another asshole showed up at one of my dad's clubs last night in Seattle. They started shit—it got bad. From what I heard, they were asking for it. But a Vitale guard got caught in the crossfire. He's in intensive care."

I pinch the bridge of my nose and can't believe this. "But, why?"

"Why do you think?" Art butts in.

I'm about to grab my dog and run to Canada. I'll go on foot, commando and hungover, if I have to. It would be better than Brand poking a bear because of me and people dying.

"If you think I'm fucking with you, Art, try it again." Brand's entire frame is tense and radiating an energy I do not like. He looks at me. "I played their game for six months—I'm done. If me moving on from fake misery starts a war with the Riccis, I'm willing to lead the army. I just told my dad the same thing. The Riccis can get ugly, but I'll make sure you're shielded from it."

I drop my face to my hands.

"Hey, asshole," Brand calls. When I look over, he's talking to Art. "You staying for breakfast?"

"I take the girls for donuts on Saturday mornings. But I'll stay for bacon because Tess doesn't do bacon. While I'm waiting, you need to tell me what your plan is. The last thing I want to do right now is call the police and report Cory for breaking the restraining order. We don't need that kind of attention after last night. You've got it on camera if we need it later."

Brand fires up another burner and spoons bacon grease into the smaller skillet. "I plan to do exactly what I'm doing now with Aria by my side. If you need an official story, we met at the auction. I had one session with her." He looks over at me and hikes a brow. "You know, for my mental health. After that, it was on."

"No, that's not true," I interrupt, looking back and forth between them. "You're not my patient and never were. Do you know how that makes me look professionally? It's against … so much. No. Just no."

Art shrugs. "But if the police ever question you again, you can pull doctor-patient confidentiality. That's huge. The only way you can break that is if you feared your patient or someone else were in danger—"

"I'm a psychologist," I snap and the pressure from my ire causes my head to pound harder. I rub my temples and close my eyes. "I completely understand my responsibilities."

"Just saying—"

Brand rips off a handful of paper towels and lines a plate before forking out the batch of bacon. "Drop the therapy part, but the rest stands. Six months is enough. I'm moving on, and the Riccis can kiss my ass."

Art reaches over me and grabs three pieces, talking around a big bite. "Aria, sorry we didn't meet under better circumstances. Tessa wants to meet you. You'll love her—everyone does. She's the only reason we have any friends besides Prince Charming, here."

I give him a small smile. It's the most my head can handle after the wine and this morning's activities.

Art walks out the front door without further drama, and Brand sets a steaming cup of coffee in front of me with a bottle of water. "Not the way I planned to come home to you this morning, Doc."

He turns and cracks two eggs in the second skillet and adds more bacon to the first.

I take a bite of bacon and try to decide if it tastes good or makes me want to hurl.

Brand continues to work on the eggs, adding more bacon grease. My college swim coach would have a fit.

"Is this a normal thing for you?" he asks without looking back at me.

"You mean, meet someone, and a week later have had all kinds of kinky sexual experiences with him? During which time I'm questioned by the police because that same man is being investigated for his dead wife's murder? Oh, and that man is the son of the biggest mob boss on the west coast and he's also wanted dead by a lot of people, whomever they are. Though after this morning, I'm guessing *those people* are your dead wife's family."

He turns around, holding the small skillet, and frowns.

"If that's what you're talking about, then no. I do not do this often. In fact, this is a first for me."

He slides the eggs onto a plate. Sunny-side up and fried in bacon grease. I guess he's not the health freak I thought he was. I wonder what else I got wrong about him.

"I was talking about drinking too much. But I'm honored to be your first for all that other shit."

I catch a fork he slides across the marble. "No. I have a drink here and there but not like last night. It was a long week dealing with you. And I needed liquid courage last night."

"For the snooping," he adds.

I point my fork at the ceiling and spin it in a circle. "Among other things."

His full lips relax into a lazy smile. "I know for a fact you don't need liquid courage to get your freak on."

I ignore that and dip my bacon in the yolk which is the perfect consistency. Of course it is. Is there anything he's not good at? "I need cream. And sugar. Though I'm surprised you even have sugar, but I know you do. I saw it in your pantry last night."

He cracks more eggs in the skillet and fetches my cream and sugar. I doctor my coffee, and he continues to be awesome at the stove. After two pieces of bacon and most of my eggs, my stomach isn't back to normal, but it's a solid eighty percent.

I might make it to my next drama.

Or sexcapade.

Whichever comes first. At this point, it's a toss-up.

He plates three eggs for himself and stands opposite me as he shovels food into his mouth.

I pick up my mug and take another sip. "Brand—"

"Doc." He bites off a piece of bacon.

I glare at him before looking around his home, the woods, and the lake. Muppet has calmed after all the action and has made the sofa his throne. I'm not sure if Brand could do anything about it at this point if he didn't want pets on his furniture. Besides, a rescue pup should be spoiled rotten. If it's not a law, it should be.

When his plate hits the counter with a clank, I turn back to him. "I need to know more, Brand. You said you owed me more, and I'm ready. Especially after what happened this morning."

He doesn't look away as he raises his coffee to his lips and takes a sip.

"If you want me to stay, I need to understand. Please, help me understand."

He licks his lips and contemplates me for a moment. "I trust very few people in this world. Art is one of them. My dad is another. If I'm at work or in a burning building, my brothers at the station. That's it."

Goosebumps roll over my skin and I hike a leg, tucking a foot under me. "You can trust me."

He tips his head and studies my features so intently, I feel more exposed than I have so far, and that's saying a lot. "You don't have to convince me, baby. I know I can. And you're right. I want you next to me and that means you need to understand."

Twenty

PROMISE ME

Brand

*T*RUST AND LOYALTY.

They mean something very different in my world.

To some, trust is talking to one neighbor about another behind their back. Trusting someone to care for your kid. Trusting someone to not fuck up your investment portfolio.

Loyalty is the other way around. Loyalty means you've got people at your back who will be there no matter how ugly or messy shit gets.

I like to know who has my back. Who will go to the ends of the earth for me. I want to know they'll do anything for me. Even kill, if it came to that.

There are very few people I'd kill for.

But I would.

And I have.

I'm not a made man. It was my agreement with my dad when I married a Ricci for the sake of my family.

The things I've done are not because someone else ordered them. I did them because they fucking needed to be done.

Nine years ago, when Art decided Tessa was the one, she couldn't get out from under the filth of her family. And that filth was dirtier than the scum of the earth. She was eighteen. Art was ten years her senior. They met at a seedy club on the wrong side of Seattle.

Their relationship was quick and intense. Tessa's older brother owned the club that was purely a front for pimping women. He had plans for his littlest sister and they did not include Art Ramos unless he was a paying customer. She had no one and no way out of that life.

Tessa avoided his scum as long as she could, but when Art found her beaten, cut, and bruised because she refused to spread her legs so her brother could profit, that was it.

Art and I took care of him. We took care of his business partners too. And then burned his club to the ground. We did this so Tessa could rest easy for the rest of her life. Art did it for her, and I did it for him.

Art married her as soon as her bruises faded. He was already climbing the ladder in one of the most prestigious law firms in Seattle.

Art won't cross me. I have his loyalty for what I did for him. In return, I know I can trust him with my life.

Can I trust Dr. Aria Dillon?

When the time comes, will she give me her loyalty?

She wanted an answer, but I made her wait. I showered off the soot from the call we worked in the early morning hours and she put herself together as best she could in her hungover condition.

Her antics last night amused me, but that doesn't mean I'm not relieved she says it isn't normal for her. I don't like drunks and I don't like people who lack discipline.

I've watched her. I was sure she wasn't those things. From here on out, I'm holding her to her word that she's not. I don't want that for the mother of my children.

"Did you ever try to make it work with your wife?"

I run a hand through my damp hair and pull her ass closer to my hip.

When I got out of the shower, I couldn't find her or the dog. For about twenty seconds, I was about to lose my mind when I thought she ran on me.

But I found her curled up on my outdoor sofa that's centered on the deck. This has the best view of the water. The dog's leash is tied to a table leg and he's asleep in a rare mid-morning sunbreak. It's late October, the weather is cool, and she's wrapped in a blanket.

I could get used to this. For the first time in my adult life, I'm dreading my next shift at the station.

I have her wrapped around me. The need to be near her, touch her, know what she's doing every moment she's not with me is immense. I almost find it annoying since I've never experienced that in my life.

I roll her to her back and tuck myself into her ass, with her legs over my lap.

In the beginning I found her oddly controlled. But as the days go by, her fidgets are coming out of the woodwork like wild bulls that were gated, waiting to be let loose. She's picking at her nail, staring at her fingers, and refuses to look me in the eyes.

I wrap my hand over both of hers and hold tight. "Aria."

Her focus turns to me.

"The answer's *no*."

Her brows pinch.

"I never tried. Why would I try with someone I didn't want?"

She sighs.

"Marcia was a business transaction. She knew it. I knew it. Both of our families knew it. If she or others had romantic notions about our arrangement, it wasn't because I let anyone believe that, and it definitely wasn't my problem."

"The night you took me to dinner … you said you hadn't had sex with your wife in years."

I shrug. "I hadn't."

"But—"

I put a finger to her lips. "We were young when we got married. I thought I was sentenced to her for life. Did I want kids? I guess. She was the only way that was going to happen. We tried for a few months. Even though she told me it was the perfect time, it wasn't happening. I found it odd, so I started snooping."

She rolls her eyes, but I keep going.

"Yeah, just like you." I tap her nose with the tip of my finger. "I found birth control pills in her bathroom. After that, I was done. We weren't even married a year—no way was I going to put up with her lies. She tried to manipulate me onto some emotional rollercoaster for her to control. I didn't touch her after that. I might not have been a saint, Aria, but she was not a good person."

"No," she whispers. "She wasn't."

"I was miserable. She was angry. She did everything she could to get my attention, usually pissing me off more. She thrived on that and wanted to get a rise out of me. I learned the best way to handle her was to ignore her. Plain and simple. The last year of her life, I refused to recognize her existence even though we lived under the same roof. That time was the worst. Nothing pissed her off more than that."

She looks out to the lake and I give her time to process my past. Whatever she wants to know, I'll tell her.

We sit like this for a few minutes before she turns back to me. "Do you regret it? Making that deal with your dad and marrying her?"

I tip my head and shrug. "For years, I regretted it. Seemed like working for my dad would've been a hell of a lot easier. But you know when something good happens and you wonder if you'd ever get there without having to go through all the bad shit leading you to it?"

She pulls that damn lip between her teeth.

I brush her bottom lip with my thumb. "I have a feeling you wouldn't be right here if I hadn't lived through the hell with her."

I lean forward and brush my lips to hers. Her breath is heavy and when I lean back to look at her, her blue eyes storm over. "That sounds philosophical."

"My psychologist is rubbing off on me. Literally and figuratively. What are you thinking?"

"That I'm sad you had to live with that for ten years. It would be selfish of me to be happy to be here knowing what you went through."

"You're selfless."

She shakes her head. "I'm not. I'm controlling. I have this need to fix people. Even I know it's … unrealistic. I know where it comes from and I still can't help it."

I reach to play with her hair. "From your sister?"

She looks back to her fingers. "Mostly. Also because I had no control over anything for most of my life. My dad micromanaged me and everyone else he possibly could." She shakes her head. "But when I saw Briar at our mom's funeral? She was a zombie. She was being shuffled from one facility to another for psych issues. But really, they were drugging her to a point she had no personality, no feelings … she didn't care if she lived or died. She didn't even know what day it was. Our parents didn't give a shit and I was too busy in school to realize what was happening. The day after I graduated, I went to Miami, signed her out of that horrid place, and moved her across the country."

"You did that when you had very little. That's brave."

"Not brave. Do you know the guilt I carry for not knowing what was happening to her for years? My own sister? We might be close now, but not while I was in school. That's still no excuse for not knowing."

"You're hard on yourself."

"A leftover habit from being Dr. Astor Dillon's perfect child. Perfection was expected." She grabs my hand and entwines our fingers. "Can I ask you another question?"

"You can ask me whatever you want."

"Why did you hate me when we first met?"

I tip my head and think back. "Never hated you, Doc. From the first time I laid eyes on you, I found you intriguing in a way I've never found anyone else."

"Feels like a lifetime ago." She turns my hand in hers and traces my left ring finger with her middle one. Up and down and around. "But I would not have guessed intrigued. If I were to describe your feelings toward me, it would have been contempt."

I lean in and give her a tight squeeze. I wait for her to look up and then lower my voice. "Why contempt?"

She holds on tight. "I don't know. That's why I asked. Then you insisted on taking me to dinner and it all changed."

"It was never contempt. But you're right, I changed. It's no secret now I'm still dealing with the Riccis. Wasn't a good time for you to walk into my life, but then I said fuck it. You opened the door, and I walked through."

She sucks in a breath.

"I got tired of waiting, Doc."

An exhale rushes from her lips and her eyes do the frantic thing they do when I've wound her up. "Sometimes I feel like you're speaking in code."

I shake my head. "No, baby. When it comes to you, you deserve the truth. I'm just here, being me, waiting for you."

"See?" she accuses. "What do you mean? I'm right here."

I lean in and kiss her again. This time I let it linger, trace her lips with my tongue as her breath quickens on my skin. I've become obsessed with things in the last week that have surprised even me, and this is one of them. The effect I have on her body. How she reacts physically to me and not just my touch. My mere presence.

I wonder when that will end?

"I like you here," I murmur against her lips. "I want you by my side, no matter what hell is swirling around us."

My phone vibrates in my pocket, but I ignore it.

"Promise me you'll stay."

She brings her hands to my jaw, focusing on the path of her fingers. "You've asked me to promise a lot in the short days we've been doing this."

I shift over her and continue to ignore my fucking phone. "After what happened last night, this could get bad before it gets better. All I can say is, it will get better, but you need to stick with me. Promise me, Aria. Promise me you'll stay no matter what happens. I want your trust."

"Ruff!"

Aria jerks, and I sit up. That bark is different from any I've ever heard from the dog before.

My phone vibrates again, and from a distance, I hear cars.

I pull my phone out of my pocket and it's my security system.

I flip through the screens and switch to the feed from the front door. "Fuck."

She pulls her legs off my lap. "What is it?"

I look through the glass toward the front of the house.

She gasps.

"Yeah," I mutter and turn back to her. Her face has paled and it looks like she's seen a ghost. "Remember when I said things will get bad before they'll get better?"

She looks to the house again and doesn't acknowledge me.

"Well, Doc. This is what I meant."

Twenty-One

NOTEWORTHY

Aria

"BRANDO VITALE, JR., we have a warrant to search your property and all its structures. This search is in reference to the death of Marcia Ricci Vitale on, or approximately near, April twentieth of this year. The search includes any and all electronics. They may be confiscated if our officers find reason to search them off-site. You may remain on the property, but someone will be with you at all times. We ask that you stay out of the way so our officers can do their jobs."

Detectives Trudeau and Osborne stand behind the officer rattling off the details of the warrant, examining me like I'm the rarest of gems at a traveling exhibit. I wind Muppet's leash around my hand one more time to keep him close since he's found himself in the presence of new people to greet for the second time today.

Brand snatches the warrant from the officer and scans it. I wonder what he's looking for when he flips the pages and reaches the end. "I need to call my attorney."

"You can call whoever you want. We're still searching." He looks over his shoulder. "Let's do this."

They push forward and Brand tucks me behind him.

"Dr. Dillon," Detective Osborne drawls, narrowing his eyes. "This is definitely a surprise."

Brand starts to punch at the screen of his phone when an officer wearing plastic gloves plucks it from his hands. "Sorry. We're going to need to submit that for evidence. If it's clear, you'll get it back."

Brand glares at him and reaches for my hand. He pulls me, I pull Muppet, and the three of us go straight to the sofa. Once he has me glued to his side with an arm stretched behind me like we're settling in to watch a movie—not that we've ever done anything so normal together—Muppet proves his loyalty, even in the short time we've been together, jumping up and sprawling over our laps.

Being questioned by the police is one thing, but being at Brand's home while they carry out a search is something very different.

"Dr. Dillon." Detective Trudeau slides his hands into his trouser pockets and looks me over. "I see you didn't heed our warning."

I'm about to open my mouth when Brand brings his hand up from behind me and dips his fingers into my hair. He leans in and presses his lips to my temple. It's sweet, but I know what he's doing—he's marking his territory. I look at him and my breakfast does somersaults in my stomach.

His stare burns into me. "You don't have to talk to them."

I nod. It's not lost on me, the longer I'm with Brand in whatever this has become between the two of us, more and more of my walls are crumbling when we're alone. I fidget, bite the skin inside my mouth, and nibble at my cuticles. I'm not proud of it, but the longer he's in my presence, the more I'm letting my freak flag fly.

But not right now.

I don't know what kind of show Brand is putting on for the cops, but the need to do everything I can to protect him is fierce. Overwhelming might be a better word for it.

I turn back to the homicide detective and scratch Muppet so he'll settle. "I know I don't have to speak to them. Besides, I'm held to a high standard—you know, doctor-patient confidentiality."

Detective Trudeau's brows almost touch his hairline. "That's a new development. The last time we talked, you convinced us you wanted nothing to do with Mr. Vitale."

I'm not looking at him, but I can hear Brand's cocky smile in his tone. "Apparently I'm also convincing."

I slide my hand over his thick, rock-hard quad and warn him with a squeeze.

This wins me another kiss on my temple and makes me wonder how much of this is him staking his claim or if he's showing the police he doesn't give a fuck. My guess is both—and I'm not sure what to think about either.

A crash comes from the kitchen. I'm about to turn but Brand stops me, tucking me tight under his arm and brings his other hand to Muppet's head. My dog is in heaven, even if he is completely self-absorbed and oblivious to the hell going on around us.

"I find this noteworthy," the detective continues and takes a seat across the room from us in a leather club chair, similar in color to my burned garlic. "That you've flown under the radar for six months since your wife's murder—until this past week."

Brand stays silent, staring at the detective.

Trudeau leans back in his chair and rests an ankle on his other knee. "Last night was busy in Seattle. Upped the murder counts for the year at one of your dad's clubs."

My phone vibrates in the deep pocket of Brand's sweats I'm still wearing. I don't move. Brand must have felt it, too, since it's sandwiched between us. His arm blanketing my shoulders constrict, and he turns to me. "This will be over soon and we can get back to our day."

"I know." I give him a small smile and try not to fidget. They can search anything in this house. I realize my things in this house fall under that blanket. No way am I bringing my phone to their attention. I have my patient information on there. If they want my phone, they're going to have to search me, which means they'll have to arrest me.

Officers work around us. Some are carrying boxes, a laptop, and they're slamming drawers in his bedroom.

Good luck to them. Little do they know, I just searched the place last night and didn't find a thing.

"I'd like to call my attorney," Brand says.

Poor Art. I hope he had time to get donuts between emergencies. Brand is just going to have to use another phone. There's no way I'm offering him mine.

"What's the number?" Trudeau digs his phone out of his sport coat.

Brand tells him the number from memory and Trudeau types it in before standing to hand it over.

Like a king, Brand hardly moves, accepting the detective's phone. Art must answer immediately. "Art, it's me. I had to borrow a phone since they took mine with their search warrant. Yeah, right now. See you soon."

The detective catches the phone that flies through the air. "You've had a good run, Vitale. But everyone slips up eventually."

"I'm innocent." They are the first words Brand has offered that weren't sarcastic since the police arrived. And those two words send a thrill down my spine. "There's nothing to slip on."

"Yo, boss."

The tips of Brand's fingers press into my shoulder, and I don't move. Trudeau, however, does. "What did you find?"

"Clothes. Women's clothes—bagged in the garage."

I release my breath slowly. That's nothing other than proof she lived here, which everyone already knows.

"Tag them and we'll take them to the lab," Trudeau orders and settles his scrutiny back on Brand. "Never say never."

Brand shrugs. "When you're done, you can return them to Marcia's parents. I bagged them, but haven't gotten around to giving them to her family yet."

"No, I suppose you wouldn't want to see the Riccis given their opinion of you. Back to Seattle—that was a lot of gunfire. One man is dead, two are on their deathbeds fighting for life, and no one is talking. Not an employee, not a patron, not even your father."

"I was at the station last night. Ask anyone there."

"Do you find it a coincidence that people die while you're at the station?"

Brand sighs, and if I didn't know better, I'd think he was bored. "The truth isn't coincidental. The truth is simply the truth, Detective."

Three officers appear in the hall from Brand's bedroom. "We got nothing in there."

Trudeau doesn't try to hide his disappointment. "Go help outside."

More officers descend from upstairs. "Nothing. Some of those rooms are completely bare."

"Weapons?" Trudeau asks.

"I'm a firefighter," Brand reminds them of something they already know. "Don't need a weapon to save anyone in my line of work."

"Fuck," Trudeau mutters and pulls a hand down his face.

Art storms in the front door wearing the same Saturday uniform he had on earlier. "Where's the warrant?"

There's no greeting other than Brand coolly lifting his chin. "Coffee table."

Art does a replay of what Brand did, flipping to the end and hesitates before nodding slowly. Then he folds it in half and tucks it under his arm. "They about done?"

Trudeau crosses his arms. "Getting there."

"You got what you wanted," Art growls. "Maybe now you'll realize why no judge in the western half of Washington would grant a warrant.

There's nothing here linking my client to the death of Marcia Vitale. By setting your sights on my client and my client alone, you've blinded yourself to the fact there's a murderer out there. Maybe you should start from scratch—this path is cold for a reason."

I sink into the sofa and Brand pulls me closer. Deeper and deeper, he's drawing me in, and I wonder if there's any way this story can end that isn't completely and devastatingly disastrous.

Twenty-Two

Ghost

Aria

TIME MAKES THE heart grow fonder.

I'm downright jealous of those hearts. To grow fonder sounds like a lovely and beautiful progression of the organ that gives us life. Falling slowly, enjoying every step of the journey, making the decision to put one foot in front of the other, and making a conscious decision to take a relationship to the next level with someone who causes that organ to pitter-patter.

I've questioned my actions over the last few weeks. My motivations, my choices, and, yes, my own heart. I've tried to push myself the way I push my patients when I encourage them to stop, think, and examine the consequences, because there are times when you turn a corner, it's too late. There's no going back.

I turned that corner a long time ago, and have traveled so far into the journey, there's no way I can find my way out now. No matter how much I know I should.

Because if I were my own psychologist, I'd beat myself over the head with every textbook I studied at Harvard until I was black and blue. It's the reason I've lied every time Russ has called or texted to check on me. He's a wonderful friend and the best mentor I could ask for. I can't bring myself to see him in person and not tell him the truth. He deserves more.

What I wouldn't give to experience the journey that simply makes the heart grow fonder. Because, in my case, time has only made mine desperate.

And we all know desperation makes us do things we'd never consider under normal circumstances.

I should donate my heart to the study of the psyche. Experts could publish journals upon journals, reporting all the ways I went wrong and the poor choices I've made along the way.

Because I'm moving forward, cementing myself deeper into Brand Vitale's life. I can't look back. If I tried to turn and find my way out now, I'd be lost forever.

Which makes me all levels of a hypocrite, pushing my patients to do what's right and healthy, while I do everything but.

Brand and I have settled into an odd normal that has included meetings with Art, as his attorney, not his childhood best friend, the way I'd rather get to know him. The search warrant was granted by a judge outside the Vitale network. It doesn't take an expert to understand what that means. Art has managed Marcia's death to this point and he's not happy a warrant was signed by anyone in the state of Washington.

Brand informed me the Vitales have control over most judges, but the Riccis have more police officers on their payroll than, in his words, *any fucking family should.*

If that wasn't the push to turn and run, I'm not sure what it will take at this point.

So, here I am. A month after buying a date and a dog, warming the bed of a mafia-son firefighter who's being investigated for his dead wife's murder.

Hypocrite. Idiot. Liar. It should be etched onto my nameplate, warning people of the mess I've become.

"Do you think he's trying?" I ask.

The situation between my patients Marin and Eric has spiraled to a new depth of ugly. Eric has not returned for couples counseling and has canceled every session we had scheduled individually. At this point, I'm treating Marin as an individual, instead of them as a couple.

Marin shrugs and has trouble making eye contact with me. "Sometimes."

"I'm afraid you're at a point where *sometimes* is not good enough. He either is or he isn't. He can't choose to be faithful one day and defy your vows the next, Marin." I shift in my chair and wait for her to look up. There's only fear in her eyes. "Instead of focusing on Eric, we need to discuss your boundaries. Boundaries can't be moved and they're not gray. It's time for you to set them in your marriage. If he chooses to obliterate them, there needs to be consequences. You've been my patient long enough, I can tell this isn't only weighing on you emotionally, but physically. We need to focus on you."

She plucks another tissue from the box on the end table and dabs her swollen eyes. After taking a big breath, she finally nods. "I know. I've been trying to make myself come to terms with it. I was hoping I could make him change. Hoping I could do something to make it better."

"Do you realize you're asking yourself to change who you are so he will quit cheating?"

She goes back to studying her fingers as if they hold the magic answer to her problems.

"He's blamed you for his choices. He's been avoiding, not only you, but your children in the last month to be with her. And now he's with her openly because he wants you to make the next move."

"He's going to use it against me," she whispers before her tear-stained face turns to mine. "He said so. He's going to use it to turn our kids against me. Friends, family. He's going to make me the villain, I know it. I want to file, but I'm afraid to. Tell me what to do."

"You're here for me to help you work through your problems, not for me to tell you what to do. My job is to help you help yourself. I don't want you to be dependent on me or anyone else. You only have control over you, Marin. I know you can handle your children and explain what's happening on their level."

She nods methodically, but her words don't coincide with her actions. "I don't know if I can."

"You'll know when it's time. I'll be here to support you and help you work through it." I sit back in my chair and hope my smile is as sympathetic and encouraging as it's meant to be. I look at the clock behind her head. "I'm sorry, our time is up. Should we meet at the same time next week?"

She lifts her purse to her shoulder and grabs another tissue. "Yes, that would be fine."

"Good." I move to take her hand. "You remember how to get hold of me if you need to? Any time, day or night."

"I do. Thank you, Dr. Dillon."

"For the last time, call me Aria."

I walk her to my waiting room, but instead of giving her the proper goodbye she deserves, my heart stutters. An unwelcome ghost is sitting there in the flesh.

She swipes her eyes one more time. "See you next week, Aria."

Marin moves through the waiting room as he stands. He takes me in from top to bottom, examining me—for what, who knows—just as I'm accustomed to. His inspection is as judgmental as ever, not that I'd expect any different, but I sure as hell didn't expect to see him. Especially here, in a place I've built on my own, from long hours and hard work.

I force myself to look back to my patient. "I'll see you next week. Don't forget … anytime."

Once the door is pulled shut behind her, I direct my attention back to the man I have no desire to speak to, let alone see in the flesh. "What are you doing here?"

"Aria, sweetheart. Is that anyway to greet me after so long?"

I pull my office door shut behind me. "What kind of welcome did you expect, Dad? The last time I saw you, we buried Mom. On the same day I learned Briar was being *treated* at that Godforsaken place you dumped her, because you were too busy to realize what was happening."

"I didn't know—"

"Stop," I interrupt and pull my phone out of my pocket to check the time. Marin was my last appointment, and Brand should be here to pick me up any minute. "Don't pretend to be the concerned parent now. You had the chance to do the right thing for eighteen years and ignored Briar, even when she was undergoing treatment. I have to live with the fact she was being drugged into a semi-comatose state and you didn't care."

He runs his hand through his hair. I realize in my shocked state from seeing him, he's changed. I didn't notice it at first, but now it stands out front and center. He's aged tremendously.

Dr. Astor Dillon practices the most self-absorbed profession the western world has to offer and he has to look the part. My father has aged as gracefully as every injectable and procedure has allowed. Besides his favorite pastime of molding me into what he wanted, he always worked out with a private trainer, had his hair dyed to cover most of the gray—but not all, because that wouldn't look authentic—and made sure his face did not match that of his age.

His goal in life was to be as realistically fake as possible.

But not today. The lines around his eyes are deeper, his hair is grayer, and I think he's lost weight.

"I'm here to see Briar. I want the chance to make things right with her, but I can't pinpoint an address. This is the only listing I could find for either of you."

The hazards of having to promote my practice I guess. At least my attempt to keep Briar's life private worked. "A phone call would have been nice."

"I knew if I called, you wouldn't see me."

"You were right." He takes a step forward, but I hold a hand out, halting him in place. "I'm protective of Briar and have done everything I can to make sure she lives a life she deserves. You're not getting anywhere near her."

He pauses and I recognize the expression taking over his face—it's one I'm all too familiar with. Nothing has changed—it brings out the same bitterness in me it always has.

But instead of snapping at me, his tone comes across desperate. "I feel horrible how I left things with you girls. Please, let me meet with her. I want to apologize and do anything I can to make up for not keeping a closer eye on the care she was receiving. I want to make it up to both of you. You're the only family I have left."

It's all I can do not to gnaw on my fingernail, because Briar does not need this. She's made so much progress since we got here and there's no way I'll allow any chance for that to be compromised. "You're getting nowhere near her. I'll make sure of it myself. Do not mistake me for the innocent girl who abided by your every wish. I might've sought your approval then, but not anymore. I don't need you, and Briar doesn't either."

My father might stand at five-ten, but it was always his presence that intimidated me into living my life by his terms. That was a long time ago.

When he takes another step in my direction and reaches for me, it doesn't have the same effect it used to. "Aria—"

"Get your fucking hands off her."

Having Brand at my side doesn't hurt either. He looks like an angry warrior about to draw the blood of his opponent.

My father takes a surprised step back and jerks his arm back to his side.

I exhale.

Without breaking his intense gaze from my father, I know Brand is talking to me when he asks, "You okay?"

A small smile settles on my lips. "Yes. But I'm glad you're here."

Brand wedges his way between my father and me in my waiting room, reaching around to give my hip a squeeze. "Is he a patient?"

"Brand, this is my father, Astor Dillon." I move to his side, slip my hand into his, and wait for him to look down at me. "He was not invited."

"Who is this?" my dad barks.

We've only been together for a month, but I know better than to answer that question and I'm right. Brand answers for me. "I'm the man who's going to make sure Aria isn't bothered by anyone she doesn't choose to be around. And from what I've witnessed for the last thirty seconds, she doesn't want you here. I've also heard enough about you to know she doesn't want you in the western half of the country."

A glimpse of the old Astor comes out to play. "How dare you talk to me like that. You can't keep me from my daughter."

"Don't test me because you will lose." Brand looks at me. "What does he want?"

I'm getting way more satisfaction than I should from this scene. I've never had anyone to stand up for me. I shake my head and lean into his arm. "Seems he wants to finally be a father, but has a keen interest in making amends with Briar. I was just telling him to stay away from her."

"He's not getting anywhere near either of you," Brand adds. He pulls his hand from mine and wraps an arm around me. After I sink into his side, Brand finally addresses my father again. "Your daughters want nothing to do with you. From what I know about you, I don't want you to have anything to do with them either. Go back to where you came from and we can forget this ever happened. Take this warning as the favor it is."

My father drags a hand through his hair. "Aria. You have to hear me out. I saw a picture of Briar on TMZ. She was with Alexander Thornton. They were ... together. It made me realize how much I'm missing out on."

Brand gives me a squeeze, and I look at him. "Your sister hooked up with Thornton?"

"Maybe." I pull in a deep breath and don't allow my father to see even the hint of surprise that's coursing through me. First of all, if Briar is seeing someone—anyone—and didn't tell me, I'll... Well, I don't know what I'll do. And second, the only Alexander Thornton I know of is the one who donated a shit ton to the center. Which means not only is my sister dating someone, she's dating a bigshot tech mogul. "Or maybe not. It isn't my news to share."

Briar met the man I've dumped all intelligent reasoning for during a drop off for Muppet. I guess I can't hold it against her for keeping things from me when I haven't shared the whole truth about Brand.

But then again, I plan to carry that to the grave.

My dad doesn't speak for a long moment as he studies me, Brand, and likely the intimate hold we're locked in.

When his silence stretches, my damn curiosity wins out. "What does it matter who she's seeing?"

"I need..." He takes a deep breath, looking even older than his years. "I've been wanting to reach out for a while. Seeing her grown and dating someone was the push I needed. I want to fix things. I *need* to fix things. With her." His expression is earnest as he takes a small step closer, his gaze darting to Brand then back to me. "And with you. Please."

There's a tinge of desperation in his tone I've never heard. It almost makes me pity him.

Almost.

Brand speaks before I have a chance and gives me a squeeze. It's the same thing he did while the police were searching his house and he didn't want me to go for my phone. "We'll talk to Briar. If she wants to talk to you, Aria will reach out. She has your number?"

He nods. "Yes, it's the same. Who are you?"

"Brand. And don't come back to Aria's office unless she invites you."

My dad looks at me and nods. "You have to give me a chance. I'll wait for your call."

I frown and say nothing as he turns to leave.

When the door closes behind him, I pull away from Brand. "Why did you agree to that? And how do you know Alexander Thornton?"

He tags my hand and pulls me back. "I said it to get him the hell out of your office. I don't know Thornton personally, but he's a giant in the tech industry. Software development and other shit I know nothing about and don't care to. How do you know him?"

"He donated to the center."

"Your sister didn't tell you she was seeing him?"

My eyes widen. "No, she didn't. I'm googling as soon as we get to the car. I need to see these pictures for myself."

"I'll make a call. I've got a guy who can dig up anyone's shit, no matter how deep it's buried."

My body tightens, a pit growing in my stomach for far too many reasons. "You think Alexander is up to something?"

"No, your dad. I don't trust him."

That's understandable, neither do I.

"I'll give him your dad's info," Brand continues. "See what we can find out."

"I can't afford that." I pull out of his hold and turn back to my office to close for the night.

"You think I'd ask you to pay for that, Doc?"

"I'm just saying, you don't need to. I'll talk to Briar and warn her, but since there's no way she'll agree to see him, I really hope he'll go back to Miami and leave us alone. He has his life there, he doesn't need to be here stressing us out."

His heat hits my back as his arm circles me. A familiar warmth runs through me when his mouth hits my neck and he tastes my skin. "I need to get you home. Unstress you. Your dog almost ran on me today."

I turn in his arms and reach to kiss him. "Muppet loves you, and I know you secretly like him."

Brand's dark eyes narrow and he leans to grab my bags. "I think you should rename him. He needs a self-respecting name. How can anyone go through life with a name like that?"

Brand holds the door for me, and I hit the lights. "He loves his name. He understands and comes running."

"Yeah, but I'll look like an idiot when I call for him."

Brand just got off a shift at the station this morning. Whenever we're away from each other for a full twenty-four hours, his homecoming is an active night. "You couldn't look like an idiot if you tried."

He opens the reception door. "You're just trying to butter me up so I'll let you suck my dick."

I bark a laugh and walk down the quiet hall to the elevator.

When he stands next to me, his hand comes to my ass. "You know you want to."

I lick my lips. "Maybe."

I lose his touch for a quick second, when his hand returns with a sharp smack. "Send me your dad's number. I need to get that going and then we need to eat. I made kabobs."

The elevator opens and when we're on our way to the parking garage, I lean into him. "What did I do to deserve you?"

His gaze lingers like a rest at the end of a complicated concerto right before the big finale. He leans in and presses his lips to my forehead. The elevator dings and we step out into the parking garage. "You saved me, Aria. Every day with you, life is easier and lighter than I've ever had."

I pull my coat together to protect myself from the chill, not knowing if it's the nip of late fall or his words.

What I don't do is question it. I take his hand and let him lead me to his house that I've all but moved into on the same property his wife

died.
    Where his wife was *killed*.
    And again, I don't look back.

Twenty-Three

A DOSE OF DESPERATION

Brand

"YOU HAVE TO see this. My sister is on TM-freaking-Z."

The dog attacks my legs as I close the back door and hold up the platter of food I just grilled. "Doc, I'm sending your dog to training. He's out of control."

"Muppet is perfect the way he is," she mutters, perched on a barstool at the island.

I set the food in front of her. "He jumps all over everyone—we can't let him out unless he's tied to us or something else."

She doesn't look away from the pictures she's scrolling through at the speed of light. "Isn't that what all dogs do?"

"Fuck no. He's going to bootcamp."

Aria doesn't have to reach far to scratch the dog on the head since he's got his paws on her lap, begging for food. "Don't you worry. You're not going anywhere."

Shit. I'm going to have to bring someone here to work with him. At this point, Aria and the dog are a package deal.

She's wearing another one of my sweatshirts over her workout clothes. Despite me trying to convince her I have other ways to burn off some energy so she'll sleep, she hits my treadmill every night before bed. At least I get to enjoy a shower with her, followed by another workout that exhausts us both. She's nothing but pure fucking gold.

Aria is in my bed every night, even while I'm at the station, and has been for more than a month. When Marcia was alive, I used to take extra shifts to get out of here. Now I'm handing over days to guys who want extra time. I love my job but I don't need the money. Doing my thing for Vitale Holdings more than funds my life without touching my investments.

I did not see this coming, this obsession. But my curiosity about the good doctor got the best of me and I couldn't give up the opportunity to know more about her. What makes her tick.

She drops her phone to the marble and looks at me. "Briar isn't answering my calls or texts. If I didn't love her so much, I'd wring her neck for not telling me about the techy multi-gazillionaire man she's been photographed with. Honestly, I wonder if she even knows she was seen, let alone photographed. If she didn't before, she will once she gets my messages. She's private, Brand—hates attention more than anything. I'm not sure if that comes from our mother forcing her into those horrid child beauty contests, or later, when she was fighting cancer. I'm worried about her, but I'm more worried about what my dad wants with her."

I dish two plates and push a bowl of salad toward her. "Eat."

A smile touches her lips, and she picks up a fork. "Do you get tired of cooking for me? If you teach me some skills, I can cook for you on the weekends. I hate being such a taker."

"I'm afraid of what you'll do to my kitchen." I grab the bottom of her barstool and pull her closer to me. "I sent your dad's info to my guy. Your choice, but you might wait to tell Briar he's in town until we know more."

"Who's your guy?"

I angle my eyes to her as I take a bite. "You really want to know?"

She pushes a mushroom around her plate and goes for a piece of steak, but doesn't look at me when she speaks. "Yes."

I wrap my hand around her thigh and slide it north. This gets her attention, and she turns hesitant the way she always does when we talk about the Vitales. "Baby, told you I'd tell you what you wanted to know. The more you ask, the more I'll give you. But that means you're in deeper. You can't know these things and then walk away."

She sets her fork down as if I just soured her stomach. "You're very direct."

"Haven't I always been?"

"Yes." Her hand covers mine, still wedged between her legs. I'm willing to cancel her nightly run and eat a cold meal. Instead of removing my hand, she presses it to her pussy and looks me in the eyes. "I always know what you want, but I don't always know what you're thinking."

"Right back at you, Doc."

She pulls that lip between her teeth.

I cup her tighter. "Give and take, baby. You want to take, you've got to give."

She opens her legs for me.

"I don't mean this," I say, even as I take full advantage and silently curse the invention of pants. I lean in and press my lips to her temple to show her what I'm talking about. "I mean this. It's been over a month. I know every part of your body like the back of my hand. I understand your work. I put up with your dog. I miss you when we're apart, but when we are, there's nothing I like more than watching you on the cameras. Yet there's still a part of you you're keeping from me. I want it all."

Her chest rises and falls quicker than it should for someone who can run daily for an hour straight. When her palm starts to sweat over mine, there's nothing more I want to do than reach for her neck and check her pulse.

"What are you afraid of?" I ask.

She exhales, and I'm forced to pull my hand away when she moves. All it takes is one foot to the floor for her to climb onto my lap. She straddles my hips, pressing that hot pussy to my cock, and wraps me with her limbs. There she whispers into my neck, "Everything."

My cock stiffens, and I know for a fact our dinner will grow cold. I put a hand to her ass and grind her on my needy dick that hasn't had her since before my last shift at the station. "Seems to me the doctor needs to get her shit right in her head. Not sure what I've given you to be afraid of."

"I feel like you've been coursing through my blood for longer than just a month. I'm afraid of this ending. I'm not sure if I could handle that."

I pull her to my chest and feel her tighten around me even more. "I could say the same. But I'm not afraid of anything. Fuck the force that tries to take you from me. No shit, Aria. I'll take them out myself and they won't live to see tomorrow."

She pulls back just enough to look me in the eyes. "Don't say that."

"It's true. I need you to—"

I'm about to give her more of me. Tell her what I've done and what I'll do again if she gives me everything, but my phone vibrates on the counter next to my plate.

Shit. It's my dad.

Palming her ass, I hold tight when she starts to move away and grab my phone.

"Be quick. I'm busy."

"Cut the attitude, Brand, and turn on the news," he bites. "I called you first but you need to call Art. Marcia's case just blew up. I'm on my way."

Fuck.

ARIA

ART IS PACING again—tonight he's wearing a suit—barking orders into his phone.

The TV is blaring, and in the back of my mind, I realize this is the first time I've ever seen it on. If we aren't eating, I'm playing with Muppet or running, or we're in bed.

Or in the shower.

Or, sometimes, on the island.

What we don't do is watch TV.

A news conference is in progress—live from the Redmond PD. Detective Trudeau is at the podium taking questions. The topic, an impending arrest in the death of Marcia Vitale.

"We know there was a search warrant issued for the address and property of Brando, Jr. and the late Marcia Vitale. Are we to assume this upcoming arrest has something to do with Mr. Vitale?"

Trudeau shakes his head, holding on to whatever professional candor he can with a condescending smile plastered on his face. "We can't comment on that. Yet. Give us an hour or two."

"Fuck," Brand hisses, standing next the sofa where I'm huddled. His stance is wide and his arms are crossed. He seems bigger than usual and I realize I have no idea what it's like for him to be angry because right now it looks like he could rip his TV off the wall and throw it through the wall of windows. "Who the hell does a press conference to announce they're going to make an arrest?"

"Why has it taken this long to move forward in the case?" a reporter asks.

The camera zooms in on the homicide detective that warned me to protect myself from Brand. Because his alibi was *murky*. Because he's from a questionable family.

Trudeau rests his hands on the podium and loses the dumb-ass smile. "We've run into roadblock after roadblock. We haven't had the cooperation we needed from the courts. But, mark my word, that's changed."

My stomach twists. I'm glad we never got around to eating. If I had food in my stomach right now, I'd be physically ill.

Brand turns to look at me. "Don't worry. We knew this was a possibility. Art has it covered."

I don't have a chance to ask why or shake him since he needs to be freaking out like I am, because his front door bursts open.

We all look toward the front of the house and Brand shifts to stand in front of me. I grab Muppet's collar to keep him close. "Son, do you know anything?"

An older version of Brand hurries into the house wearing slacks, a dress shirt that's open at the collar, and a long wool coat. His hair, which was probably once dark like Brand's, is now more salt than pepper.

A tall, elegant woman sashays in behind him, wearing a smart dress that hits her below the knees and fits like a glove everywhere else. Her hair is perfectly highlighted in a cool blond, and her heels click across the wood floors. "Brand! Please tell me Art is prepared. And I think you should change your clothes. Go put on a shirt from the station. Remind them they're fucking with one of their own."

"I'm good, Mom. They've been watching me for months. They know who I am, no need to remind them."

"This'll be your first arrest. That shitstorm in college doesn't count," his dad goes on. "Play it cool. Don't be cocky, but don't kiss anyone's ass—"

"For God's sake, don't kiss anyone's ass," his mom echoes.

His dad doesn't miss a beat. "Art's going to follow you downtown, and so will we. That fucking cop thinks he can showboat this, but we made the necessary calls. There will be a hearing tonight and Art will post bail. You'll be released and back home in a few hours. The press will be there—maybe national outlets if they can scramble. We'll meet you outside as a show of our support and as a *fuck you* to the Riccis. Don't worry, this'll die in no time."

"I know what to do, Dad."

"Umph." Muppet is too strong and wiggles out of my hold, jumping down and running before Brand can grab him.

"A dog?" his dad growls.

"Oh my God, you got a dog!" his mom squeals and bends at the knees on her spiked heels, letting Muppet kiss her all over the face.

Okay, so Brand is right. Muppet has no manners. If Brand gets out of this mess, I'll let him send Muppet to whatever bootcamp he wants.

Brand moves forward to extract my unruly dog's tongue from his mother's face. When he does, his parents spear me with a probing glare.

I really wish I hadn't changed out of my work clothes.

"Your father told me you were seeing someone. Hell, everyone in town knows you're seeing someone, but you haven't invited us to meet her. I've given you your privacy, but I'm done." Brand's mother looks at her son. "Are you going to introduce us?"

Shit. I stand, wanting nothing more than to run or disintegrate into thin air.

Brand takes a big breath. "Mom, this is Aria. Dr. Aria Dillon. Doc, this is my mom, Eloise, and my dad, Brando Senior. You can call him Brando or Senior. He answers to either."

His mom steps forward and takes my hand. "You can call me Eloise."

I shake her hand and then Brando Senior's. "It's nice to meet you."

"Maybe I should stay here with Aria until you two get back," Eloise smiles brightly, not at all worried about her son's impending arrest for murder.

"You know we need to make an appearance," Senior says, as if they're swinging by a cocktail party.

Do I need to remind everyone that Brand will be charged with murder? We're not talking about something mundane like jaywalking.

Eloise clears her throat and walks to Brand. She puts her hands to his jaw, and for the first time since she waltzed through the front door, she looks like a concerned mother instead of a mobster's wife who's been to this party before. "Don't worry. It will all get straightened out. We know you're innocent."

Tears prick the backs of my eyes and it's all I can do not to be stupid and blubbering in front of Brand's parents.

She pushes up on the red soles of her shoes—hers are not dupes—and presses her lips to his cheek. "Art will get you out of this. I know he will because if he doesn't, I'll kill him myself."

"Thanks for the show of support, Ellie," Art deadpans and grabs the remote to turn off the TV.

Brand pulls his phone out of his pocket and stares at the screen before turning to me. "They just turned in. Don't worry and stay here. I'll be back."

Art moves in beside us. "I arranged to have someone watch the house. She'll be fine."

Brand doesn't look away from me when he nods and continues speaking to me in what seems to be code, because it makes no sense since he's the one being arrested. "You'll be fine. I promise. I don't want you to worry."

I don't have a chance to say anything. With his parents and Art watching, he wraps his arms around me and puts his lips to mine. It's not chaste or mildly affectionate. It's completely passionate with a dose of desperation.

He only breaks our kiss when a rap hits the glass door. His thumbs swipe the escaped tears streaking my cheeks.

With his forehead pressed to mine, he whispers, "I'll be back and I'll take care of you."

I hear the door open but he doesn't let go of me.

"Brando Gian Vitale, Jr., we have a warrant for your arrest for the murder of Marcia Vitale. You have the right to remain…"

I don't hear the rest.

Brand steps back, cooperating yet never breaking eye contact from me as they handcuff him. My vision drowns in tears. Even Muppet realizes this isn't the time for his antics because he whines at my feet.

My hearing tunnels and I can't look away as they lead him out the door. I barely acknowledge his mother when she places a light hand on my arm and repeats her son's wishes for me not to worry.

Then they rush out the front door.

Art follows after rattling off more instructions that I don't comprehend.

Then, I'm alone in Brand's house. I look around the space. It's larger, emptier, and colder than normal. And tonight, I know Brand isn't watching me on his high-tech security system. I feel more alone than I ever have.

Fear has eaten away at me in life.

But nothing like this, afraid of the unknown, of Brand's future.

A future that's tied so tight to mine, I've lost the point where one ends and the other begins.

I crumble to the floor in a pile of exhausted emotions.

Twenty-Four

SCARED

Aria

A HAND SLIDES over my hip and my body before it palms my breast. I'm groggy from exhaustion more than sleep. The last time I looked at the clock, it was after three in the morning. Art responded to a couple of my texts assuring me he knew how to do his job and to *chill*. I have no idea how long I've been dozing, but it feels like a week has passed since they took Brand away in handcuffs.

My exhale is full of relief when his touch hits me. "You're home."

I try to roll but he twists my nipple and his bare chest hits my back. His lips touch the skin under my neck as his words rumble down my spine. "Don't move."

His damp hair brushes my cheek. I guess I was sleeping deeper than I thought if I didn't hear him come home and shower. Eucalyptus and mint envelop me—the scent of his body wash I've become as obsessed with as I am him.

Everything about Brand consumes me. I knew I was on my way to an unhealthy fixation, but when he was taken away tonight, I realized just how bad it is.

He presses his hungry cock to my ass as his fingers feel their way from my breast to wrap around my neck.

"Arch, but do not touch yourself."

Oh.

I missed him. I'm in so deep, I'll do whatever he says, no matter the consequences. This isn't like me, and I'm not proud of myself, but I arch.

With one swift shift of his hips, he takes me.

"Good girl."

Powerful.

Greedy.

Hungry.

And, for the first time, bare.

We've never discussed it past my telling him I'm not on birth control. He should buy shares in the condom company because we've gone through so many in the last month, I'm sure its profits have climbed exponentially.

"Brand." He's inside me for the first time, skin to skin. I stretch to his thickness when he starts to move with force. I'm beyond wet and ready. I know I should tell him to stop—that now is not the time to be reckless—but I can't make myself. I'm not sure if I'll ever be able to tell him to stop, not when I crave anything he'll give me.

My need for him is depraved and so very, very wrong.

"You're always ready for me, aren't you?" His hand tightens around my neck, pulling me to meet his every thrust. "From the day I told you if you were in my bed, you'd be here naked. When I tell you to touch yourself. Even in the beginning when we were new, and I touched you and exposed you without asking … you did it all. For me."

My lungs beg for a breath when I admit, "I'll do anything for you."

"I know you will." His teeth sink into my shoulder and my pulse races below the firm hold of his hand on my throat. "From now on, you'll do exactly as I say."

My clit is swollen and lonely and desperate. "I'm scared."

"You should be," he grits as I take every forceful and beautiful onslaught of his cock, touching every spot inside me that matters. "But I won't let anything happen to you."

I try to shake my head even in his tight hold. "I'm scared for you."

He doesn't answer, he can't. I can tell by the way he's taking me—faster and harder. Deep down, I pray there's a desperation in him that runs as hot as mine. If not, I don't know what I'll do.

"Please, Brand."

"Ask," he demands, one angry word gritted between thrusts.

I arch to take every inch of him I can. Under the grip of his hand, I beg, "Please make me come."

I pull in a full breath of air when he releases my neck and drags his muscled hand between my breasts, over my abs, and slides his fingers between my legs.

"Oh, yes," I moan, guilt plaguing me for wanting anything from him after what he's gone through in the last few hours.

He pulls out of me and I huff in protest.

"Baby," he growls, pressing his face into my messy hair.

It only takes two more firm rotations around my clit and I come—moaning, gasping for air—as he thrusts against my bare ass, coming between us. He holds me tight, pressing his chest to my back, his cum hot and sticky, gluing me to him.

I've fantasized about him for what seems like so long. I welcome anything he'll give me, and have come to love it all. I have to wrap my hand over his between my legs to stop him because I can't take any more.

I welcome it when he gives me his weight, doing everything I can to ignore reality and not think about what happened after they took him away from me tonight or what might happen when the sun rises.

Murder charges.

The Riccis.

The Vitales.

The organ that has betrayed all moral reasoning, blurring right and wrong into a lovely utopia over the last month, steadies, but I don't let go of his hand still wedged between my legs.

He doesn't move or utter another word.

I break the silence. "I rescheduled my patients. I want to be with you tomorrow."

Every muscle in his body tenses and he presses his lips to the top of my head. "Go back to sleep. We'll talk in the morning."

I nod and relish the heat his body is feeding mine.

I need to believe he's telling me the truth. That he'll take care of this. That Art will take care of him and make it go away.

And this utopia he's given me doesn't turn into something that nightmares are made of.

An ugly, black dystopia.

Twenty-Five

A MILLION FUCKING PIECES

Brand

*I*T WAS WORSE than we thought.

Actually, it was the worst of all the scenarios Art and I considered possible.

They blew my alibi into a million fucking pieces. Art is a damned good attorney, but there's no way even he could put that shit together again. No way any judge on the Vitale payroll would accept it. Even we could see there was no light at the end of that tunnel.

I wasn't at the station the night Marcia was killed.

Somehow the police got their hands on the real surveillance feed of the station that night. The video was taken care of, or so I thought. The real one showed a utility truck arriving to work on our systems since the storm blew shit out far and wide. No one was there, and the generator made sure the cameras were humming away perfectly.

Along with the real surveillance, they have the statement to prove it from the utility company.

The month prior to that night was bad. Bad between the Riccis and Vitales, and really fucking bad at home. Marcia wanted out of our contract, but her family wouldn't let her break it. Saul Ricci did everything he could to stir shit up—poking at my family through our businesses, at me, and doing everything he could to renege on his agreement without actually being the one to renege. He's that much of an asshole and his daughter was that much of a bitch.

She did everything she could to piss me off and it worked. But, like everything else in my life, I practiced restraint and control, no matter how much I wanted to rip her fucking head off every single day.

I put my self-discipline to work.

I ignored her.

And that fed the monster in my late wife.

Marcia Ricci Vitale—still fucking kills me the she-devil carried my name for even a minute, let alone a decade—did not like being ignored. She, like every other narcissist, fed off attention and when she got none, she went fucking crazy.

I came home from the station one morning, and she'd torn my bedroom apart. My mattress was sliced, shit was thrown at the walls, and she even overturned my dresser. Shit was broken all over my bathroom—bottles, mirrors, the glass shower doors were shattered. My closet and clothes were trashed.

She sat on the damn sofa watching and waiting for me to blow up. She sucked on a cigarette right here in the house, flicking the ashes to the floor, not taking her beady eyes off me as I walked right back out of my room and straight to the kitchen. I grabbed a bottle of water and protein bar as I dialed the cleaning service. I arranged for them to send a crew out to clean that shit up, and while they were at it, to fumigate my house from the cigarette smoke.

Then I called Anna, my oldest sister, and told her I wanted to redecorate my bedroom and bath. Right in front of Marcia, I informed Anna she was in charge and there was no budget. Then I grabbed my duffle and left, never once glancing at my wife.

I slept at the station for ten days.

A week after I moved back home, I walked in on some asshole fucking Marcia on my sofa.

I ignored them both and proceeded to make myself a steak.

She told him to ignore me, but the asshole couldn't focus enough to finish, even when I insisted he shouldn't stop fucking my wife on my account.

But I didn't utter a word to her.

He ran out, and she screamed so much I thought I was going to have to call the builder for a new wall of windows.

It went on and on and on.

Her non-stop drama put the entire Bravo lineup to shame. Meanwhile, the Riccis were pressing into Vitale territory. Organizing underground fights in areas of Seattle controlled by my father. Booking penthouse rooms under other names, hosting high-stakes games in our own fucking hotels, and then throwing it in my dad's face so he had to take care of that shit in front of customers. Then they paid off someone at the city to get my construction permits pulled.

My dad handled it the best he could—not the way he would with anyone else. Especially any other organization he was not contractually tethered to by the church.

Because all the other shit that went down didn't matter, no one fucking messes with contracts made in front of God. It might be whacked, but it is what it is.

So me ignoring the fuckfest happening right under my nose—and on my oil-brushed leather sofa that cost me ten Gs that I later threw out—was the straw that broke the bitch's back.

Because Marcia stopped.

All her shit.

Just. Fucking. Stopped.

And the Riccis pulled back.

For two weeks, my house was perfect and quiet—the way a multimillion-dollar home situated on a mountain in the woods, on a pristine lake that goes on as far as the eye can see, should be. Marcia and I lived together the way any married couple would who agreed to the shit we did, but still hated each other.

Tolerantly.

Separately.

Silently.

I thought she finally got the message.

That should've been the biggest red flag waved during my ten-year prison sentence.

And that's where I made my biggest mistake.

Twenty-Six

DENIALISM

Aria

I OPEN MY eyes and hear tiny voices that can only be attached to tiny humans. High-pitched screaming and laughter rings through Brand's normally serene home, even through the closed door to his bedroom.

Besides me, his bed is empty.

Adult voices dance with tiny ones, followed by one of the happiest barks I've heard come from my dog.

How many people are here?

I sit up in bed, hold the sheet to my bare chest, and look across the room to the full-length mirror resting against the wall. My eyes are puffy, my hair is a rat's nest, and I smell like sex. There's no way I'm leaving this room in my current state.

I throw back the covers and hurry to Brand's bathroom. As the shower warms, I dig through my things that have made their way to his house and ended in a pile on the floor in his closet. There's something about the empty one across the bathroom meant for the master's mate … I can't bring myself to walk in there, let alone dump a pile of clean clothes. And Brand hasn't invited me to. He also hasn't complained about my mess in his perfectly organized closet.

Who am I kidding? For the last month, Brand and I have danced around so many topics, I could write an entire paper on our incredulous relationship based on denialism. Which makes last night's reality the slap in the face I feared, but deep down, knew it might be unavoidable.

I shower as fast as I can, throw on a pair of jeans with a sweater, and dry my hair to damp. My need to know what happened last night and what might happen in the future outweighs whatever vanity runs through me. Skipping makeup doesn't seem like such a big deal right now, no matter who I have to meet outside of Brand's room.

I take a deep breath before opening the door.

When I turn the corner to his big family room, all eyes land on me.

And there are a lot of them.

I'm not sure who's chasing whom, the slew of tiny kids or Muppet, but there's a tornado swirling. It looks like a preschool. Pillows are thrown on the floor, dog toys are flying through the air, and piles of dolls and cars are everywhere. Muppet is in dog heaven and now I feel bad I don't have a backyard or kids to entertain him. I've never seen him this happy.

"Doc."

I look across the kitchen. Brand is drinking a cup of coffee with a hip leaned against his island. His mother is holding a spatula at the stove, his father and Art are sitting at the bar, and Tessa, Art's wife, whom I've met twice, is spooning their youngest something orange while trying to get the baby to sit still on the marble.

I have no idea who the rest of them are.

Brand lifts his chin.

I move because it's better than everyone staring at me.

He doesn't have to ask when he holds his arm out. I go to a place that has become my favorite on earth—his side.

His arm wraps around me. "Sorry for the reunion from hell. These are the Vitales. I held them off as long as I could, but there's nothing like murder charges to bring your family knocking."

I don't ask what I really want to know—if murder charges happen often in his family. Knowing what I know so far, the less I ask, the better.

Denialism at its best. Another sport I could medal in.

I look around the room and try to smile. "Good morning."

More eggs and bacon are frying and Eloise asks, "How do you take your coffee?"

"Cream and sugar," Brand answers for me and keeps talking. "My sisters—Anna, Lilly, and Cammie, their husbands Henry, Nolan, and Zig. You remember Tessa—she and Art are honorary members. I'm not going to bother with the kids—too many and they won't stand still long enough anyway. As you can see, cute but pains in the ass."

As if on cue, one of the boys slams into our legs. "Is that your girlfriend, Uncle Brand?"

Brand frowns at him. "Yes."

The little boy cackles like a hyena. "Do you kiss her?"

"Yes," Brand answers. "Go wear out the dog."

The little guy runs off and Eloise replaces him, handing me a steaming mug of coffee. "I'm making eggs and Anna brought pastries."

"I heard you like sweets and I know my brother doesn't keep that shit in his house for fear he might gain an ounce of fat." The woman who must be Anna smiles and tucks her long, dark hair behind her ear.

"Always the suck up," the shorter one says to her. "I'm Cammie, the youngest. You'll like me the best because I'm the fun one."

The third woman throws a kitchen towel at Cammie. "You show up and don't do anything. That doesn't scream fun, that makes you lazy and a taker."

Cammie laughs. "She's obviously the middle child. Brand doesn't count since he's the only boy."

"My boy tells me you're a doctor," Senior says.

I offer the first words I've been able to squeeze in. "Of psychology. Not an M.D."

He talks around another bite of pastry and wipes a drip of jelly off his lip. "Impressive. And convenient."

Brand sighs, but doesn't say anything.

"Move off that barstool." Eloise snaps her fingers at her husband as she sets a plate of eggs and bacon on the bar, cooked to perfection, just like Brand's. "Let Aria sit and eat." She looks to me and frowns. "Drink your coffee. You look tired. Last night was a long one."

I try not to take offense from the *tired* comment and rethink my choice of going makeup free. "Thank you for breakfast, Eloise."

"You're welcome. Brand told me you don't cook."

Her son smiles at me. "Sorry, but it's true."

"We need to get back to Brand's defense," Art interrupts. "We're already painted into a corner. They know your alibi is a lie. That doesn't look good."

I swallow hard and look over at Brand. He slides the box of pastries toward me and shakes his head. Any other day, I'd dig in, but I'm not sure my stomach can take it while I'm listening to his defense and wondering what the hell happened to his alibi.

Eloise cleans her mess. "We need to get these kids out of the way. Let Brand and Art figure this out."

"I've got a meeting anyway." Senior reaches over me and grabs another pastry while talking to his son. "I'm a man of my word and stuck to our agreement when she was alive. I've even done my part to keep the peace for your sake since the big event, but I'm done. The Riccis are going to see what it's like to experience blowback for a change."

Half the people in the room verbally agree with him and the other half don't seem fazed by his threats. But they do listen to orders and start gathering tiny humans. Muppet will be disappointed.

"I'm going to take the kids home so you can work," Tessa says, wiping the orange mush off the baby's face. She picks up the little girl and goes to Art, pressing a kiss to his lips.

He kisses her back before blowing bubbles on the baby's neck, making her squeal. So normal. So loving.

I'm so jealous.

I say goodbye to everyone as Brand's mom and sisters hug and kiss him. It takes a good five or ten minutes, but when they leave, the house is once again quiet. Instead of tranquil the way the massive lake home normally feels, today it's eerie.

Brand walks back to the kitchen after locking his front door. "Sorry about this morning. They're a pain in the ass. I've kept them away since you've been here for that very reason."

"It's okay. I wish I could've met them under different circumstances. Tell me what happened last night?"

I pick up my coffee and Brand moves to the other side of the island to pour himself another cup. "We'll get to that, but first I need to fill you in on your dad."

My mug hits the marble. "I almost forgot about him."

Art sits next to me and flips through the screen on his phone. "Brand has a PI who's got access to a lot of information. He didn't have to dig too deep to figure out your dad's shit. Did you know your old man's partners severed him from their practice?"

I drop my fork. "What?"

Art continues. "I'll send you the report, but yeah. Happened five months ago."

My eyes go big and I sit back in my barstool. "That practice defined him. There's nothing he loves more."

Brand doesn't sugar coat the news. "There's something he loves more—blow and hookers. And not just any hookers. Fucking high-dollar ones. It's a habit he can't seem to break even now that he's unemployed. My guy was able to peek into his bank accounts and there's not a lot there."

My mind is blown. I've always known my dad is an asshole, but cocaine? And thanks to his nips and tucks, he's still a good-looking guy. Why would he pay for sex?

"My guy is digging for more," Brand keeps going. "But right now, looks like your old man is on his way to broke with some very expensive habits."

I rub my swollen eyes and sigh. It's all overwhelming and I have other important things to focus on right now—none of them have to do with my father.

I look between Brand and his best friend. "I've got to warn Briar, otherwise I don't care about my dad right now. Tell me what happened last night. What is this thing with your alibi?"

A stare hangs between the two men when Art finally says, "You know how I feel about this. If you want her to know, you're going to be the one to tell her."

I look at Brand. "Tell me what?"

He crosses his arms and his words don't waver. "They confirmed I wasn't at the station the night Marcia died."

A weight presses on my chest, and my lungs struggle to find air. "Where were you?"

"That doesn't matter," Art interrupts, but I don't look at him. I can't.

Brand's dark eyes burn into mine. He says nothing. No explanation. No reason as to how his alibi was obliterated.

"The important thing is," Art goes on, "I don't think they have evidence. I'm waiting on discovery."

I blink. "How can they charge you with no evidence?"

Brand shrugs.

Art's answer is curt. "They can and they did."

"On what grounds?" I'm no attorney, but I do watch TV. They can't charge him without probable cause, right?

"Circumstantial." Art drops his phone on the counter.

"Can they do that?" I press.

"Yes. Brand is officially unaccounted for during the time she died. On top of that, they hated each other. The Riccis have always been relentless when it comes to Brand, but they upped their game the day you showed up on his arm."

"Watch it," Brand bites.

My heart seizes.

Art keeps talking despite Brand's warning. "It doesn't look good that my boy here has been lying about his alibi all this time. In fact, it's pretty fucking bad, but we have a plan."

I look to Art. "Plan? What plan?"

Brand shakes his head. "We're going to see how this shakes out. The plan is a last resort. I don't want to go there if I don't have to."

"You make my job really hard, you know that?" Art complains.

"You're compensated well enough."

"Yeah, but you're paying me to get the charges dropped. It could be a walk in the park, but you're making me forge through a burning forest to get the same outcome."

"I have faith in you."

"You should. I'm the only attorney on the face of the earth who would go this route for his client. I don't want you to go to prison for that bitch."

Prison.

"I doubt it will come to that."

"I'm glad you doubt it, because I'm not so sure."

Oh, shit.

"I have my reasons," Brand says, far too calmly.

"It would be fucking great if you filled me in on them."

"Doc."

My breaths are too shallow—I need oxygen.

"Aria."

I shake my head and can't bring myself to look at him.

"You okay? You're pale."

"No," I whisper. "I'm not okay."

"Fuck," Brand grits. I finally build the nerve to look at him.

He moves around the island and grasps my bicep when I sway. His beautiful black eyes sear me, and just like so many other times since I barged into his life, I can't tell what he's thinking.

This is too much.

"I…"

His strong jaw tenses and he gives me one shake of his head.

I force my words, but they come out hoarse and weak and thick with emotion. "I need to—"

I wince when he squeezes my arm tighter.

Brand looks over my head to his attorney, who I'm sure hates me for turning his friend's life on end. "Get out."

"Fuck that. We have work to do. I barely got you out on bail."

"Brand," I beg.

"Quiet," he growls at me. His tone is a whip—sharp and painful.

Brand turns his glare to Art as he rips me off of my barstool. "I said get the fuck out. Now."

Another barstool scratches across the floor and Art's voice rises. "What the hell's going on?"

Brand yanks me to his chest and keeps arguing with Art. "I'll throw you through the glass if you don't get out."

Tension sits heavy in the space that was once full of life and love for the man I can't quit.

"I don't know who you are anymore. If I have to step in and save you from yourself, I will. I don't give a shit what you're keeping from me. There's no fucking way I'm going to sit by and let my best friend go to prison over a Ricci. That bitch got what she deserved."

I let out a sob as the glass door slams.

"I'm over this," Brand grits and doesn't hesitate. He moves and pulls me with him.

"What are you—"

"When I tell you to quit talking, Aria, I mean it."

He drags me to his office, a place I haven't been since the night I snooped through every inch of his house. I try to twist my arm out of his hold, but there's no use.

"It's time. My back is against a wall here. I didn't want to do this now. I wanted to wait until you were in so deep, you had no choice but to stay. Thought I'd have a ring on your finger or my baby planted inside you. Maybe both. But you pushed me. I can't protect you if you fuck this up."

Baby? Ring?

I'm all of a sudden regretting everything. Every single thing that brought me to this moment. He's different and has never treated me like this. Not even in the beginning when I was sure he hated me.

"Brand, you're hurting my arm."

He pulls me around the desk before finally letting me go with a warning. "Don't move. I'll fucking run to the ends of the earth to bring you back. Try me and see what happens."

He pulls his phone out of his pocket and jabs at the screen. Multiple clicks sound from inside the wall and his bookshelf—the one in which I touched every object and even flipped through his novels—shifts from floor to ceiling.

He steps back and swings it open.

I stare, in awe of what's in front of me. This time I don't have the wherewithal to complain when he grabs me again and pulls my back to his front. His arm circles my chest and his hand wraps around my neck like a noose. There's no way he doesn't feel my pulse racing under his thumb when his lips hit my ear. "At first I thought it was a coincidence that your name is Aria. In Italian, it means *air*. You don't know how many times during those six months I've beat my head against the wall to keep myself from you."

Six months?

I suck in a breath and his hand tightens on my throat. My heart speeds and I know he feels it too.

"That's right." He lowers his voice answering my thoughts. "Six months. It's time we clear the *air*, Dr. Dillon."

Twenty-Seven

SECRET

Aria

"SIT."

Brand dragging me into the secret room located within the walls of his house is like entering a different world—something from a movie. It looks nothing like the rest of his rustic-modern lake home. The walls are black, safes line one side of the room, and computer screens cover the wall behind the wide desk. There's a constant hum from the technology buzzing, doing its thing … surveying, watching. The lights are bright and harsh. If there were an Instagram filter for eerie, this would be it. The room is like ice, and the hairs on my arms rise as goosebumps prickle my skin.

Live feeds play out in front of me. The front and back of his house, the main rooms, buildings I don't recognize that are still under construction, and more that aren't. My brain clicks and calculates quicker than normal, running through every scenario of why I'm here, why he's chosen now to show this to me, and, most importantly, how to escape.

Because this is too much.

When I don't do as I'm told, he rolls a sleek, black desk chair out and puts a heavy hand on my shoulder, pushing me into it. Then he leans his ass against the desk next to me and crosses his arms.

I pull the inside of my lip between my teeth and bite down hard. "This is … what is this?"

"I have a lot of responsibilities, Aria." He's towering over me, and

I try my best to read him. It's been an emotional day, a lot of which he spent being charged and processed in the courts for the murder of his wife. "I might have made a deal with my dad all those years ago to step back from running the family, but that's only known between him and me. To the rest of those who play in the world we operate in, I'm his successor, and they don't want him to have one. They're ready for the Vitales to go away forever. Not to mention, I'm not good at making friends because I don't give a fuck. I've told you this—a lot of people don't like me, and some of them want me dead."

I look back to the camera focused on the back of his house, on the banks of Gray Mountain Lake, and his dock. My stomach starts to roil and it's everything I can do not to be sick.

"You know who wanted me dead more than anyone?"

I can't look at him, nor do I guess, because I already know.

I jump when he touches me—a finger and thumb pinching my chin. He forces my face to his. "My dead wife."

I hold his dark stare that's more ominous in this secret room. He's a different person. Not a hero and not even the son of a mob boss who wants nothing to do with that life. He looks very much in control of every aspect of the world he operates in.

I tremble, but he won't let go of my chin. As if he feels it too, he drags a heavy thumb over my bottom lip, forcing my jaw to go slack.

He finally lets go and turns to the desk. Typing in a password longer than the one I used to turn off his security system, he brings the largest screen to life. About ten clicks of the mouse—menus inside menus within more menus—a screen pops up and he enlarges it.

I've lost all feeling in my extremities and sink in the chair. "Oh my God."

"Yeah," Brand agrees and leans in from behind me, his face so close to mine, I actually feel his warmth in the cool room. But unlike every other time we're close, he's not offering me comfort. I'm not sure anything could. "I'm unfortunately out of time, which means we need to address the very cold, dead body in the room, Doc."

He reaches for the mouse and clicks *play*. It's all I can see and it makes me physically ill.

There's no audio, but I don't need it.

I know.

I remember.

The scene playing out in front of me is one that has haunted my mind and subconscious since the night it happened...

Twenty-Eight

AGENDA

Aria

Seven months ago . . .

MY MERC SPEEDS through the storm on winding roads I've never seen before. I can barely keep up with her taillights through the sheets of rain pelting the earth.

I should've done something. I've let it go on too long. My only excuse is I thought for sure it was just her being her. Because this shit doesn't happen in real life. It only plays out on Dateline *and bad Lifetime movies or in psychology journals.*

It sure as hell doesn't happen in the mountains of the Pacific Northwest.

I assumed she was craving attention. She's transparent and has tried to bait me more than once. No one expects such a trying case right out of the gate when they start practicing.

I know there are patients who come to therapy for reasons that don't include bettering themselves. Not everyone desires to learn how to cope with life in an effort to be mentally healthy. Some are forced into it—by a loved one, work, or even mandated by the courts. Others, like her, have self-serving goals that don't have anything to do with becoming a better person. Rather, they have everything to do with furthering an agenda.

A dark and calculating agenda.

I have no choice. She's said it's happening and there's nothing I can *do about it. I waited too long. Reporting a patient is not a quick or easy process. She spit all kinds of bullshit about doctor-patient confidentiality. She has no idea what she's talking about, because when it comes to this, no amount of patient privilege is protected by the law.*

Or it wouldn't be, if I had acted sooner.

I might as well be playing Russian roulette with my patient.

Spinning and shooting. Spinning and shooting.

She's all blanks. Or she was. I was sure of it. I never believed she had any ammunition bolstering her threats.

Until today.

Today, I believe her with everything I am.

And I've waited too long.

I physically tried to stop her from running out of my office, but she's no slouch. I might be strong, but she has at least forty pounds on me and a set of nails sharper than a tigress. She fought me off and I'm sporting the scrapes and dried blood on my neck to prove it. I grabbed my keys without thinking and was out the door without my purse or phone.

Decisions like this ... their consequences are haunting.

She might be scrappy, but I'm a runner. I had no trouble catching up with her.

All the way here, I've scolded myself for the mistakes I've made and am continuing to make. I sped after my patient, out of Redmond and into the mountains, twisting and turning through the storm that everyone says is unusual for this part of the country. She was my last appointment—it's late and dark from the downpour.

I hit my brakes as Marcia Vitale radically veers off the road ahead of me. I follow her Volvo crossover onto a narrow lane, through the forest, and bury my nerves. The stakes are too high.

I have to put a stop to what I should have weeks ago.

A home comes into view through the storm, standing like a giant in the massive forest. I screech to a halt, the brakes complaining in the rain. I'm out and running through the downpour before she has the chance to open her car door.

"What have you done?" I scream through the thunder as lightning strikes.

She climbs out, slams the car door, and charges me. "Who the fuck do you think you are? You can't follow me to my house! Do you know who I am?"

I grab her arm. "You're a sick woman, and I should've stopped you weeks ago."

She tries to shrug me off. "Fuck you!"

"Have you done it? Am I too late?" I demand, holding tight to the sleeve of her blouse.

"I've been at it for days, bitch. I won't have to put up with his shit much longer." Her hand connects with the side of my face—my vision tunnels. She pulls away so hard, I'm left with a scrap of silk in my hands.

She turns and moves for the front door.

I kick off my heels and go after her, barely catching the strap of her purse.

I yank and it's enough. She trips and falls on her ass, and I throw her purse into a hedge of deep bushes.

I push away my hair that's glued to my face and look down at her. "Been at what for days?"

She climbs to her feet, puts her hands to my chest, and shoves. "I'm not telling you jack shit. You served a purpose in case this ever comes back on me. I was being treated, couldn't help myself. I don't need you anymore."

I stand my ground. "If you think I can't see through your bullshit just because I'm fresh out of school, you picked the wrong doctor. Anyone would be able to see who you really are. I took you on as a patient because I thought I might be able to help you—get through to you."

And fix you, but I don't dare admit my own demons.

She looks to the side for her purse and keeps talking. "I don't need help. I need out! Dammit, now I can't get into my fucking house. I hate this place!"

She starts for the side yard, through the rain and mud, and I follow. "Marcia! Stop! Talk to me!"

Beyond the vast property, a lake comes into view with sheets of rain pounding on the body of water. She continues moving toward the back of the house. If she gets inside, I'll never know what she's done.

I grab the back of her shirt and yank. "Tell me, dammit! What did you do to him?"

She whips around and comes at me like I'm her prey and she hasn't eaten in days.

Marcia Vitale is always put together. From her blond-streaked hair, perfectly smoothed into long waves or coiffed into an elegant updo, to her heavy makeup, and nails like talons. I recognize every handbag, shoes, and article of clothing she dons. It's not hard—she might as well be a younger version of my mother and a perfect candidate for my father's practice.

But not tonight. Tonight, she's a mess. Makeup streaking her face with the rain, her hair glued to her head, and her clothes act as a second skin.

She tries to jab at me again. I narrowly dodge her and back up deeper into the dark night. "Don't judge me. You don't know what I've been through. I was offered to the most eligible bachelor. Handsome, rich, powerful. I thought I could win him over, but he has no interest in me. None. I'm in a fucking prison and there's only one way out. My brother told me what to do and I'm doing it. I want my life back!"

She comes at me again, forcing me farther into the darkness. Her expression is wild, her eyes crazed as they stare me down.

"Please, Marcia. Tell me what you did. I can still help you."

A smile slithers over her face like a snake, causing a shiver to course through me that has nothing to do with the cold rain.

"I don't need help," she seethes. "I've taken care of everything on my own. A little Visine in those fancy fucking water bottles of his is doing the trick. It's slow, the way it needs to be. He's not himself, I can tell. Even if he doesn't give me the time of day."

"You're poisoning him?" I scream through the storm. "You're a monster!"

"Maybe," she sneers. "But I'll be a free one soon. And you can't do shit about it."

Lightning strikes way too close, but we both ignore it. I grip her arm to stop her. "I'm not bound to keep your heinous crimes a secret! You're nothing but a narcissist, and I knew it from the beginning! And now a murderer! You think you can use me—to feel better about yourself and what you're doing—but you're wrong. I'm going to the police like I should have weeks ago when you admitted you fantasized about killing your husband!"

She freezes. The whites of her eyes shine through the dark night like a wild animal. "You can't! It's the rules and shit! What we talk about ... I'm protected!"

I shake my head and lose grasp on all professionalism. I take another step toward her. "You're an idiot, Marcia. How fucking stupid can you be? If you or someone else are in danger, I'm bound by law to report it."

Whatever monster lives inside her comes to life—the same one that brought her to murder her husband.

She comes at me.

Slapping me.

Shoving my weight no matter how hard I try to keep my feet beneath me on the slippery ground.

Nails scrape my skin.

I stumble and fall, screaming when my elbow catches my weight as I land on wood. We're on a long dock, projected far out into the water.

I scramble to my feet but she comes at me again. "You're not going to the police. Do you hear me? My family will come after you. They'll come after you and everyone you care about and take you out one by fucking one. You're a nobody. No one fucks with a Ricci and gets away with it!"

Images of Briar fill my vision, the only family I have and the only person I care about more than myself.

Marcia pushes and I stumble.

As I topple, I reach out.

My fingers touch silk and grab hold.

But that silk does nothing to stop my fall. Only this time I don't land on wood, I'm submerged and Marcia follows, her scream swallowed by water.

I push her off me as we both surface for air.

Her arms flail as she screams, "Crazy bitch! I'm going to fucking kill you!"

She comes at me and pushes my head under. I wrestle to get out of her hold, but she grabs a chunk of my hair and twists.

I bring my knee up and kick, forcing myself back. My face barely surfaces for air, but it's filled with rain water. I cough and sputter and take the second I'm given to suck in a breath when her nails dig into my face and push.

I go under.

I struggle to get away, but she fists my sweater and wraps her hand around my hair again.

She's going to kill me.

I have no choice.

I wrap my legs around her waist and pull her in tight. Then I take us both farther into the quiet darkness.

I have no idea how deep it is, but I take her down far enough that she can't get her head above water. She finally releases her hold and the power returns to me. Little does she know, my lungs are strong and conditioned. I can hold my breath with the best of the best.

Her nails connect with my skin as she fights to get away. My legs tighten and we sink.

I won't let any harm come to Briar. I'll do anything in my power to *stop it. I already failed my sister once by not protecting her from our parents when I could have.*

When I should have.

I don't believe a thing Marcia said about her husband during our sessions. Not anymore. Not when she just admitted to poisoning him. I might be too late to save him, but I won't allow her to hurt anyone else.

I can't see a thing in the dark water, though she's right in front of my face, struggling under my hold. She might've had the upper hand on land, but not here. Water is my haven and always has been. It's beautifully quiet. All I hear is the vague tip-toe of rain dancing above us.

I don't think of anything but her husband, of Briar, and how if Marcia couldn't kill me herself, she had people willing to do the job for her.

Her body jerks and her struggles fade.

I exhale a few bubbles.

I'm fine. I could stay like this for at least another minute. Maybe more.

I allow my mind to relax as I hold tight, the reality of what I'm doing coursing through my veins as my patient gulps water instead of the oxygen I'm keeping from her.

Her fight for life becomes erratic.

I wait.

Exhale another few bubbles.

Marcia's weight begins to drag me deeper.

But I don't let go. Not until I can't go another moment without a breath. I do what I always do while I'm under water. I push away reality—something I know I'll have to deal with when I finally surface.

It's like I've trained for this. It might be morbid and vile, and yes, even criminal.

But there's no turning back now. If there's a chance I can still save her husband, protect Briar, and myself, I'll deal with the consequences...

Twenty-Nine

SCIENCE

Aria

DURING AN ACTIVE drowning, a high concentration of carbon dioxide with the low concentration of oxygen in the blood triggers the brain to take a breath.

If that happens beneath the surface, copious amounts of water are inhaled.

As water reaches the airway, the larynx closes.

The victim loses consciousness before water enters the lungs. Life-giving oxygen is prevented from being distributed to the needed tissue to reach vital organs.

I have memorized the details, the science behind drowning. They are the things that keep me awake at night, have made me suspicious of every patient that graces my office, and have even infiltrated my dreams.

I stare at the screen and watch the image of one surface after two went under, reliving the night that changed me.

Forever.

I watch myself swim to the bank, the rain pummeling me as I crawl to shore. With my hands and knees still in the water, I remember the feeling of my stomach churning to the point of dry heaves. It was late and I hardly had time for a bite of lunch that day. Emotion took over and I could hardly see through the storm. I remember forcing myself to climb to my bare feet and stumble over rocks and gravel, through Brand's yard, and around his house. It wasn't until then I realized how cold it was.

Adrenaline has a way of protecting the body from things like that.

Drunk on guilt and remorse for doing all the wrong things, I forgot about the shoes I kicked off in front of his house at that moment. I wasn't thinking of anything besides my actions. I staggered to my car and got the hell out of there.

I wonder about those shoes every day.

I had no idea a stray pair of shoes could haunt you in your sleep.

Or if my skin was found under Marcia's nails.

Or if there were security cameras on the mansion of a lake home surrounded by forest and water.

Yes, I followed the death of Marcia Ricci Vitale like it was my second area of study.

I also spent months waiting. Looking over my shoulder, through my rearview mirror, and scrutinizing my surroundings. I could never shake the feeling that someone was watching me.

Following me.

I finally chalked it up to being a murderer. It doesn't feel good to take another life, even if it starts in self-defense. Being me since that night has been an agonizing and arduous experience.

The only balm to my remorse was Brando Vitale, Jr.

The moment I got home, I researched him and found out he was a firefighter and paramedic at Station Six. I couldn't risk anything being tracked back to me, so I called from a line at the center and asked for him. They told me he was off duty, but was scheduled for that coming Thursday.

I checked the obituaries. Scanned the news. I obsessed over the life and wellbeing of a man I knew nothing about.

I came up empty handed.

Then, there was breaking news.

Marcia's body floated ashore on the banks of Gray Mountain Lake and it was reported that her husband was devastated by the demise of his beloved wife.

Brando Vitale, Jr. made a statement.

Which meant he was not dead. After what happened, I couldn't bring myself to make a report, let alone reach out to the widower. I might have been a coward, but I was so scared. As the days clicked on, I fell deeper and deeper, and the consequences of my actions weighed on my every thought.

When I saw him on the news, grieving the death of his wife, he vowed to find the party responsible. He also noted that he, himself, was being scrutinized, even though he had an alibi.

He was on duty the night his wife died.

Or, was murdered.

Days turned into weeks, and weeks into months … reports about Marcia's death became fewer and farther between.

Five months passed, and I was finally able to sleep a bit better. No one ever came to question the fact Marcia was my patient. She always paid in cash, even though I accept most insurance plans. When I offered to bill her insurance, she blew me off and told me she paid cash for everything. Who was I to argue? I needed the money and was happy to pocket the payment I wouldn't report on my taxes.

Later, I realized she might not want a treatment paper trail if her plan didn't work.

Lucky for me, it made it easy to shred her records.

Poof.

Like it never happened.

I had no ties to Marcia Vitale.

I thought I was free.

I *was* free.

Until I became brazen.

And, to be utterly honest, obsessed.

I tried to reason with myself. To rationalize my internet stalking and driving by his station as normal, a way to ease my conscience. I never came into direct contact with him until the night of the auction. You'd think after I drowned a woman, she would be the one to flood my thoughts, but no.

It was her husband who possessed me.

Obsessed doesn't do justice to the amount of space Brand monopolized in my head.

I told myself it would be hard for any psychologist not to be consumed. Brando Vitale, Jr. is a hero, a widower, and the most beautiful human I've ever seen.

My brazen curiosity turned into audacity, and eventually, into bravery. I couldn't help myself.

I had to know.

Was he worth it?

Because I needed him to be worth it.

I thought I knew everything there was to know about him from my stalking.

I was an idiot.

I knew nothing about the man he really is.

And if I thought I was obsessed before, I'm a goner now.

There's no way I'll allow him to go down for something I did. I'll walk into the police station and tell them the truth if I have to.

I'd walk through floods and fires if it meant he were safe.

This is what obsession looks like. My heart swells for him. There's nothing I wouldn't do.

The video freezes at the end, motionless on my Mercedes taking off into the dark storm with the license plate in full view.

The quiet buzz of the room roars through my head and I feel my tears drip from my chin. I hadn't realized I was crying.

Brand slides a hand up my neck the way he does so often. It's a touch I've come to love—domineering, controlling, possessive. Like everything I've experienced when it comes to him.

When I focus on him, I forget the world around me. He makes my reality fade away.

But not anymore.

He knew the whole time. From the moment we officially met at the auction, he knew.

His thumb presses in on my neck and my heart churns.

"I'm sorry." My words are raspy and rough. I can't bring myself to look at him.

"Are you?" He sounds surprised.

He knows everything, even if he doesn't understand what led to that moment. I'll need to make him understand but what I won't do is lie to him. "No. I'm not. But it doesn't mean I wanted that to happen. I didn't mean for *any* of this to happen."

He says nothing and desperation sours in my belly.

I wrap my hand over his on my neck, and my tears stream harder. "She was my patient. Once I realized what she was planning…" I finally have the nerve to look at him. I can't read his expression. "She told me she wanted to kill you weeks before. The way she was … I thought she was all talk and no bite. I waited too long, and once I realized she was going through with it, I had to stop her. You couldn't hear on the video, but I swear. She told me she was poisoning you. She said it in front of your house, right in the middle of that storm. She even told me her brother told her how to do it. Then she threatened me—and Briar—if I tried to stop her. I had no idea who the Vitales were, or the Riccis for that matter. But then she attacked me and I—"

"Shh." He brings his other hand up and presses a finger to my lips. "I know."

I let out a breath but can't pull in another. This is not the first time I find myself suffocated in his vicinity. "You do?"

He nods. "I know everything."

Thirty

ENDS OF THE EARTH

Brand

WHEN DR. ARIA Dillon strutted into the ballroom the night of the auction, I thought I was going to lose it. To see her made up and so fuckable that every other firefighter in the room was probably sporting a hard-on from her mere presence pissed me off.

I told her the truth that night.

Most of it, anyway.

I didn't want to be there. My brothers at the station insisted it was time I showed my face in public. I had a shit few months and it had everything to do with Marcia, but nothing to do with her death. The night Marcia died at the hands of her psychologist was the night my world shifted. I had no idea who Aria Dillon was before that night and I had no idea Marcia was even going to therapy, no matter what bullshit reason she had for it in that fucked-up head of hers.

My dead wife had shit for brains and it showed in everything she did.

The storm blew the electricity out the night she died, but I'm no idiot. I have a generator and my security system works on backup batteries that last for days. I told the police it was out because I don't work with them, ever, and I wanted to know more about the woman who was willing to throw down with my dead wife. The brunette beauty raced off into the dark night battered, bruised, and scraped to hell and back.

It took my PI about three minutes to look her up by a simple search of her license plate. If she came to my house that night with the intention of killing Marcia, she had to be the most stupid human on earth.

After a while, I knew that was not the case.

I watched her. Followed her. Hell, who am I kidding? I became a fucking stalker. For months. When I was no longer sicker than hell, or on shift at the station, I was on *Doc Watch*.

I wanted to know why a psychologist would risk everything to murder my wife.

It didn't take long to learn that Dr. Aria Dillon is straight-laced. She works—a fucking lot—spends some time with her sister, goes to the gym once or twice a week, but other than that, she's at the center, her private office, or huddled up in her shit apartment. She waits at a four-way stop too long, always uses her blinker, and never edges her old Merc even one mile per hour over the speed limit.

The woman was boring as hell.

Until she waltzed into my life and dropped fifteen grand on me and a dog.

"I have an alibi, Doc."

She looks like she's fighting for a breath, even as a glint of relief hits her icy eyes. "But you said—"

"*That* alibi," I interrupt, "was bullshit. The night Marcia died, I left the station with my brothers, but not on a call. They were rushing me to the hospital."

Her hand spasms in mine. "What?"

"I didn't know if I was having a heart attack or seizure. It was bad. My heart rate was all over the place. They put me in the back of the rig and took me straight to the hospital." I pause and cup her face when what I really want to do is feel her pulse thrum under my touch. I'm fascinated by the feel of it when she comes alive for me. Instead, I wipe her tears away. "Tetrahydrozoline can fuck you up. When they ran a toxicology report, that's when I knew. I'd been feeling off for days. It was building in my system. The doctors told me if I weren't as big as I am and in shape, I probably would have been dead the day before."

She stands and moves between my legs, the chair rolling off behind her. Her hands frame my jaw and mine go to one of my favorite places in the world—her ass. "That night, she told me she was poisoning you."

"I was in the hospital for two days. My cardiologist wanted me to stay longer, to be monitored for lingering symptoms. They were flushing me with fluids, and I could do that at home. But I needed to show my face in front of the media."

"I saw you on the news," she whispers. "I've never been so happy to see anyone walking and breathing in my life, and I didn't even know you. You were only a stranger to me, but you were alive."

I pull her tight to my cock. Nothing has made me harder for her than knowing this shit isn't standing between us. "I looked like shit, but, yeah. I was alive."

"I thought you were upset by her death. I knew you were innocent." Her blue eyes wander to the side. "Obviously."

"By the time they got me stable enough that I could focus on something besides dying, I caught up on the notifications from my security system. I left my main cell registered to my name at the station so I couldn't be tracked being taken to the hospital, but I always keep a burner on me for … other things. I switch out my burners all the time." I pull her face to mine and take her mouth. It's like I'm tasting her for the first time all over again. I tip my forehead to hers and breathe her in. "I had Art get his ass over here and make sure the scene was clear. Your shoes, her purse. There was even a tear from her shirt. I wanted the chance to figure out who the hell you were on my own. Best decision I ever made, baby."

She wraps her arms around me and presses her face to my chest. "Thank God you were okay."

"My brothers at the station know I didn't do it. I asked my cap to put me on administrative leave and with all the shit in the news directed at me, it was easy for him to do. I couldn't let it get out that I was sick and made them promise not to leak the truth."

She pushes back from me. "Wait. You have an alibi. A real alibi. With medical records and a hospital stay and everything. Why would you lie only to have it blown out of the water?"

I shake my head and feel the tension return to her body. "You don't understand this yet, but you will in time. It can't get out that I was poisoned. I won't allow the Riccis to know they got to me. Initially, no one could see me as vulnerable, especially them. And now I have you to protect."

She tries to push out of my arms, but I don't let her. "That's crazy. You have to tell the police."

I shake my head. "This will go away in time."

"No." Her expression hardens as more tears well in her eyes. "You can't take that chance. If you don't tell them, I will. I'll tell them what really happened—that it was me."

"No, you fucking won't." I know my expression matches my tone. I won't allow her to, even if I have to tie her up. It's why I brought her in here now, to clear the air between us. I was afraid she was about to open her mouth. "I've protected you this long, even without you knowing it. With you by my side and in my bed, no one will fuck with you. Especially the Riccis. I won't be found guilty on circumstantial evidence and you are not going down for Marcia being a crazy bitch. You wore her marks for over a week, and some longer. That was bad enough."

Her breath catches. "How do you know that?"

"Because I had you followed. And as soon as I felt good enough, I followed you myself. Even in the beginning when I was trying to figure you out, it stirred something in me to see you bruised and battered, especially by the woman I hated more than anything. When I look back on it, that was the beginning."

Her face softens. "I had no idea."

"I had to know why you did what you did. Watching someone for months on end, but not being able to approach the way I normally would have, had a way of getting under my skin. *You* got under my skin."

She falls into my chest. "I never followed you because I didn't have the nerve, but I wanted to. I learned everything I could about you. Studied every picture I could find online. I would even drive by your station. It was wrong because I had no idea you didn't love your wife, but I dreamed about you." She tips her head to look into my eyes. "I made you into a fantasy. You were perfect—*we* were perfect. Because, in my head, you deserved so much more than her. I wanted to be everything she wasn't—for you."

Even with all the shit swirling around us, I can't stop my lips from tipping. "I was perfect, huh?"

Her smile mirrors mine. "Yes. And then I met you."

I tip my head. "Not so perfect in the flesh?"

She shakes her head. "You're nothing like my fantasy. You're better. Dark, intense, controlling. You're all the things I never knew I wanted. No, you're all the things I never knew I needed. The real you is more of a fantasy than anything I could dream."

I ask the question I've been wondering since the night we first spoke. "Why did you come to the auction?"

"Because I had to know. I had to know if you were worth it. I never intended on talking to you that night, but I wanted to see you in the flesh. Then you approached me and you were so miserable. You were nothing like I imagined."

"I was shocked you were there. It didn't matter how much I might have wanted you, the timing was shit. The Riccis were still hot on my ass. I knew the moment I was seen with another woman, it would blow up in my face."

She runs her hand down my chest and stares at her fingers. "When that other woman started to bid on you, something came over me. I had no claim on you other than what I'd created in my head, but I lost control. So much so, I spent fifteen-thousand dollars I don't have even though it scared the hell out of me to speak to you."

I force her to look at me. "I knew I had to have you. No matter how that auction ended or how bad the timing, I couldn't stop myself. And, baby, that feeling was foreign. I've never wanted anyone, let alone needed them."

"This is surreal," she whispers.

"No," I disagree. "This is very fucking real. No one is going to prison and no one is leaving. Ever."

I grab the hem of her sweater and yank it over her head. My fucking family barged in first thing this morning, and I did all I could to keep them from waking her. I wanted to sleep in with her, wake her with my mouth and fingers, and forget what happened last night for just a few more hours. Forget how my dead fucking wife keeps suffocating me—no, us—from the grave.

I pop her bra, and like so many times before, without hesitation, she's standing before me almost naked. My doctor—always hungry for anything I give her. And I can't wait another second.

"Never wanted anyone, baby. Then you came barreling into my life and I couldn't get you out of my head. Consumed isn't a strong enough word for how I felt, and trust me, Doc, there was nothing healthy about my fixation. It got to a point that I thought I might go crazy if I couldn't have you."

She steps out of her jeans and kicks them to the side. Even with the pending murder charges, there's nothing in her eyes but pure relief—identical to what's coursing through my veins. I pick her up and she wraps her long, toned legs around my waist. I take three steps and put her back to the wall of safes, full of firearms, ammo, cash, and the shoes she left behind the night she fled my house.

I reach under her to play with her pussy and her fingers dip into my hair. "Brand."

"There's nothing between us." I plunge two fingers inside her and watch her eyes fall to half-mast. "No more secrets. I know everything about you. By you being here right now, you accept me and my way of life. I'll take care of this but you have to trust me, baby. Tell me you understand and you'll do as I say."

I circle her clit and she gasps. "If something happens to you—"

I kiss her, plunging my tongue in her mouth to shut her up. Her knees draw north, opening herself to me. My dick is begging for her.

But not until she agrees. This can only happen on my terms.

I let go of her mouth and lean back far enough to look into her eyes. "Nothing is going to happen to us. A lot of people are paid a shitload of money to make sure that's the case. Now that you're mine, I'll do anything—any-fucking-thing—to protect you. Tell me you'll do exactly as I say. It's the only way I can keep both of us safe."

She thinks about it while pressing onto my hand, wanting me as much as I want her. Her fingers come to my jaw and she nods, but it's her words that almost bring me to my knees. "I couldn't walk away when I should have and I really can't now. I'll do anything for you because I love you."

My hand stops and my heart seizes for the second time in my life. But this time, it's not from the poison my dead wife fed me, it's the love of the woman who saved me in more ways than she knows.

"Fuck. Just when I don't recognize myself, you make me fall deeper." I let go of her pussy to free my cock. "Never wanted to be tied to anyone or anything and now the thought of you walking away hurts more than I can bear."

I take her in one thrust, needing our connection, needing to be close. Needing to tie her to me forever.

"Fucking you without a condom," I breathe as I angle an arm up her back and cup her head. "And I'm not pulling out."

She doesn't answer but she does sink down on my cock as much as she can in the little room I've given her to move. She nods and wets her lips.

She's all in.

"Never loved anyone," I mutter against her mouth as I push inside, knowing this is it. "Looking back, I think I loved you before the damn dog brought us together and I didn't know what the hell was going on with me."

"You're worth all the fear, anxiety, and sleepless nights. I'd do it again to be right here. To be yours."

She arches, and I angle my hips, thrusting, pushing her closer to the edge, memorizing every feature of her beautiful face as she reaches for her orgasm. Her bright blue eyes peek through heavy lids, her full lips slack, lost in me as much as I'm lost in her.

I pull her down as I thrust into her and she finally moans, falling as her pussy clenches my dick, begging for everything I have to give her. And I give it. My balls tighten and I let go.

I come inside her for the first time with nothing between us. I want everything with Aria—sooner rather than later.

When I catch my breath, she's wrapped around me, spent, with her face stuffed in my neck. I stand like this, holding her in my secret room that only a handful of people know about, and now she's one of them. I wait for my heart to steady, thinking how it wasn't long ago I thought it might be fucked up forever.

But now, figuratively and literally, it could not be stronger. And it only beats for the woman in my arms.

Her tears wet my skin.

"Baby." I put my hand to her head and pull her back to look at me. "What's wrong?"

She shakes her head. "Nothing. Everything. It's been intense and stressful and now I know that you know—you've always known. I'm not sure what I feel other than relief. I was so afraid you'd hate me if you ever found out. But I couldn't bring myself to tell you or make myself leave you."

"Never going to let you leave me, baby." I look into her blue eyes that I'm ready to call home forever. "Couldn't love you more. You're pure and brave and selfless. I don't deserve you but, since I'm selfish, I'm going to keep you forever."

She presses her lips to mine and her salty tears dance with our tongues.

Today is the beginning. I'll go to the ends of the earth for her.

Just like she did for me when she saved me from hell.

Thirty-One

THE FAMILY

Brand

I'M NOT SURE if it's her lack of sleep from last night or the emotions from what she just went through, but she's exhausted.

She got dressed and I made her rest on the sofa. After I assured her no one else knows what happened the night Marcia died and promised her Art will get me out of these charges, she finally settled.

She's more concerned for me than herself, which is whacked. I need to manage that closely so she doesn't do anything stupid—like admit the truth. She was about to spill the facts to Art. I could see it in her eyes, and there is no way I'll allow that to happen.

Art might've taken care of the scene that night by my orders, but no one has seen that video but me. He asked, and I told him to mind his own fucking business. I kept the video because I had no idea who the woman was or why she came to my house that night. It came in handy today when I needed to prove to her I've known all along.

Art wants me to come clean and use my hospital records. I get it. It is my foolproof get-out-of-jail card. All charges would be dropped in a heartbeat. But the longer they fixate on me, no matter how cold the trail is, I don't have to worry about them snooping around Aria. I'm balancing on a tightrope with nothing below me but the fiery pits of hell.

But to protect Aria, I'll do it.

I drag my fingers through her hair when my front door opens. Art's eyes dart from Aria to me and I shake my head.

After making himself comfortable in the club chair opposite us, he studies me for too long. Finally, he speaks in a low voice so as not to wake her. "Never thought I'd see it. Didn't mean I never wanted this for you. But this right now," he motions to Aria who's asleep with her head rested on my thigh, "is a surprise."

I shrug and say nothing. It surprised the fuck out of me too.

"Tess chewed my ass when I got home. Told me to think about my friend before my client. You helped me when I needed it—when Tess needed it. Aria's it for you, isn't she?"

I nod and keep at her hair when she sighs in her sleep.

"That night," he starts. "The shoes, Marcia's purse—"

I shake my head and speak low, but firm. "Stop. I'll tell you what you need to know. But that's something you'll never know."

He looks out to the water and scrapes a hand down his face. "This is why you're being difficult?"

"Yes and no."

He looks back and frowns.

"Cory told Marcia what to do—how to poison me."

Art frowns. "Aria told you this?"

I don't confirm or deny this because it's something Art and I already assumed—Aria simply confirmed it. I was leaning toward making this decision but having her in my life now has given me the final push. "Marcia might've been the one doing the deed, but her brother gave the order. We're officially at war with the Riccis. I might not have been active in the past, but that's about to change. They're about to learn once and for all I'm off limits." I reach out and wrap my hand low on Aria's hip. "Now that I have more than myself to protect, I'm rethinking things."

"Rethinking what?"

"My role in the business. My role in the family."

"No shit?"

I nod. "I want you by my side."

Art's eyes wander around the room for about five seconds. He answers exactly how I knew he would. "I'm always by your side."

I thought so, but it's good to know he's all in like I thought he'd be. "Appreciate you."

He shrugs. "You'd be a dumbass not to want me."

Finally, I smile. "I'm no dumbass."

He goes from cocky to inquisitive. "You sure about this? You've never wanted any part of it."

Marcia came close to taking me out. I've never felt more helpless than I did when I was told tetrahydrozoline was coursing in my blood. I look down at Aria and think about the step we just took in the safe room. "I plan to do everything I can to protect my family. I have more at stake now and know exactly what I need to do. I've been talking to Dad over the last week. He knows I'm moving in this direction and is ready to start making the transition. He also knows you're coming with me."

Art frowns. "Asshole. What if I refused you?"

"Like you'd refuse me."

He lifts his chin to Aria. "Will she be good with this?"

"She will." As if on cue, Aria shifts and rolls to her back. When her eyes flutter open, I push the hair out of her face. "You feel better?"

She nods. "I was exhausted."

"Hey, Aria."

She jerks and pushes to her ass. "How long have you been here?"

Art smirks. "Long enough to listen to you snore."

I reach around her waist and pull her to me. "You don't snore. Well, you weren't just now."

She looks straight at Art and doesn't mince words. "How do you plan to get the charges dropped?"

Art smiles and shifts his eyes to me. "Apparently I work for both of you now."

She wraps her hand over my thigh and squeezes. "I have to know. What's the plan?"

I stretch my arm across the sofa behind her, lift my feet to the coffee table, and turn my focus to my life-long friend and attorney. "From now on, you can talk freely—no more secrets."

Art nods. "Okay. Let's get this done."

Thirty-Two

THE REST OF FOREVER

Aria

I NEVER TAKE days off. It's not like I have vacation time. I work for myself—contracting at the center and building my practice so I can have something to call my own. I can't afford to go anywhere, so why bother?

The last time I took personal days was seven months ago when I was in an *accident* and needed some time to recover. I couldn't sit across from my patients when I was bruised, battered, and looked like I'd been in a catfight.

Which was basically the truth.

How can I expect them to trust me for advice, guidance, and self-enrichment techniques when I'm basically a fraud?

I hid out for two days after I drowned Marcia Vitale. I was scared. Afraid of the police, afraid of the Riccis, and quite honestly, afraid of my own shadow.

I was afraid of who I'd become.

I refused to see Briar until every mar on my skin was healed. If she saw me sporting even a scrape or bruise, she would've pressed me for answers and there was no way she could know.

Brand and Art talked and planned and strategized late into the evening. I told them, as long as Brand and I can put this behind us once and for all, I would go along with what they thought best.

When Brand made dinner, I decided I really need to learn how to cook. I'll start next week when I'm not mentally drained. Over grilled pork tenderloin, roasted Brussels sprouts, and baked potatoes, Brand informed me of two things. One, I was moving the rest of my things into his house. He was serious as a homicide when he said he wanted his closet back and it was my job to fill the empty one that's never been used since he built the house.

And two, he paid off my credit card. He said it was the easiest fifteen grand he's ever spent in his life. I didn't argue, nor did I ask how he got my credit card information. I was too overwhelmed to care.

Then he made love to me.

It wasn't bossy, dirty, and he didn't have to push me out of my reality.

It was beautiful and deep and lit places of my heart I didn't know existed. After he came inside me with nothing between us for the second time, he said he was going to have to marry me soon—seems his family priest isn't fond of pregnant brides.

He also explained that he decided to step up, play a bigger role in his family—as in the biggest role. How that role was always meant to be his and it will protect us and our future family. He added that I stepped in to save him before I even knew of him and he'd die doing the same for me. And how he needed me to be okay with everything because he wants me by his side forever.

The whole thing made me nervous. But then he pulled me into his arms and told me he didn't know what he did to deserve me after the last decade. Growing up with parents who had their own fucked-up marriage, I knew I would accept anything so long as I had him.

There was no way I would argue with forever.

Then I fell asleep in his arms and wondered what I did to deserve *him*.

I know what I did will always haunt me. But we're alive and we're together. Being present with him is the only place I want to be.

And I'll never have to worry about Briar being in danger.

What people will never know about Brand and me is our love affair started long before we first met. There's something beautiful about that—how it will only be ours. Let the world think our whirlwind romance started at the auction. The truth is for us and us alone. I'll take it to the grave and I know he will too.

"If you have this number, why are you calling instead of texting? Leave a message. I probably won't call you back."

The tone beeps. "Briar. You're not returning my texts and you won't take my calls. What the hell is going on with you? We need to talk, and not just about you and the techy gazillionaire, though you'd better be prepared to spill about him." I sigh and look out my window. It's dark and cool and drizzling. My last appointment for the day canceled, and I'm waiting on Brand to pick me up, which has become a thing when he's not on duty at the station. I close my eyes and pull in a big breath. "I wanted to tell you this in person. Dad is in town. Brand did some research and I need to fill you in on what's going on. But Dad is the one who saw you on TMZ. Call me. I need to talk to you—"

Shit. It cut me off.

I should be updating my patient files but I'm too anxious. Brand and Art have spent the day strategizing. I feel left out and want to know what's going on. Art is still waiting on discovery from the DA's office. Neither of them seem worried and that freaks me out.

My phone vibrates and I put it to my ear instantly. "Briar?"

"Sorry to disappoint you, Doc."

I exhale and fall to my sofa, wondering what it's like for my patients to sit here and tell me their secrets. "I'm sorry. She hasn't called me back. All I've gotten from her is an *I'm fine* and she'll *get with me later* text. I finally had to leave her a message about Dad, but I'm worried. She's cut him out of her life and never looked back. I just need her to be aware."

"Sorry to pile it on, baby, but I've got more bad news. More like, disturbing news."

I tense. "Is it your defense?"

"No, it's your old man. My PI dug deeper and has some contacts in Miami. Some scary people are after him. Turns out a hooker OD'd when they were partying together last month. Not only does your dad owe his supplier, the chick's pimp is pissed."

I groan. "Could it get any worse?"

"Don't ask questions you don't want the answers to because, yes, it does. Here's the best part—the pimp is after your dad. He wants him to pay up for the revenue he lost being down a girl. And since we're talking top-of-the-line call girl, that's a shit ton. I have a feeling this is why your dad wants to see Briar if he thinks she's tied to Thornton. The man bleeds money, but that's just a guess."

"As if my family could be more fucked up. I'm so sorry."

His car door slams and locks beep in the background. "What are you apologizing for? You didn't pay for a hooker and feed her so much blow she bought it."

I fall to the side and my head lands on a pillow the color of oatmeal.

"I'm sorry because you have more important things to worry about than my asshole father paying for sex and all the consequences that come with it."

I hear a smile in his tone when he goes on, "Do I need to remind you that you paid for me?"

"I can't believe you went there. Do I need to remind you that you're actually the one who paid for it?"

"I'd give everything I have for you, Doc. Open the door, I'm here."

I pull myself to my feet and grab my bags. Emotional exhaustion is no joke. The last few days have taken it out of me. If I could only put into practice a little bit of what I preach to my patients, I might fare better.

When I unlock and open my reception door, I'm still in awe of what I see. That the tall, dark Italian hero standing before me is mine.

"Hey."

He leans in to kiss me. "The days get longer and longer when we're apart. Thinking we need to do something about that."

I yank my bag up my arm and flip off the lights. "I'm not sure what that will be. We both have jobs."

"We'll get it figured out after Art gets the charges dropped." He takes my hand and we head to the elevator. We step inside and he pulls me to his chest. "I don't like what's going on with your dad. He's still here and drove by your office twice today."

I sigh.

"I've got someone on him. I want to know where he's going and who he's seeing. I also want to make sure he stays away from you and Briar."

"He can't do anything to me. I realized that a long time ago."

"Don't underestimate a junkie."

"I still can't believe he's spiraled into that mess. It's unreal. I'll call Briar one more time tonight. This is too important. I'll go over there if I have to."

"We can swing by there on the way home."

"Thank you." I look at him and squeeze his hand as we exit the elevator. "Enough about my dad. Is there an update on the case?"

As much as Brand tries to convince me he's got it all under control, the guilt is heavy for what he's going through. I'm still trying to process the balance of not providing his real alibi with the desire to keep that information from the Riccis.

He says I'll understand in time.

I'll have to—I have no choice. The only alternative is to walk away from him.

And that's not an option at this point. Nothing is more important than him.

Thirty-Three

In a Heartbeat

Brand

I ROLL ARIA away from me and get out of bed. After throwing on a pair of shorts, I grab my phone and walk out of my bedroom.

Art – Call me ASAP.

Not the text anyone wants to get in the middle of the night from their attorney. But Art's always been a workaholic and a night owl. It's why I want him at my side when I finally transition and take over.

It barely rings once when he answers. "I've got good news and bad news."

I stare at the full moon shining off the lake from the dark of my house. "It must be good if it couldn't wait 'til tomorrow. Give me the bad."

"Evidence. I got the coroner to email me his report directly. I'm just now going through it line by line. Brand, there was DNA collected from the body."

I grip my phone so tight I might crack the damn thing. "Fuck."

"Yeah," he agrees. "But DNA is not on the discovery list. It was hair. Long, dark hair—knotted around her fingers, even after being in the water so long."

"Dammit," I bite. "What's the good news?"

Art sighs. "That there's DNA evidence. And since you were in the hospital that night and have never had long hair, I'm going to go out on a limb here and say it's not yours. That DNA is your get-out-of-jail-free card and my fuck-you card to the DA for not including it in discovery.

That shit's illegal."

I've never once been worried about getting the charges dropped. I knew Art would find a way to get me out of this without having to use my real alibi. And there's the fact I'm not guilty of anything.

But someone else is.

"Art—"

"I know," he interrupts. "I mean, I don't because you refuse to confirm it, but I can assume. I need to finesse this. If you don't want to use your real alibi, we need this evidence."

"*She* was here when they searched the house, Art. She'd slept in my bed, her things were in my bathroom. They combed through my stuff."

"They didn't take her things that day. They were after you. The Captain goes to church with Saul Ricci. They play golf, sit at the same poker table, and have known each other for years. Their goal that day was you. You're the one under arrest and they aren't looking anywhere else."

"Brand?"

I turn and pull my hand down my face. Aria is standing at the mouth of the hall to my room, wearing my station T-shirt and nothing else.

She tucks her messy hair behind her ear. "What's wrong?"

I've never felt the need to protect someone so much in my life. If I do nothing else, I need to cushion her from this. She's battled enough demons since the night Marcia died. "Nothing. It's Art. Go back to bed and I'll be right there."

She tips her head and frowns. "Art wouldn't call you at three in the morning if nothing was wrong."

I don't take my eyes off her when Art keeps talking. "You go take care of her however you think best. She's proven she's tough, so my guess is she can take it. Let me do my job. They took a sample of your DNA when you were charged. We'll run it through the county first. There won't be a match and then I'll do something about the evidence. I'll demand a dismissal. We know this judge, it should be enough for him to save face and take care of you."

"Let me know."

"Later."

I disconnect the call and watch Aria move through the dark room lit only by the reflection of the moon. "Sorry I woke you. If Art calls in the middle of the night, I know it's important."

She stops in front of me. "What's going on?"

I toss my phone on the sofa and pull her to my chest. "I'd tell you, but I'm afraid you'll have to hit the treadmill for an hour and all I want to do is carry you back to bed."

Her eyes widen. "Tell me."

I pull her tighter so she can't move. "They have DNA evidence."

I'm glad I have a good hold on her because her knees buckle, and she whispers, "What?"

"It's okay. It's on the coroner's report, but not a part of their discovery. They weren't planning to use it because they know it's not going to match mine and I'm their target."

She shakes her head. "But—"

"No buts. Art thinks this is enough to get the case dropped. They have nothing on me and have been fucking with the only evidence they do have. This is plenty for the judge to throw out the case and then Art will fix the rest."

Her eyes close before her forehead falls to my chest.

I put my lips to the top of her head. "Let's go back to bed. No reason to think about it until tomorrow."

"This is wrong. It was self-defense. I think it's time I—"

"Art and I will fix this." I pick her up and put my hand to her bare ass. She wraps her legs around my waist and I head back to bed where we should still be sleeping. "I promise, once this is behind us, life will be easy."

She crawls into bed and I follow after dropping my shorts. I fit myself to her back as she pulls a pillow into her chest, but she doesn't say a thing.

"Doc, what are you thinking?"

She pulls in a big breath and her body tenses. "I wish there were another way for us to get here. I'm afraid this will always follow us, nipping at our heels."

I press my lips to the crown of her head, dip my hand under the T-shirt she didn't take off, and splay my hand over her abs. "It won't. Art will get the charges dropped and take care of the rest. Not many people I trust in the world more than him, but you moved to the top of that list, baby. I need you to trust me as much as I trust you. Promise me you'll let us handle this."

She runs her fingers along my arm and wraps her hand around mine. "I just don't want this to haunt us forever."

"I won't let it. We're moving forward. Never loved anyone and now I have you. Nothing will stand in my way."

She burrows deeper into my chest. "I love you."

"Love you, too, baby. Go to sleep."

It takes her a while, but her breathing finally evens, and her grip on my hand loosens.

Fucking Marcia. If I could kill her myself to take that memory away from Aria, I'd do it in a heartbeat.

And I'd enjoy it too.

Thirty-Four

Aria

BRAND'S DNA DID not match the evidence that was wound around Marcia's fingers.

Well, no surprise there.

It's been two days—it's only taken this long because Art had the DNA tested by three independent labs, in addition to the county's. In his words, he was *not fucking around with this*, but in the same breath added, *it's a part of the plan.*

I know it's only been two days, but it feels like years. Art scheduled a news conference in which he will announce the results of the DNA test, as well as informing the public how the DA didn't bother testing the evidence because they knew it wouldn't match.

That's what happens when you're on a manhunt for the wrong man.

Or woman.

I won't be waving my feminist flag today. This is the one time I'll happily set my equal-opportunity-loving heart aside and allow everyone to think Marcia's murderer was a man.

Just not my man.

Another thing to scratch off my list of shit to worry about is my father. Brand's PI followed him to SeaTac last night. He was booked on the first flight to Miami. I never heard from him again during his stay in Redmond, and at this point, I hope to never see him again. He didn't find Briar, for which I'm grateful. Probably not as grateful as Dad should be.

Turns out I'm not the only one with a protective man.

"You're so beautiful."

Brand's brows pinch as he spears me with his dark eyes through the mirror while expertly knotting his tie. "Never been called beautiful."

We're in his closet, which is once again neat and orderly since my mess has overtaken the once empty space across the bathroom. Muppet is curled at my feet. As the days click on, he's always near me if I'm home. "That's a shame, because you are. You were wearing a suit on the news the first time I saw you. I knew nothing about you other than the lies Marcia spewed during our sessions, but I knew in that moment you were beautiful. I wish I could go with you today—you deserve to have someone at your side."

He tightens the knot and adjusts his collar before turning to me. "There's no one I want by my side but you, baby, but it's too risky. I don't want any extra attention on you. The Riccis know who you are and that's bad enough. Art will get the charges dropped, then we'll start making plans. I'm ready to put this shit behind us."

When I move, Muppet whines and rolls to his back. I slide my hand down Brand's silk tie and push onto my toes. It's a needless effort, because he leans and takes my mouth, his arms crush me to his chest. "I'm going to wrinkle your shirt."

"When I get home, you can do whatever the fuck you want to my shirt, then wear it the rest of the day."

I smile. "Thank you for what you're doing for me."

He nudges my nose with his. "There's nothing I won't do for you. Today is no different than when I had to make an appearance after I checked out of the hospital. This is for the media, but it's also for the Riccis. They think they can fuck with me through the PD, but they have no clue about the moves we're making or the changes that are coming." His hands frame my face, and his expression darkens. "I've got plans for Cory Ricci. It might not happen tomorrow … I need to wait for the right time. But he's going to pay for the part he played in trying to kill me and threatening you."

"He didn't do anything to me."

Brand stoops. The only thing in my vision is him. "You were in my house. Not only that, you were wearing my clothes. That in and of itself means you're under my protection. Cory is an asshole and always has been. He has no respect for me, which I could deal with before, but I'm sure as fuck going to make sure he never threatens you or makes a move on me again."

I don't have a chance to respond. He turns me in his arms, fitting his chest to my back. We're framed in his full-length mirror. I'm wearing another one of his station T-shirts and a pair of panties. My hair is a mess and I need a shower. Brand looks like a model straight from Milan. He's ready to conquer the world.

Or, at least, the media.

It's Monday. I need to get ready, but my first appointment canceled and I'm taking advantage of the extra moments with Brand. Every time I leave this haven he invited me into, I count down the hours until I can return.

As he wraps an arm around me, the contrast between his sleek and shiny appearance compared to my disheveled one is stark. Yet, his words make me feel like his queen when his gaze penetrates mine through our reflections. "Obsessed over you for months, trying to figure out your story. Then I officially met you at the auction when you strutted in wearing your confidence and fuck-me shoes." He presses his lips to my messy hair. "All that, and this look is my favorite—you swimming in my clothes and thoroughly sexed. As soon as these charges are dropped, we're having a serious talk about our schedules."

I don't answer because I can't think about anything past the charges being dropped. It's plagued my mind and stirred a hurricane in my gut. I can barely eat the healthy meals Brand prepares for me when he's home.

"It's time for you to ditch the apartment, Doc," he adds.

I pull my teeth between my lips, and he immediately gives me a squeeze.

"You trying to tell me something?" he asks.

"No, of course not," I shoot back. "I just think with the Riccis … I don't know. Keeping it one more month can't hurt."

His jaw hardens. "The Riccis have no bearing on my decisions. You're here, and we're going to make it more official in the near future. Make the call today and give notice. I don't want you anywhere but here."

I pull in a breath and nod.

"Good, baby." He brings us face-to-face and kisses me one more time before grabbing his jacket off the hanger. "I'll touch base with you later, but don't worry. Today is the start of big things. I feel it."

I watch him shrug his jacket up his broad shoulders before reaching down to give Muppet a scratch on his way out. "Wishing you good luck seems trivial, but good luck. And I love you."

He turns back one more time and gifts me with a heart-stopping smile. "Love you, too, Doc."

And, he's gone.

I WALK MY patient to the waiting room of the Redmond Mental Health Center and shake his hand. "I'm happy with your progress and I hope you are too. I'll see you next month unless I hear from you sooner."

Brand texted me earlier and said his news conference went as planned. Art already filed a motion to dismiss all charges in light of the new evidence. I haven't had time to call him about the details, but I've been lighter all day knowing this might come to an end soon.

But now my phone is lighting up like a firecracker, and that's never good.

When I get back to the small office space I use while seeing patients at the center, I go straight to my phone.

My heart sinks.

I press go and will the connection to be speedy. I've missed at least five calls and even more texts over the last forty-five minutes.

I hear the tremor in her tone when she answers. "Hello?"

"Marin. What's wrong?"

She sniffs. "I can't talk right now. I've got laundry to catch up on."

Shit. *Laundry*.

"Are you at home?" I open my laptop to find her file.

Kids are crying in the background and a male voice yells.

"Yes."

"I'll call the police and send them to your house. Can you confirm this is what you need me to do?"

"Yes," she sobs and Eric growls for her to get off the phone.

"Marin? Are you there?"

The line goes dead.

Shit!

I hang up and dial nine-one-one. I explain who I am, why I'm calling, and give them Eric and Marin's address, reporting a domestic emergency. They assure me they'll send someone right away. I tell them I'll meet them at the scene to be there for Marin after the police have the situation under control.

Grabbing my bags and coat, I race out the door and barely pause at the front desk. "Can you please cancel my last appointment? I have an emergency."

The receptionist's eyes widen. "Sure. Do you need any help?"

I shake my head and call over my shoulder, already halfway out the door. "I have help on the way. Thank you!"

I race through the parking lot. Getting to work late means parking in BFE. The weather is as dreary as ever—overcast and wet. I slosh through puddles when a man appears out of nowhere.

I stop in the drizzle, just shy of my car since he's blocking the driver's door.

He's tall and tan and well built. His collar is open at the neck under an expensive navy suit. Maybe not as nice as Brand's, but it still fits his athletic frame perfectly. His dark blond hair is perfectly styled, even in the light rain. "Aria Dillon?"

I shake my head and feign confusion. "No."

"Really?" He glances between me and a soggy piece of paper. "You sure look like her and you're running to her car."

I take two steps back. My only thought is he could be a Ricci, which isn't good. "Sorry. You're mistaken."

"I don't think I am." He advances. "Been waiting on you for days. The good doctor is hard to catch on her own."

I grip my phone and continue to move away. "What do you want?"

He shakes his head, and when his lips tip on one side, my insides turn. "Don't worry, sweetheart. I just want to talk."

I'm sandwiched between a row of cars and it doesn't matter how fast I try to retreat, he moves faster. I throw out the first thing I can think of that might make him back off. "I'm meeting my husband and am already late. He's a cop."

He shakes his head and clicks his tongue. "That's a lie, and we both know it. But you're cute. I mean, you're hot as promised, but your attitude? Cute … for now, but we'll break it."

Fuck.

I turn to run when an engine revs. A van is racing toward us.

I slip my phone into the back of my pants to free my hands.

I'm out of options.

Throwing my bag at him, I move. Tires squeal on wet pavement, and the van screeches to a halt. It knocks me to the side, and I stumble. My palms skid on the pavement before I'm able to push to my feet.

I scream and scramble around the front of the van.

A man and woman are two rows over and he starts to run for me as she heads for the building, yelling for help.

That's when a strong arm circles me from behind.

"No!" I scream and kick, my boots connecting with his shins.

He growls—his breath is heavy on my skin. The smell of stale cigarettes rolls off him in waves. "Shut the fuck up, Dillon. I don't have time for this shit."

It doesn't matter how much I struggle, yell, or thrash.

He throws me into the van and climbs in after me.

The good Samaritan yelling for me is cut off when the side door slams shut, sealing my fate.

The asshole grabs a roll of duct tape and starts for me. With my back to the wall of the van, I bring my leg around and my boot connects with his temple.

"Bitch!"

I scramble for the door, even though the van speeds off. I'll jump if I have to. My hand grips the handle as my scream echoes off the metal walls.

This time from pain.

A needle lands deep in my thigh. I'm thrown to the floor as he leers over me. He's too fast and too strong for me to fight.

My stomach turns and my head spins.

"There you go. That'll quiet you. We'll get you started on the good stuff later. I need you desperate and begging for your next hit."

I try to push myself up, but my arms noodle. My hand slips out from under me, and I slump against the side of the van on the dirty floor.

"Let's get the hell out of here."

Thirty-Five

THE END

Brand

I REMEMBER LIKE it was yesterday. The news I got while I was in the hospital wondering if my fucking heart was going to suffer permanent damage, or if I'd live to see the next day. My kidneys weren't looking good, either, and my liver had seen better times.

Dad and Art were by my side when their phones lit up in unison. The news came in fast and furious.

Marcia was found dead, floating in Gray Mountain Lake behind my house.

Not that it was a surprise. I'd already seen the surveillance video.

We'd already put the rest together by that point. Art had all the open food and beverages in the house tested. She was poisoning the filtered water I kept in the reusable water bottles. I guess that's what I get for doing my part to save the Earth.

Did I wonder how the events came to be that I saw on the surveillance? Yes.

Was I upset?

Fuck no.

Whoever the chick was who took on my crazy-ass wife, unshackled me.

Even while being treated by my new cardiologist, I felt lighter and freer than ever. That was the day I promised myself I'd never be with another woman who I didn't trust in every way possible. Especially with my own life.

I wasn't sure that would ever happen. At that point, I was a skeptical asshole and pledged to live my life alone.

Aria charged into my world in the most violent way possible. The beginning of my life started with death—the irony of that will stick with me forever.

She's the one I could trust with my life.

Loving her was even easier.

That phone call about Marcia was a born-again moment. My do-over.

But this phone call…

This news…

This might be the end of me.

Thirty-Six

PAY

Brand

"I'LL FILE FOR all charges to be dropped tomorrow."

"Good. I have a private appointment with the jeweler later today. I'm ready to move on, and the sooner I can do that, the better." I look at my phone and frown at the unknown caller, but answer anyway. "Vitale."

"Aria's been kidnapped," a woman says, by way of greeting.

I look at Art. "Who is this?"

"It's Briar. Brand, the center called. Someone attacked her in the parking lot and—"

My body goes rigid. "When?"

"This afternoon. We've got the thingy pinging on the map and there's a van but it's not a smart van so Alexander can't hack into it and—"

I can tell she's trying to keep her shit together, but her words make no damn sense in a time when it's really fucking important that they do.

"Flower," I hear someone say in the background.

"What the fuck happened—" I bite but a man interrupts.

"Vitale?"

"Who is this and what the hell happened to Aria?"

"Alexander Thornton. Aria was kidnapped in the parking lot. There were witnesses and police are looking at the surveillance now."

I turn to Art and can't believe this is happening. "Aria was taken."

Art doesn't hesitate. He grabs his phone and pulls out a side drawer in his desk, producing two Glocks, and tags his jacket.

We're out the door as I question Thornton. "What do you know?"

"We have a make and model of the van and a description of the guy. I have technology the police don't have or can't use without a warrant. I tracked her phone. Looks like she might still have it on her—it's moving, pinging towers heading east on ninety. They're almost to Ellensburg." He tries to calm Briar who's crying in the background. "Flower, shh. We'll find her. I promise."

"The police are on it?" My gut turns—I'm not used to feeling helpless. I'm also not a fan of the police, but right now I'm desperate enough to know when I need them.

Thornton continues. "I'm not sharing my technology with them. Told them Aria's location is linked to Briar's phone. They're scrambling highway patrol in that area. I called my pilot and we'll be ready to take off soon. There's room in the chopper if you can make it here quick."

Art and I exit the elevator and run through the parking garage. "Tell me where to meet you." He gives me the address as Art and I climb in my Tahoe. "I'm in downtown Redmond now. I'll be there in less than ten."

Art hangs onto the dashboard as I speed out of the parking garage and take a sharp left. "What the hell happened?"

"She was in the parking lot at the center. I don't know anything other than she was taken. The minute I get her back, heads will roll."

"Who was that?"

"Thornton."

"Thornton? As in Alexander Thornton?"

"Yeah. Don't ask because I don't know much." I grip the steering wheel so hard, I'm afraid I'll rip it from its column. "Art, if something happens to her—"

"Focus and drive. You've been through too much not to get her back."

I pass two cars and take another turn. He's right. Nothing can happen to her. And when she's safe, someone will pay for this.

With their life. They'll die, and I'll enjoy making it happen.

Thirty-Seven

RINGS AND BABIES AND WEDDINGS

Aria

I MOAN.

My body is heavier than a ton of bricks, and my brain is pounding from the inside out. When I try to put my hand to my temple, my arms won't respond.

I can't move.

The memory of what happened outside the center seeps through my foggy brain.

My mouth is taped and my hands and feet are bound. My head bounces on the metal floor with every bump. I force myself to swallow over the bile bubbling up my throat so I don't choke to death.

That is, before I fall to my death in some other way. Because I'll die fighting before I succumb to whatever plans this asshole has for me.

Something vibrates against my ass. Something very different than the van taking me who knows where.

My phone.

"Over two days in the car is a fucking long time—I'm already hungry. We need to stop soon. I have to piss."

"Sure thing, Duke. We're coming down from the pass. Can't wait to get back to warm weather. It's fucking cold here."

I focus on my breathing and try to remember how much battery life I had left on my phone when I last checked it. Maybe fifty percent? It has to last long enough for … for something.

There were people in the parking lot. Someone must have reported what they saw. Brand will find out eventually.

Brand.

He'll be sick with worry.

With *rage*.

He texted earlier that the press conference went well. He said it was the first step to putting everything behind us, once and for all, so we can start our lives together.

That was before he added that tonight we'd celebrate, and he'd do everything he could to make sure I was pregnant, if I wasn't already. That rings and babies and weddings would be in our near future, and he didn't give a fuck what order they came in, as long as they happened fast.

I have no idea what this guy shot me up with, but I can't take a chance that he'll do it again.

I have to do everything I can to stay alive and get back to Brand.

Thirty-Eight

Horrid

Brand

"THERE!" I POINT to the highway below us that comes into view after clearing the last mountain range. I'm riding shotgun next to the pilot. Thornton, Briar, and Art are in the back.

"Her cell is pinging right below us—it's got to be her. I'm showing it has twenty-one percent with no activity for two hours." Thornton leans forward and talks to the pilot through the headsets. "Duncan, do you have enough space to land in the middle of the highway ahead of them?"

Duncan studies the earth below us. "Traffic looks light. I should be able to if I can find a stretch long enough. The last thing we need is a big rig coming over a mountain and not being able to stop. When I land, get out and move off the highway."

The mountains have had a decent amount of snow already. Art and I are still in suits and Briar isn't dressed for this weather.

"It doesn't matter where he lands, Alexander. Just get to her," Briar pleads.

Art nudges my shoulder and points out the windshield. "He's speeding up and there's a turnoff ahead. He realizes he's being followed. There won't be a place to land on that two-lane highway."

"Fuck." I look to the pilot. "Can you dip and slow him down? We can't let him turn."

The pilot shakes his head and pushes forward. "I haven't done shit like this since I was in the Army."

I hang on as the pilot surges over the van and swings his tail around. Briar lets out a scream when we dip like we're on a rollercoaster and not her boyfriend's personal helicopter.

"Prepare for landing—it's gonna be a quick one," Duncan warns, though I'm not sure why he bothers. Quick is an understatement and the landing is not soft. But he did what was needed.

The van carrying my future hits the brakes and veers onto the shoulder. I unhook my seatbelt and rip off the headset as I watch it hit a patch of ice.

I throw open the door and draw my gun as the van spins and tips.

"Aria!"

ARIA

I ROLL INVOLUNTARILY when the driver hits the gas.

"A fucking chopper? Is it the police?" the driver asks.

Please let that helicopter be for me.

"Can you get past him?" Duke yells and looks out his window to the sky.

"Oh, shit!" The driver slams on the brakes and I lurch forward, the buzz of helicopter blades whirl above us.

The van swerves back and forth. I grunt, slamming against metal again.

"Ice!" the driver screams, but it's too late.

The van slips unnaturally to the side—everything in me wants to scream and brace and run for my life.

But I can't do any of it.

"Hang on!"

As if.

We skid to an abrupt stop, but the van is top heavy. I look out the windshield and the horizon tips.

I groan, landing on my side—my temple smashing against the sliding door that's now pinned to the snowy earth. Pain shoots through me. I don't know what hurts the most.

"They're coming!"

Shouts ring from everywhere as I search for my equilibrium.

The men scramble from the front of the van, stumbling over me. They kick the back doors open and the frigid mountain air crawls over me.

"What are you going to do with her?" the driver asks.

Duke grabs me by my bicep and drags me out the back of the van.

"Aria!"

My entire body tenses. I know that voice.

Briar.

A sob racks through my body from the pain and knowing my sister is close. I used to be terrified I would have to watch her die. First from the toxicity in her body and then from the toxicity in her mind. Now I'm scared it'll be her watching me die.

"Stop!"

My eyes jerk to the side.

Brand.

My hero is standing in the middle of the road in the same suit he wore when he left me this morning. He's lost the jacket and tie, but gained a gun, which is pointed at the man using me as a shield.

I thought Brand was beautiful this morning, but nothing compared to now. My emotions claw at me.

I thought I might never see him again—the man I killed for, obsessed over, and now love. My vision clouds—tears flood my eyes and stream down my face. I shake my head, the damn duct tape blocking all the words I want to scream. I want to tell him I love him. How I can't wait to start our lives together. And that I can't wait to give him all the children he'll let me.

Brand studies me from head to toe with wrath brewing in his dark eyes. In all we've been through in the short time we've been together, he's different. I realize the lengths he'll go to for me.

No matter how I come out of this, someone is going to die.

I know it.

"Get your fucking hands off her," Brand threatens. "If you don't back away, I'll tear you apart limb-by-limb, if I don't put a hole through your head first."

"Uh-huh." Duke moves and drags me with him. "Astor Dillon fucked up when he killed one of my best girls. My business took a hit because of him. Her daddy offered her as payment for his debt, and boy, he didn't disappoint. She'll bring in a pretty penny once I break her."

What?

Dad bartered me in exchange for his debts?

Sold me, like a used car?

Oh, God. No!

How could he? How could any parent do such a thing?

He's vile and sick.

Brand's lethal stare jumps from me to the man my father sold me to. His own daughter, using me as payment to this pimp. I'm not sure my father was ever capable of love, but even this is something I never expected.

Art appears from the shadows on the other side of the van, his own gun is drawn, closing our showdown into a scary triangle. I wince when Duke pulls me tighter and takes two paces back.

Brand shakes his head. "That's where you're wrong. She's mine, and I'm a scary motherfucker. You have three seconds to let her go before your brains are blown all over the road."

"No fuckin' way." Duke jerks me, and my bruised body aches. "I'm not leaving without her."

Brand doesn't take his eyes off Duke. "You don't fuck with a man who's already been to hell once. I'll take you down."

"I'm out of here," the driver quips and pads through the snow.

Duke jabs the barrel of his gun into my ribs, and I whimper.

"This'll be over in a minute, baby."

"I've got your back, brother. Clean shot," Art drawls—cool, collected, confident. "Say the word and this is over."

Duke twists toward Art. I do the only thing I'm able to with my wrists and ankles bound—I fold at the waist.

The moment I do, a single shot rings out, echoing off the mountains and carrying through the canyon.

Duke falls to the ground, pulling me with him.

Art disappears into the darkness, and Brand races to me. He kicks Duke's gun across the pavement and falls to his knees. Twisting to his ass on the wet, snowy ground, I'm in his lap staring at his agonized expression.

"Fuck, baby. This is going to hurt. I'll be fast." He rips the tape from my face, and even with the pain, nothing has felt so freeing. I let out a sob as Brand works at the tape on my wrists and ankles. Finally, he pulls me to his chest—warm, strong, and … mine. A place I want to stay forever. "I've got you. What did he do to you? How are you hurt?"

I say nothing—clinging to him and crying into his chest.

"Aria!" I turn to my sister, barely visible for my tears. Briar is crying and wraps her arms around me. She doesn't speak, but the fact she's hugging me means everything.

Brand places a hand on the side of my face and forces me to look at him. He lifts one of my eyelids to inspect me, and runs a hand over my temple, causing me to wince. "Baby, answer me. What did they do to you?"

I shake my head, wanting to forget the entire thing. "He shot me with something but I think it was just a sedative. I'm not sure how long I was out, but I hit my head."

I jerk in Brand's arms when a man I've only seen once at the center and then in the TMZ photographs with my sister, stoops next to us. Alexander Thornton is tall with dark hair and intense eyes. If I didn't know he was a tech guru, I might find him a bit menacing.

"Police and ambulance are on their way." Alexander looks to Brand. "That gun registered to you?"

"It's registered to me. I shot the bastard and I dare anyone here to say differently," Art says, taking the heat off Brand. He's also dragging the driver alongside him—bleeding from the mouth and nose with his hands tied behind his back. "Got this one." Sirens ring from between the mountains as Art tosses the driver to the ground. "Stay there, asshole. I ruined my shoes chasing you through the snow."

"I'll check you over once the ambulance gets here. No one's touching you but me." Brand presses his lips gently to my forehead. It's like a balm to my soul, and I never want to leave his arms.

Briar squeezes my hand. "That's it. I'm moving in with you so I can watch over you at all times. I'll sleep in Muppet's dog bed. Ask Alexander, I'll fit."

"That's not going to happen, pet," Alexander mutters, standing and shrugging off his jacket to wrap it around her shoulders.

"Hey," Brand calls for me.

I angle my face to his and burrow deeper into his warm chest.

"You scared the fuck out of me, Doc. Starting tomorrow, things are going to change."

My lids fall shut as the sirens get louder. Since there's no possible way for things to get worse, I'm okay with change.

He wraps his arms around me in the middle of a highway in the Washington mountains. I don't care where we are, as long as we're together.

Thirty-Nine

Aria

BRIAR SITS ON the sofa next to me while Muppet's head rests on my lap.

My dog still jumps on guests, begs for food, and runs off every chance he gets, as if he doesn't care that we're providing him a life of luxury.

He's also spoiled rotten, as he should be, and loves me most.

I knew he would.

Even so, he starts puppy boot camp next week. I agree with Brand—our baby needs to learn some manners.

As we watch the live press conference following Brand's special hearing in court, Briar wraps her hand around mine. It's not the first time she's initiated contact, but it still means just as much.

Art speaks, standing front and center, with Brand at his side. "We're pleased justice has prevailed. Despite detectives and the District Attorney's office ignoring vital evidence in Marcia Vitale's case, all charges against my client have been dropped. Brando Vitale, Jr. is innocent—proven not only by one lab, but four. In fact, I call upon the city council, the mayor, and chief of police to scrutinize these poor investigative methods. Taxpayers, citizens, and, most especially, victims deserve more. I don't think I'm going out on a limb here saying the evidence omitted by the prosecution is a Brady violation. But that's for another day."

I sink into the sofa and lean my head on Briar's shoulder. But I don't take my eyes off my hero.

"Mr. Ramos, what do you have to say about the only DNA evidence in the case being lost?"

Art shakes his head and contemplates that question for a dramatic moment before answering. "That evidence was being transported by police officials to the county lab. The fact that the only concrete evidence in the case has been lost ... *misplaced*," he stresses, and I force myself to keep breathing. "Is an atrocious mishandling, especially when the evidence in question was left out of case files. We wouldn't have known about it had I not combed through the coroner's report. My client and his family are deeply upset."

"Do you find it coincidental the evidence was lost?"

Art tips his head. "You said it, not me. My client has been targeted since the beginning. I'm not the one who should be fielding those questions. I do know that justice has been done today. Mr. Vitale is innocent—all charges have been dropped. Thank you for your time."

Brand and Art move from the microphones, but that doesn't mean the questions stop.

"Mr. Ramos! Are you going to file a defamation lawsuit against the department?"

"Mr. Vitale! Are you involved with another woman?"

"Are you in a relationship with the psychologist who was abducted outside of the Redmond Mental Health Center last week?"

"When will you return to Station Six?"

"I think my headache is coming back—I might be sick."

Briar reaches for the remote, and I decide I'm done with TV for good. I much prefer the bubble Brand has created for us without anything or anyone from the outside trying to taint our beauty. I only need my hero and my naughty dog.

It's been five days since Duke kidnapped me and shot me with ketamine. I suffered a concussion and was bruised from head to toe.

I thought I had problems sleeping before that dark day—now, it's downright impossible. I'm too sore to hit the treadmill and have dealt with a nagging headache that comes and goes. I'm so exhausted, the thought of running turns my stomach.

"We need to talk."

I look over at my sister. Briar has been by my side daily since the big event—caring, nurturing, and hovering. We've officially switched roles. She's become the motherly sibling, while I have withdrawn into my head. I haven't been back to work even though my concern for my patients nags at my conscience. I'm afraid to go back until I can be my best for them.

Marin and her children, however, are safe. Brand loaded me into the ambulance that day and I called to check on her on our way back to Redmond. I've spoken to her multiple times. Eric was arrested and served with a restraining order due to his threatening behavior toward his wife and children.

Marin also has a new attorney—Art Ramos.

When he saw how upset I was, Brand made it happen and is paying her legal fees. Just another reason to love him more than I ever thought I could love anyone.

So much, it hurts at times.

"Aria," Briar calls for me.

"Sorry, what?" I yawn and wish I felt this tired when I want to sleep. I know if I try to take a nap right now, I won't be able to.

The cycle is mentally and emotionally exhausting.

"I said we need to talk." Taking a deep breath, her voice is soft instead of filled with its usual snark. "I know what it's like to need a break. To need to check out and withdraw and do nothing. And that's okay. Don't put pressure on yourself to get back to normal right away. Take your time. Feel your feelings. Heal."

"How'd you get so smart?" She nailed how I'm feeling.

"I learned from watching you," she shoots back with a quick smile before returning to somber. "It's also how I know you'll ignore your needs so you can hurry back to fixing the world. And how I know you're afraid."

I angle my gaze to her. "I have nothing to be afraid of."

"Bullshit. Dad got to you. He came here to get to me, and like usual, you protected me. But there's no way that bastard will try again, Aria. Because this time, we have Alexander and Brand to protect us. Alexander is keeping an eye on him, and Brand said he's assigning a guard to you when he can't be with you. He'll never allow anything to happen to you again. Your man is downright scary."

"Brand isn't scary."

"He is to everyone but you."

I choose to say nothing, because I don't have a good argument for that. Brand has become a bit scary protective in the past week. Having a paramedic for a lover is no joke. I wonder if this is how Briar has felt all this time having a psychologist for a sister, watching her every move.

Until today, Brand hasn't been far from me. He hasn't gone into the station, he only takes meetings with Art here at the house, and he's managed the contractors for his new construction site from my side. He's touched every inch of me without really touching me. There's been no sex—he hasn't allowed it.

He also refuses to sleep unless I sleep, which means we're both drained.

Everyone thinks I'm worried about my dad and what happened to me. I won't tell them, but the murder charges against Brand have been at the top of my worries. More so than being sold to a pimp. The evidence being officially *misplaced* while being transferred between labs is almost as good of news as the charges being dropped against Brand.

I can even handle being under the scrutiny of the press for being with Brand.

I look at my fingers that are mangled from chewing on them the last few days, despite Brand doing all he can to stop me. My nervous habit has surfaced with a vengeance. "I'm relieved the charges have been dropped against Brand. I can't help but worry about Dad trying something with me again. Or even worse, with you."

She reaches over and grips both of my hands in her one. "Dad's been dead to me for years. After what he pulled, I'd be surprised if Brand didn't change that figurative into a literal."

My body tenses and my eyes widen.

"Alexander has filled me in on rumors about the Vitales—and I don't care about any of them." She smiles, but there's an edge to it. "Actually, I think I like it. That man loves you. He went apeshit when you were taken. I might have been upset, but I'll never forget his anguish before we found you. He has the resources to keep you safe and isn't afraid to use them. Nothing is going to happen to you again and there's no way in hell anything will happen to me. Alexander will make sure of it."

I give her a small smile. "Despite my being a mess, I'm happy for us. Who would have thought we'd end up here when we packed and moved as far as we could from Miami?"

"Not me. You're so normal and boring, I thought you'd settle with a guy who wears sweater vests and says 'darn' when he's really mad," she teases.

Boring. If she only knew what brought Brand and me together...

But she never will.

I smile. "I love you."

"I love you too. Which is why I'll voluntarily answer my phone if you need someone to talk to. Or I'll come over, day or night. I'll even bring salsa. You've been my rock for a long time. Now it's my turn."

"I thought Alexander was your rock now?"

She hikes a brow and a sly smile creeps over her beautiful features.

"He's my hard everything else, but you'll always be my rock."

She gets a text and anxiously grabs her phone before I can pry further into her private life. I don't have the energy anyway.

"Alexander is waiting outside. Are you going to be okay until Brand gets home?"

Muppet rolls to his back and paws at me to keep scratching him. "I don't need a babysitter, but thank you for hanging out with me today. Brand should be home soon and he has someone outside while he's gone, even though I think it's overkill."

I cringe at my own choice of words as they slip through my lips.

Briar stands and leans over to press a kiss to the top of my head. "I'm back at work tomorrow, but I'll call you. I know how you feel about taking meds, but it might be time for you to take something to help you sleep."

She took the week off to be with me. I didn't think it was possible to love her more, but I do. I try not to focus on the fact Briar and I only get closer with every drama. "I'm sure I'll sleep better now that the charges are dropped against Brand. I haven't had a headache today—at least there's that. And Brand and Alexander are keeping tabs on Dad. There's no legitimate reason for me not to sleep now."

She reaches to give Muppet a good scratch before swinging her backpack over her shoulder. "I hope you can convince your brain of that when your head hits the pillow."

I roll my eyes and am silently grateful the small action doesn't shoot daggers through my skull. "Enjoy your evening with Alexander. Maybe someday life will settle and we can focus on being a happy family, once and for all."

She throws her sarcasm over her shoulder on her way out the door. "As if. You and I are like damaged princesses, riding off into the sunset with our brooding knights, leaving scars and death in our wakes. We're like fairy tales for the dark web."

Briar knows nothing and yet she's spot on.

"Love you," I call.

My sister shoots me with her stunning, blue-eyed gaze, but adds a smirk that is all Briar. "Love you too. And I'll swing by the store on the way home to stock up on sweater vests for our men. You know, since we're both normal and boring now."

Everything is relative.

The Dillon sisters are far from normal.

Forty

RESPECT

Brand

*S*HE SLEEPS.
Fucking finally.

I don't think it's a coincidence that the first time she falls into a deep sleep happened after the murder charges against me were dropped. Between that and the kidnapping, it's been too much. As strong and smart as my psychologist is, there's a breaking point for everyone, and she met hers the moment she was kidnapped.

Being bartered as payment to a pimp by your father would do it for most people. I tried to assure her the charges against me would be dropped. Not only did they go away, but the only damning evidence in Marcia's murder case was *lost* being transferred from one lab to another by the county.

And, just like that, Marcia will never haunt us again.

Aria is safe, and Art is the master. His attention to detail is like none other, which is why he's the only person I want by my side as I take over the Vitale family. That transition started the moment I was exonerated today.

I have one more thing that needs to be taken care of before I officially take the helm.

Arrangements are being made as I crawl into bed, anxious for some sleep myself. The last week has been shit.

If I'm not in bed with Aria, the dog is. At least he knows who's alpha in the house because he jumps off as I crawl in. I've given up on getting him to listen or obey. He leaves next week for boarding school for ill-behaved canines. Aria loves him, and I love her—there's no price I won't pay to make her happy.

And having a dog who doesn't escape every chance he gets will make me happy.

My phone vibrates before my head hits the pillow.

Art – All set. A charter is arranged. I'll pick you up at five—we take off at six. If all goes as planned, we'll be home tomorrow night in time for me to put my kids to bed.

Me – See you then.

I'm not wasting any time. This would've been done last week had I not had murder charges to focus on.

I select another contact and send one last text before trying to get some sleep.

Me – Let me know if the location changes. I'm getting this shit done tomorrow.

I wonder if the man ever sleeps because he hits me back instantly.

Thornton – Done. Told you I would've happily taken care of this last week.

Me – Grateful, but I have a feeling you're a lot like me. If that's the case, you know this is something I need to do myself.

Thornton – I get it. I'll handle my end and be in touch tomorrow.

I drop my phone on the charger and finally settle behind her. She stirs and tries to roll, but I slide my hand over her hip and splay my fingers over her lower abdomen. "Go back to sleep, Doc."

Her body slumps into mine. "Hmm. Sleep."

I don't tell her I'm leaving tomorrow, not because I don't want to. There will never be secrets between us. I've been in one sham marriage from hell and grew up watching my parents live side-by-side in their own cesspools of lies.

But not me.

And not us.

I know what I've got in my bed. I don't want anyone else.

Aria's breaths become steady. This is why I can't tell her right now.

She'll know soon enough. And when it's done, we can start our life together.

Forty-One

PULSE

Brand

"DÉJÀ VU, RIGHT, man?"

I look at Art as we take the last of the steps to the second floor of the motel. "Pretty much. Never saw this coming."

"Sucks it took so long for you. You're practically ancient."

I shoot him a glare. "We're the same age, asshole."

"Yeah, but I've had nine years with Tessa and you had ten with a psycho from a horror movie. A decade is a long time to waste."

"You're telling me," I mutter.

We're in a shady as fuck part of town and I wonder how the doctor of nips and tucks feels about his new zip code.

Not that it matters. He won't have to worry about it much longer.

His new digs also make it easy for us to slide in and out. No one gives a shit about their neighbors in places like this.

I hand a pair of medical gloves to Art and bang on the door three times. As much as I want to break it down and torture the fuck who would be my future father-in-law if he lived to see next week, I have a new role and need to be careful.

Art slides his gloves on with a snap, and we flank the door.

When nothing happens, Art's gaze shoots to me. "Are we going to go Rambo on his shit or what? I don't get any action like this in the courtroom and who knows when an opportunity like this will present itself again since you'll delegate the fun shit now that you're boss."

Art lifts his hand to take a turn at the door when I try the knob. *Click.*

Art shakes his head with disappointment. I pull my Glock and peek around the doorframe.

There he is. Astor Dillon, huddled in the corner between a dilapidated desk and the wall. I keep my gun trained on him as I enter with Art at my back. The door quietly shuts behind us.

"You and I need to have a talk."

Astor is in rough shape—been worked over in a bad way. Cuts and bruises cover his face, but not enough to mask his fear.

His head jerks and looks like he's in withdrawals. "No-no. I don't have anything to say to you. G-get out."

"I didn't properly introduce myself in Aria's office that day. You have no fucking idea who I am. When you fuck with Aria, you fuck with me. And when you fuck with me, you fuck with everyone at my back. No one fucks with us and gets away with it."

Astor pushes back against the wall. If he could bury himself inside it like a dirty rat, he might. "I wasn't going to let anything happen to her, I swear. When they got here, I was going to get her away from them— help her escape. I'd never really let him pimp her out. I just needed to buy some time—"

"Shut the fuck up. You trafficked your daughter—the woman I'm going to marry and the woman who will be the mother of my kids. I don't like repeating myself, Dillon, but you fucked with the wrong man. Now get out of the corner."

Art walks around me and yanks him to his feet by the bicep. He pushes him onto a chair in front of me and drops a brown paper bag on the table. "Smells like piss in here. Let's get this over with."

I empty the bag on the table and watch Astor's eyes widen. "What's this?"

"The one thing that pisses me off," I start as I pick up a band to tourniquet his arm, "is I'm afraid you're going to enjoy this before you finally bite it. But I'm ready to be done with you. You've got so many track marks, no one will question it."

He tries to rip his arm from my hold. "Question what?"

Art trains his gun on Astor, and I yank his arm back. "Question the fact you'll be dead in a shit motel room, overdosed on cheap heroin cut with fentanyl because you can't afford the good stuff anymore. Consider this a favor you do not deserve. But your daughters need you to go away quietly, not with your brains blown to bits for the PD to have to go through the motions, only to write you off as being exactly what you are—a disgraced piece of shit, who not only owes a pimp, but his supplier too."

"This is easier," Art adds. "And, the older I get, I don't like messy."

I flick the cheap lighter to a flame and heat the heroin my guy bought. The Vitale organization is quickly getting used to me—I think they like my understated ways of doing business. When I told my soldier what I needed and what it was for, his sly smile showed me he approved. He had what I needed within three hours, promised it came from the shadiest of suppliers, and should do what I need it to do in quick fashion.

Months ago, Aria set me free.

I'm doing the same for her.

No one will ever control her again. I could have sent a number of people to do this, but it's something I needed to handle myself.

It's time for Aria to breathe easy, quit working herself to the bone, and fucking sleep, because she shouldn't have a worry in the world. I'll make sure of it going forward.

"You can't do this." Astor looks back and forth between me and Art. "I'll do anything. I'll make it right. No one will ever touch Aria again."

"You're right, she's mine. No one will ever touch her again. I have an army behind me to help make sure that's the case. Briar falls under that umbrella, too."

Astor struggles to pull away from me, but stops when the barrel of Art's gun is pressed to his temple.

I fill an entire syringe with the deadly mixture. "You're welcome for not blowing your brains out. You deserve a hell of a lot worse than what you're getting."

I find a weak vein. Astor sucks in one of his last breaths of air on earth.

Air.

My Aria, who gave me life, will be free—once and for all.

Astor closes his eyes as the poison does its job, giving him one last hit before sending him where he belongs.

I carefully set the syringe on the table next to him, because fentanyl is deadly. Art and I take a step back.

"Enjoy hell. It's where you belong. Not that you care, but Aria and Briar will be alive and thriving. Your grandchildren will never know who you are. If Aria isn't pregnant already, she will be soon."

Art turns to me. "No shit?"

"Yeah. I'm done wasting time."

"Congrats. Finally, someone will call me Godfather."

"Our kids together…" I shake my head. "If they're anything like we were, we're in trouble."

Art frowns. "I only have daughters, and they're perfect. No way will I let them do anything like we did. And if you have boys, they'd better stay the fuck away from my girls."

Astor groans, interrupting our moment. Art and I take another step back as Astor fails to sit prone, and falls to the ratty-ass carpet.

"You're the paramedic. How long do you think it'll take? I'm ready to get the hell out of here."

I shrug. "Shouldn't be long. I gave him a bigger hit than anyone should take, even if it wasn't laced."

As I stand here and watch the life seep out of Aria's father, a peace falls over me I didn't experience even when I discovered I was a widower. Until this moment, I don't think I realized how on edge I've been since Aria was taken.

But right now, in a shitty motel room in Miami, I know Aria is free for good.

I exhale a stale breath, one I've been hanging onto for way too long.

We wait another five minutes and not a word is exchanged between us. I don't look away from the man who almost stole my future.

I lean down and press my gloved fingers to his neck.

Nothing.

I carefully pick up the syringe and fold his fingers around it.

Prints.

Then, we wait longer.

I'm not leaving here until this is done for good.

No pulse. Not one beat.

He's gone.

I look to my friend. "Let's go home."

Forty-Two

OCEAN OF JOY

Brand

I LEFT HER a note this morning, telling her I had business to take care of out of town. She's texted me twice—once to tell me she made waffles out of canned cinnamon rolls without burning them, and the second, a picture of the dog asleep on my fucking pillow.

She sends me more pictures of that dog—as if I like it half as much as she loves the thing.

But she never asked me where I was. Didn't question what I was doing. Even when I called her when we got back to our charter for our return flight, all she said was she missed me and is ready for me to be home.

Trust.

Loyalty.

It hasn't taken long for those two things to run so deep between us, I don't know where one ends and the other begins. We're bound by them—stronger by the day—and when I tell her what I did, I hope she sees my act for what it was.

Obsession. Protection. Love.

She'll have them all from me as long as I'm breathing.

Art's Tesla disappears down my lane. I look through the windows to find her eating microwave popcorn out of the bag, tossing kernels to the dog every other bite. That shit is full of chemicals. I mentally add an air popper to my Amazon cart.

The man I assigned to watch the house when I'm not here approaches me from where he was waiting in his car. "Hey, boss."

I shake his hand. "I'm home for the night. Appreciate you coming over last minute."

"No biggie. I'm getting paid no matter where I am. Quiet day. Dog got out once—I helped her chase him down."

I shake my head. "I'll touch base tomorrow."

I open the door and immediately grab the dog by his collar. Forget dog bootcamp, the shithead has me trained at this point.

Aria's face lights up, and I wonder if this is how I'll feel returning home for the rest of my life. "You're back."

I shut the door behind me and go straight to her. "Told you I would be."

She tips her face to mine. "I know. I'm happy you're home."

I kiss her and push the jumping dog off me so I can sit next to her on the sofa. "You look good—rested."

She shifts to her knees on the sofa and I put my arm around her waist when she faces me. "I am. I slept forever. I think I made up for the week. Surprises me since you left so early."

I pull her closer. "We need to talk about that."

She shakes her head. "I need to talk to you about something first."

"No, Doc. Mine can't wait." She opens her mouth to argue, but I beat her to the punch. "Art and I flew to Miami today."

She tenses before sitting back on her feet. "Why?"

I don't pause or mince words. I know she can handle it. "Your dad is dead. He overdosed."

Her eyes widen, but otherwise, she doesn't seem affected. "Really?"

"Yeah. I'm sure someone will reach out to notify you soon." I lower my voice. "Baby, you need to act surprised."

She falls onto my chest and fists my shirt. The blue eyes I became obsessed with when she was nothing but a stranger to me storm over. "You did this, didn't you? You made sure he'll never touch me or Briar again."

I twist her onto my lap and hold her tight. "I did. I'm not taking another chance when it comes to you. From here on out, we can all rest easy. I hope you understand why I had to do it."

She looks at me as the emotion overflows from her eyes. "You did it for me. I'm not upset. I'm grateful. And relieved. I feel like a burden I've never been able to shake has been lifted." She presses her lips to mine and I taste her tears. "Thank you."

"I'll never keep a secret from you. You'll know everything about my business, my family, and everything I'm willing to do to keep you safe. And baby, today proves it—I'll go to the ends of the earth for you."

She doesn't want the details and she doesn't question my tactics. She tips her forehead to mine. "I love you even more and I didn't think that was possible."

I lift her chin and kiss the tip of her nose. "Love you too."

She changes the subject and her next words come out in a rush. "My period is late."

I freeze.

"Almost a week. I just realized it today. With everything going on and the concussion and not sleeping…"

"You're pregnant," I state.

She tips her head. "I don't know. My head has been so cloudy, and I've been worried about you being charged with murder. My period has been the last thing on my mind."

"You haven't taken a test?"

She rolls her eyes. "Your guard wouldn't let me go anywhere and I don't exactly have pregnancy tests packed in my overnight bag."

I lean to pull my phone out of my pocket.

"What are you doing?"

"I'm Instacart-ing a pregnancy test."

A small smile creeps over her face. "Get two. No, three! Just to make sure. And get me some chips and salsa while you're at it."

I add the five most expensive tests to the cart, along with chips and salsa, and press purchase. They should be here in under two hours. I toss my phone to the sofa next to us and cup her ass with my hand. "You need dinner, not just chips. And no more microwave popcorn. That stuff is shit—not good for you and even less healthy for a baby."

Her smile swells, just like the hope inside me. "You can make it for me. I like lots of butter."

I add organic butter to my mental list to go with the air popper. But I ignore all talk of popcorn. "We're getting married. No matter what the results are, and it's happening soon. Whatever kind of wedding you want, I'm good."

She leans into me. "I want something small, with Briar standing next to me. I can't wait to be your wife. I've dreamed of it far too long. I'm ready to live it."

"There's something else," I add, worried about how this is going to go over. If anything, I'm more worried about this than telling her I offed her old man. "This week while you were recovering, I paid off your student loans."

She pulls away from me and sits up straight.

I shake my head. "Don't be upset. It was a lot, yet it's nothing for me. I easily make that in a slow month. It was the best money I've spent. I'm tired of you working yourself to the bone and want you here more. Quit your job at the center. Pick your patients. Or quit altogether. But you need to cut your hours."

"I can't believe you did that. And I really can't believe you make that much money a month." Her tears form again and I realize her emotions are swinging like a pendulum. "It's crazy that you can pay off a loan like that at the drop of a hat."

"I'm also quitting the department."

"You are?"

"Haven't hidden anything from you. You know my family, our business. I'm taking over with you by my side. It was my legacy and now it's ours—I want it all."

Her expression relaxes, and the knot in my chest immediately loosens. "My place is by you, no matter where you are or what you do."

I put my hand to the back of her head and twist. When I have her under me on the sofa, I realize today is the day.

The first day of our lives together. Better than what my parents gave me. Better than the train wreck Aria grew up with. And better is an understatement when it comes to the last decade of my life.

Trust.

Loyalty.

Love.

ARIA

"YOU NERVOUS?"

I exhale. We're in our bathroom, staring at the timer on my cell.

Brand's chest is glued to my back, and his big hand is wrapped around my neck. His thumb is pressed on my vein. Instead of answering, I ask, "Why do you do that? Your hand on my neck?"

His words are heavy—hot, sensual, and possessive, in a way they'll stay with me forever. "You're cool as a cucumber on the outside, but this," his thumb presses in, "shows me how you really feel. Any emotion from you makes me hard. Your heart races for me, and I like to feel it."

I close my eyes and relax into his hold. He's right and it's scary. My heart only beats for my hero.

But at this moment, my pulse is sprinting for a much different reason.

"Answer me. You nervous?"

"Yes," I croak.

"Don't be."

My chest rises and falls far too quickly. "Easier said than done."

He turns me in his arms and I bury my face in his chest. He presses his lips to the top of my head. "Why are you nervous?"

"I wasn't until I peed on that stick. But now, all I can think about are my parents. I don't even know what a good mom looks like."

"You'll be perfect."

"You don't know that, Brand. My family was so fucked up. It's all I know."

His arms tighten around me and he's about to argue when the timer dings.

I grip his shirt tighter. "I can't look."

"You're really not going to look?" I hear a smile in his voice, dammit.

I shake my head. "No."

"Bravest woman I've ever met is afraid of a pregnancy test," he mutters.

He holds me to him with one arm and the other reaches.

He pauses.

I hear the test clank in the sink.

Then his hands find my face and he takes my mouth. His kiss is deep and long and intense. I relish in it even though I'm not completely sure what it means.

Finally, he lets my mouth go and tips his forehead to mine. This time, it's his voice that's laced with emotion. "You're going to be perfect, Mama."

I can't see him through my ocean of joy.

My heart bursts.

Epilogue

Aria

$\mathcal{B}$RAVERY IS IN the eye of the beholder.

I'd like to think I was brave when Marcia threatened me and my family. When she told me she planned to kill her husband.

And, even more, when my bravery turned into brazen curiosity about the man I killed for. Because I had to know.

Was he worth it?

Oh, yes. He was so worth it.

I hate to say I'd do it again, but…

For him, I'd do anything.

And for Briar. And, now, for our growing family.

Brand is the head of the Vitales. He still manages the holdings corporation, but he runs everything else too. He does what he has to do, and people respect him.

Even the Riccis.

Hate and respect can go hand-in-hand. It took me a bit to realize that.

The Riccis might hate him with a vengeance, but they respect him … now. They didn't always. Especially Cory Ricci.

Cory met his demise. He'd made many, many enemies over the years, and someone poisoned him.

Turns out tetrahydrozoline is deadly when you ignore the symptoms.

Life and death.

It's a delicate balance.

I look over at my sister, sitting in the rocker opposite mine on our porch. She's got her eyes glued to the kids as they run and play in the front yard. It worries us to have them too close to the water. "Thank you for being so brave."

She throws me a frown. "Brave? Does Brand know you're smokin' crack while baking his baby?"

I shake my head. "You're the bravest person I know. You've been through so much, but look at you now. No one could survive what you did without a backbone of steel and the bravest of souls. You might not feel it, but it's how I see you. That's all that matters."

She hikes a brow. "Pregnancy makes you sappy."

"I'm barely pregnant." I run my hand over my small bump. I just hit my second trimester, even though my bump has grown faster the third time around. I feel like a baby machine, but what am I supposed to do when Brand sweet talks me into unprotected sex? Because nothing makes him happier than making our family bigger.

Briar picks up her lemonade and turns her natural beauty to me, beaming. She's the most gorgeous she's ever been, and it has nothing to do with her beauty-pageant looks she still has after all these years. "Whatever you say. I'm brave … you're barely pregnant. The shrink knows best."

"I do."

I smile and take a bite of my cookie. I still don't cook much but I have learned to bake. My boys love sweets, just like me, and my health-freak husband has given in. Our kids will have everything in moderation. No one will control them the way Briar and I were controlled growing up. Matteo is four and Domenic is almost two. Brand wants a girl, but I don't care, as long as it's healthy. I've perfected being a boy mom and love it.

I sigh. "Have I ever told you I was scared to death when we left Miami to move here?"

"You think you were scared? I was a hot mess, minus the hot, but with extra mess. I didn't wanna fuck up and let you down. You had no idea what you were getting yourself into when you took me under your wing. If that's not bravery, I don't know what is."

I look back to the kids playing—carefree having known nothing but the love of their family for their short lives on earth. So different from what Briar and I had. Muppet romps around the yard with them. He hasn't run away in years. Even Brand likes him now, but just like in the beginning, my expensive rescue dog loves me most. "I think it's safe to say, we both took life by the reins and made our way out of hell the moment we said goodbye to Miami. We did okay."

Briar motions between us. "We fucking killed it."

She's right.

Still, she's wrong.

There's nothing normal about being married to the head of an organized crime family or a weirdly-private tech guru worth billions.

No, there's nothing normal about any of that.

But it works. And I wouldn't want it any other way. I pity the person who challenges Brand Vitale or Alexander Thornton in anything.

When it comes to the Dillon sisters, our husbands will stop at nothing to keep us safe.

That will never change.

"BRAND."

I fist my pillow and raise my hips for more. But when it comes to him, I'll always want more.

"Please," I beg.

He gives me what I want. His lips close around my clit and I'm pushed to the place only my husband can take me. Bliss, euphoria, and ecstasy don't do it justice. My mind clears and my soul soars to a place where there's nothing but him and me.

Together, we're perfection. Ask me before I met Brando Vitale, Jr. if I thought there was such a thing as perfection.

I would have said no.

Perfection doesn't happen in the real world, the place I help people cope with the ugly and the hard.

But when it's just us, and now our boys and growing unborn baby, perfection is very, very real.

The universe is a funny place.

Death brought us together.

Our path is what it is—we were meant to be. Had we come together any other way, we wouldn't appreciate what we have.

My lungs beg for air as Brand makes his way up my body, his lips trailing—over my hip, our growing baby, my breasts.

He takes my mouth when he sinks into me, slow and methodical, like I'm made of the most delicate crystal. My body forms to his and I wrap my leg around his lower back to press in. I want more but he's like this when I'm pregnant.

The taste of me lingers on our lips when he finally fills me completely. "Never ceases to amaze me—you come fast and hard when you're pregnant. It's going to be difficult to hold me off for another when there are so many benefits to keeping you knocked up."

I exhale and hold him to me, sliding my hand into his hair. Now that his firefighting days are behind him, he keeps his beard manicured and his hair a bit overgrown. His Italian rugged looks are more beautiful the older he gets. "Don't hold back, Brand."

He shakes his head and nudges the tip of my nose with his. "Don't ask for what you know you're not going to get, baby. Love you and my new miracle too much." He pulls out and slides back in, painfully slow. "You know how I feel about our miracles. Don't know what I did, but I keep getting handed one after another. I'm going to protect them and you with everything I have."

"I know, but…" I don't have the words to profess how much I love and hate that. Not when he angles his hips and presses my sensitive clit every time he fills me, robbing every lucid thought from my brain.

"No buts." He kisses me again and slides an arm under my back, rolling us. He pushes me up and I moan, pressing down on him, getting what I want. I start to move the way my body needs when his hands come to my hips. "Easy, Doc."

I look at every inch of his large frame lying below me. "You're impossible."

"You're insatiable. How did I get so lucky?"

"It's the hormones." I slide up and down on his thick length as fast as he'll allow. "You know how much energy I have in the second trimester."

He lifts his powerful hips and feels his way to my breasts. "Take what you want. I'll watch."

I lean back, grip his thick thighs, and take what I need. "Finally."

Brand drags a heavy hand down my chest, over our bump, and straight between my legs. "Even after planting my third baby in you, some days you still seem like a dream I don't deserve."

I move.

His thumb moves faster.

I didn't think I could handle another orgasm, but…

My head falls back and I gasp.

Brand lifts his hips, and his other hand goes to my waist. "There you go. Get me there, baby."

I moan and can't move another muscle, but Brand takes over. He bucks into me over and over and over before holding me on his cock.

So full.

So perfect.

My hands land on his pecs before I fall to his chest. He cups my ass and head, holding me to him as we recover before he starts to play with the ends of my hair. "Thank you, baby."

I smile against his skin. "For what?"

He presses his lips to the top of my head before lifting my face to his. His dark gaze sears into mine. "For saving me."

He doesn't say it often, but every time he does, it seizes my heart so I have to work for my next breath.

Because I don't need to escape reality to find a silent peace anymore.

I only need him.

If you enjoyed *Deathly*, this author will be forever appreciative for your review on Amazon.

Continue with the Dillon sisters in Briar's story by Layla Frost – *Damaged*

I'm chatty and want to know you! Join my Facebook group
Brynne Asher's Beauties

Thoughts and Acknowledgements

I'm one lucky girl to have a friend like Layla Frost in my life. When she told me at the end of 2020 that she was writing something fucked-up and different, I said, "Ahhh, I've had this idea for a book. Maybe we could…"

And that is how the Dillon sisters were born.

I stepped outside my norm to write Brand and Aria's story, and nothing has felt so refreshing and right. *Deathly* was a pleasure to create and the words flowed like they haven't in a long time. I'll be forever grateful to these characters for the experience. I miss them already.

First and foremost, thank you, Layla Frost. Collaborating with you is an honor and a pleasure. I hope we can do it again very soon.

Michele, *Deathly* is the first book, of ALL MY BOOKS, that I made you read without telling you the twist ahead of time. I can't lie, I loved surprising you. I hope you don't kill me if this becomes a thing. You begging for chapters certainly motivated me to write faster. Please don't break up with me.

Heather Stewart Soligo, thank you for putting up with my raw words and pimping my books far and wide. I'm lucky to have you in my life.

Kristan with edit llc you reeled me in when I tried to italicize this entire book. That's what good friends and editors are made of. This is not an exaggeration.

Carol, thank you for answering all of my firefighting questions.

Sarah and Layla, what would I do without you? Answer: I'd talk to myself all day, make myself crazy, and be lonely as hell. Thank you for your friendship and all your support.

Penny, Carrie, Laurie, Ivy, Dana, and Gi, thank you for your eagle eyes and valuable input. But even more, thank you for always supporting me, my work, and for making me feel normal when I stalk you while you read.

Annette and Michelle with Book Nerd Services you are quite literally the best and most loyal women in our book world. I'm honored to be a part of your circle.

Emoji, thank you for wearing all the funky socks I buy you and pretending Trader Joe's frozen dinners are homemade for the sake of our marriage and my sanity. I love that you read my books just because you're nosy and want to know what's in my head. Living life with you is better than any fictional happily ever after. When are you buying me a cow?

To my kids who will never read this, you're the most loveable money suckers on earth.

Zoe, may we all channel your Zen. The words flow when you're by my side.

To my Street and Review Teams, I could not do this without you. Thank you for sharing, loving, and supporting me.

Lastly, to my Beauties. You are quite literally my favorite part of this author gig. I love your chatter, your interaction, and your love for books that brought us together. You're my bright spot on the Freakybook and I love you for it.

Daily, I pinch myself just to make sure this is real. That this is my life. That I get to write stories that *you* want to read.

Fairy tales really do come true.

Hugs and butt touches,

BA xoxo

About the Author

Brynne Asher lives in the Midwest with her husband, three children and her perfect dog. When she isn't creating pretend people and relationships in her head, she's running her kids around and doing laundry. She enjoys decorating and shopping, and is always seeking the best deal. A perfect day in "Brynne World" ends in front of an outdoor fire with family, friends, s'mores, and a delicious cocktail.

Printed in Great Britain
by Amazon

58455804R00175